I0784668

Garet Garrett

Cinder Buggy: Historical Novel

OK Publishing 2021

Garet Garrett
Cinder Buggy: Historical Novel

Published by
MUSAICUM
Books

- Advanced Digital Solutions & High-Quality book Formatting -

musaicumbooks@okpublishing.info

2021 OK Publishing

ISBN 978-80-272-7317-1

*A pot-metal body
on two little wheels,
absurdly,
bow-leggedly
walking away to the dump
with the slag, the
purgings of iron, the
villainous drool of the furnace —
that is a cinder buggy.*

*It is also a sign
that what man refines
beyond
God's content
with things as he left them
will very soon perish
for want of the dross
from which it is parted.
Why hath each thing its cinder? —
even the sweetest desire?*

I

A generation has fled since a stranger was seen in the streets of New Damascus on an errand of business.

The town has nothing to sell except the finest wrought iron in the world. As the quality of this iron is historic and the form of it a standard muck bar for use in further manufacture you order it from afar at a price based on what is current in Pittsburgh.

Sellers of merchandise miss New Damascus on purpose. It is a catalogue town. It buys nothing because it is new, nothing it does not need, has no natural pride in waste whatever.

Strangers are not unwelcome, only they must not mind to be stared at. The town is shy and jealous and has the air of keeping a secret.

There are no sights to see. Once people came great distances, even from Europe, to see the New Damascus blast furnaces. They were the first of their kind to be built in this country, had features new in the world, and made the scene wild and awesome at night. All that is long past. There is only a trace of the mule railroad by which ore came down from the mountains. Where the furnaces were are great green holes. Nature has had time to heal her burrs. No ore has been mined or smelted at New Damascus for many years. Yet the place is still famous for its fine wrought iron. The ore now comes from the top of the Great Lakes, stops at Pittsburgh to be smelted, and arrives at New, Damascus in the form of pigs to be melted again, puddled and rolled into malleable bars. That may be done anywhere. It is done at many places. But it is so much better done at New Damascus than anywhere else that the product will bear the cost of all that transportation. The reasons why this is so belong to tradition, to the native pride of craftmanship, to that mysterious touch of the hand that is learned only in one place and cannot be taught. The iron workers here, descended from English, Scotch and Welsh smiths imported to this valley, are the best puddlers and rollers in the world. Therefore as people they are dogmatic, stubborn and brittle.

There is the old Woolwine mansion on the east hill, there is the Gib mansion on the west hill. Nobody would recommend them to the sense of wonder. Besides they are disremembered. They were once very grand though ugly. They are no longer grand and have been made much uglier by architectural additions of a cold ecclesiastical character. One is a nunnery. One is a monastery. The church got them for less than the walks and fences cost. Only a church could use them. All that the indwellers knew about them is that the woodwork polishes easily and must have been very expensive. The grounds are still nice.

The river is lovely, but nobody has ever cared for it esthetically. The town is set with its back stoop to the river, as to an alleyway or tradesmen's entrance, facing the mountains where its wealth first was.

Sights? No. Unless it be the sight of a town that seems to exist in a state of unending reverie. This is fancy. New Damascus appears to be haunted with memories of things confusedly forgotten, as if each night it dreamed the same dream and never had quite remembered it.

In the Woolwine library there is a memory of distinction in sixty parts, —bound volumes of the NEW DAMASCUS INTELLIGENCER back to 1820. There was a newspaper! An original poem, a column humorous, a notable speech on the slavery question, the secret of Henry Clay's ruggedness discovered in the fact that he bathed his whole person once a day in cold water, and the regular advertisers, all on the first page. One of the advertisers was a Wm. Wardle, bookseller, stationer, importer of all the current English imprints, proprietor of a very large stock of the world's best literature, periodicals, and so forth. Wm. Wardle's name is still on the lintel of the three-story building he occupied until about 1870. The ground floor now is rented to a tobacconist who keeps billiard tables in the back for the iron workers, the upper floors are in disuse, and there is no bookshop in New Damascus. Well, that is a sight, perhaps, only nobody would think to show it to you, because much stranger than the disappearance of that important old bookshop is the fact that no one can remember ever to have missed it.

If you mention this curious fact to the First National Bank president he helps you look at the faded name of Wardle above the tobacconist's sign and says, "Well!" precisely as he would help you to look at one of the great green holes where a blast furnace was and say, "Well, well!" never having seen it before.

"What do people now read in New Damascus?"

"Magazines," says the banker. "I find if I read the Sunday newspapers I get everything I want."

"How do you account for the fact that New Damascus, an iron town, has fewer people to-day than it had fifty years ago?"

"You've touched the answer," says the banker. "It *is* an iron town. Always was. When modern steel making came in fifty or sixty years ago anybody might have known that steel would displace iron. New Damascus stuck to iron."

"Lack of enterprise, you mean?"

"Something like that."

"Yet New Damascus had the enterprise to roll the first rails that were made in this country."

"Yes, they rolled the first American rails here, —iron rails."

"And having done that there was not enough enterprise left merely to change the process from iron to steel?"

"Well, there was some reason. I've heard it said a committee of New Damascus business men went out to investigate the steel process. They reported there was nothing in it. Then the steel rail knocked the iron rail out completely. There isn't an iron rail made anywhere in the world now."

"And nails. New Damascus was once the seat of the nail industry. What became of that?"

"Same thing. They made iron nails here, —what we call cut nails. The cheap steel wire nail knocked the iron nail out. Then, of course, you must remember that when the Mesaba ore fields were opened we had to close our mines. We couldn't compete with that ore. It was too cheap."

"That wasn't inevitable, was it? Since New Damascus stopped, other towns have grown up from nothing in this valley, —towns with no better transportation to begin with, no record behind them, hauling their raw material even further."

"Yes," says the banker. "Well, I don't know. There's something wrong in the atmosphere here,"

The banker on the next corner has another explanation.

"It's the labor," he says. "People who've been around tell me, and I believe it's true, that labor here is more independent, more exacting, harder to deal with, than labor anywhere else. In other mill towns you'll find Italians, Hungarians, Polacks and that like. All our labor was born here. Jobs go from father to son. Foreigners can't come in."

"That's strange. One never hears of any serious labor trouble at New Damascus-not the kind of trouble they have in other mill towns."

"Not that kind," says the banker. "There's a very peculiar thing about labor in New Damascus. It can live without work."

"How?"

"I don't know how. It just does. When anything happens these people don't like they stop work. That's all there is to it."

"Is it a union town?"

"They don't need a union."

Bankers in New Damascus are like bankers anywhere else. They know much more than they believe and tell only such things as ought to be true. It is scandalous for labor to be able to live without work. That offends the economic law. It ought not to be so. Yet in so far as it is there is no mystery about it. The town is invisibly rich and has a miserly spirit. There are as many banks as churches, —and the people are very religious. The banks are full of money that cannot be loaned in New Damascus. It is sent away to Pittsburgh, Philadelphia and New York to put out at interest on other people's enterprise. If you ask why that is the answer is cynical.

"Perhaps," says the banker, "we know each other too well."

But you see how it is that labor may live without work. Everybody has something by, —a home, a bit of land, a little hoard to sit upon. Spending is unfashionable. Carried far it is sinful. Living is very cheap. Three mornings a week the farmers come in with fresh killed meat, sausage, poultry, eggs, cheese, butter and vegetables and turn the main street into an open air market; and there is an ordinance which forbids the shopkeepers to buy any of this produce before ten o'clock. By that time there is nothing left, or if there is no dealer wishes to buy it, since the demand is already satisfied.

But there is still the question: What happened to New Damascus?

Ask John Tizack, the tobacconist, in the old Wardle building. He meets you with the air of a man of the world and pretends to be not in the least surprised when you say: "I've asked everybody else and now I ask you. What's the matter with this place?"

"Neighbor," he says, "I was born here, my father before me and his before him. I began as a lad in the mill here. Everything in New Damascus came out of that mill. I say everything. That isn't exactly right. Them mansions on the hill, —they came out of it. The library, that row of fine houses you may have seen on what we call Quality Street, all the big and little fortunes you see people living on here, came out of that mill. When I was twenty-five I says to myself, 'I'll see a bit of the world before I die. Some of it anyhow.' That was thirty years ago, —yes, thirty-two. I've been to New York City and Buffalo and around. Now I'm back. I'm going to die here. This ain't a bad business if you look at it right. Not so bad. And you want to know what's the matter with this place? You've been asking everybody else. What do they tell you?"

"This and that. No two alike."

"S'what I thought," he says. "I couldn't agree with them. There's men in this town, merchants, mind you-well, you wouldn't believe it. There's not ten business men in this town been as far away as Philadelphia. I know what I'm saying. I won't mention any names, but I happen to know the president of the biggest bank in town was never in New York City."

"Is that what's the matter?"

"Now wait," he says. "You see the kind of place I got here. No profanity. Nothing at all. I know the boys that come here every night. Iron workers you might say, but they're gentlemen, in a way of speaking. They play billiards, smoke, talk. Not one of them under thirty. Went to school with most of them. Their fathers was born here like mine. And they don't get treated right. Now I'm telling you. They're the best iron men in the country, bar none, and they don't get treated right."

"So that's it?"

"No, that ain't it either. I'm just telling you some of the things that's wrong with this place. You asked me the straight question, didn't you?"

At this point he gives you a piercing look. Are you also a man of the world? He seems to doubt it. You may be one of those people who go around talking just for the excitement of it.

It is necessary to remind him that he was apparently coming to something else, —to the point, perhaps. He waits for you to do so. Then with an air of extreme asperity, meaning that you shall get all you came for, he clears the top of the showcase and leans at you with his bristles raised, looking first toward the back room, which is empty, then towards the street, which is clear, and lastly at you in a pugnacious way.

"You asked me, didn't you?"

"Yes."

"Do you happen to believe in any of them unnatural things?"

"Such as what"

"Such as hants and spells?"

"More or less."

"All right," he says. "Now neighbor, take it or leave it. Suit yourself. I've seen my share of this world and I know what I'm talking about. That's what's the matter with this place."

"What?"

"What I'm telling you, and I'm going to die here. There's a spell on it. Nobody can help it. There's a spell on it. Now that's all."

"Who put it on?"

"Oh, well, n-o-w," he says, becoming irresponsible. "That's different. That's very different again. I'm not telling you anything I don't know. Who put it on? I tell you frankly I don't know. Maybe you'll be smart enough to find that out. To speak the truth, I don't know as it's anything I want to meddle with."

There is a difference, you see, between a banker and a tobacconist. A tobacconist believes more than he knows and tells things that ought not to be so.

Still, there is the fact. New Damascus, having cradled the metallurgical industry, ought to have grown up with it and simply did not. A town that rolled the first American rails smaller now than it was fifty years ago! Why? If it had died you could understand that. But it is not dead. Its health is apparently perfect. There is not a sore spot on its body. It functions in a kind of somnambulistic manner. The last thing you hear as you fall asleep at the old Lycoming House is the throb of its heart. That is the great engine of the Susquehanna Iron Works, muttering —

> *Wrought iron*
> *Wrought iron*
> *Wrought iron*

It never stops.

II

When in 1879 Gen. Aaron Z. Woolwine founded this place all the best Palestinian names, such as Philadelphia, Lebanon and Bethlehem, were already taken in Pennsylvania, so he called it New Damascus; and this name when he thought of it was perfect. The Damascenes were famous artificers in metal. He imagined even a geographical resemblance, —a plain bounded on one side by a river and on the other three by mountains representing the heights of Anti-Lebanon.

He resolved a city and that its character should be Presbyterian, and entered in his diary a prophecy. With ore, coal and limestone in Providential propinquity, with a river for its commerce to walk upon and with that spirit of industry which he purposed to teach and exemplify, aye, if necessary to require, New Damascus should wax in the sight of the Lord, partake of happiness and develop a paying trade.

Besides capital and imagination he brought to this undertaking a partner, three sons and a new wife.

For thirty years he fathered New Damascus. He saw it become the most important point of trade between Philadelphia and Wilkes-Barre, with five notable inns, two general supply stores, three tanneries, six grist mills, two lumber mills and the finest Presbyterian conventicle in that part of the state. The river was a disappointment. It was high and swift in flood and very low in the dry season, all very well for lumbering and seasonal traffic, but not a true servant of steady commerce. To bring the canal to New Damascus he entered politics and continuously thereafter represented his county in the legislature. He did not live to see the rise of the iron industry. That was left to the wonder of the next generation.

One of the disasters of his old age was with stone coal, the name by which anthracite was first known. All the coal around New Damascus was anthracite. For all that could be made of it commercially it might as well have been slate or shale. Nobody knew how to burn it. The fuel of industry was soft coal, which ignites easily; and wood was burned in open grates, not in New Damascus only but everywhere at this time; and as anthracite or hard coal would not burn in the same furnace and grates that burned either soft coal or wood people were sure it would not burn at all. General Woolwine knew better. Wherever he went he carried with him samples of hard coal, even in his saddle bags, begging people to try it, but the notion against it was too strong to be overcome by propaganda. Only time and accident could do that. Once he freighted a large quantity to Philadelphia, resolved to make it burn in some of the large forges there. The result was a dismal failure. Others before him on the same crazy errand had been arrested for obtaining money under false pretences, selling black stone as coal, and the prejudice was irreducible. He abandoned the stuff in Philadelphia; it was broken up and spread in walks. Later, —too late to benefit him, —the secret of burning anthracite in furnaces was discovered by accident. A perverse foundryman, who believed less in hard coal than in the probability that what everybody disbelieved was for that reason true, spent a whole day trying to make a fire of it. Then he left it in disgust and went home to supper. Returning some hours later he found an amazing fire, —hotter than any soft coal fire he had ever seen. The secret, beyond having a strong draught, was to let it alone. In a little while everybody was saying that you could burn stone coal if only you let it alone. That simple bit of knowledge, derived from trial and error, was worth more to Pennsylvania than a thousand gold mines.

In the last few years of his life General Woolwine, by his efforts to exploit stone coal and in various schemes of the imagination, lost a considerable part of his fortune by not attending to it. He was not a sound man of business in that sense. Ideas obsessed him. The idea that stone coal would burn was an obsession on which he made large outlays of time and money. He pursued the idea to failure. A more practical man would have first invented a grate suited to the fuel. A more conservative, selfish man would have sat on his anthracite beds until someone else had invented a grate. Yet he was never discouraged. The day before he died he wrote in his diary:

"As I lay down this life I am moved to reflect on its beauty and fulness to me. I have used up my strength in works. Nothing have I withheld from the Lord. I have walked in the faith. I have imagined civilization in a wilderness. Then I have seen it with my eyes."

That was all he said of New Damascus. Other memories crowded in.

"In 1774," he wrote, "I married a pious, sensible woman, who bore me two sons. In 1781 I married an eminent, worthy woman, who bore me a third son. In 1788 I married a delightful, affectionate woman, whom God was pleased to spare me to the end. She bore me my one daughter, Rebecca."

The two sons by the first wife were already dead. This he did not mention in his testimony. The third son, born of the eminent and worthy woman, was at this time thirty-seven and unmarried, unlikely to perpetuate the line or to grace it if he did. All the Woolwine vitality went into Rebecca, born of his union with the delightful affectionate woman. Rebecca had married Phineas Breakspeare, the inn keeper, and was for a long time estranged from her father on that account. He forgave her on the head of a grandson, his namesake, Aaron Breakspeare.

The founder's affairs were left in a somewhat involved condition. Everyone was surprised that the estate was not greater. His partner had large claims upon it and the accounts were in confusion.

The widow survived the General but one year. The third son died the next year. The whole estate then passed to Rebecca, who had buried her inn keeper; she held it in trust for the founder's grandson, Aaron.

Here ends the Woolwine line. The name disappears suddenly from the annals of the county.

III

Nowhere in the annals of the county nor in those lymphatic biographical histories, quarto, half or full leather, profusely illustrated with steel engravings, which adorn the bookshelves of posterity, is there any mention of General Woolwine's partner and man of business. This was Christopher Gib, cold, and logical, with a large broad face, dull blue eyes, a long bleak mouth line and a hard apple chin. People feared him instinctively. He inspired them with dread, anxiety and a sense of injury; yet in practical matters, especially in great emergencies, he commanded their utmost confidence. Those who complained of his oppression were certain to have been weak or wrong. That made no difference, —or made it worse. In every dispute he was technically, legally, perhaps morally right. By all the rules of law his acts were blameless. Nevertheless they outraged that subtle sense of the heart, higher than the sense of right and wrong, to which human conduct is referred for ultimate judgment. He acquired his rights fairly. His way of making a bargain was to let the party of the second part propose the terms. Then he would say yes or no, and that was final. Higgling disgusted him. But having made a bargain he insisted upon it in a relentless, dispassionate manner. No one could say he was unjust. But from one who is never unjust you shall not expect generosity. Human beings do not crave justice; they accept it. What they long for is understanding through sympathy. Christopher Gib had no chemistry of sympathy. It was left out of him. Therefore he had no emotional understanding of people and people had no rational understanding of him. His tragedy was invisible. He was denied what he could not give, namely, bread of the sweetened loaf without price, for which everyone hungers. Contempt for all the sentimental aspects of life was the self-saving device of his ego. He treated people as children. The more they disliked him the more bitterly he took his due.

He was ten years younger than General Woolwine and dominated the elder man in all their joint affairs, as a rational nature may dominate a romantic one. They quarreled a great deal; — one in a low, cynical voice; the other in loud, righteous tones. These disagreements were private. Outwardly to the end they maintained an appearance of unbroken amity. As to his ideas the old founder was immovable and pursued his own way. In matters of business he would sooner yield than continue the argument. One neglected business; the other lived for it. As the Woolwine estate declined that of Gib increased. There was no inequity in this. It was inevitable. The General drew out his profits and spent them; Gib reinvested his in undertakings outside the partnership. At the beginning the coal and iron lands were divided between them in the pro-portions of one-third and two-thirds, according to the amounts of capital respectively invested. The one-third was Gib's share. In the end the proportions were exactly reversed. The Woolwine estate owned one-third and Gib two-thirds. It was all perfectly correct and legal.

At the age of fifty Gib married Sarah, of the Withy family, that came from New Jersey and built the first grist mill in New Damascus. Sarah was a dutiful, reconciled woman of strong, uncomplaining fibre, who could not fold her hands until the work was done. She never under-stood her husband. He never understood her. It wasn't necessary. She was thirty-five and had once loved a young man who never even suspected it.

Of this inarticulate union came one son, named Enoch, born on the same day with Aaron Breakspeare, Rebecca's child, grandson of the founder.

Christopher Gib lived fifteen years more, growing steadily richer and more misunderstood. Then he built himself a tomb, the walls of which were three feet thick, reinforced with bar iron, and died in the night alone.

IV

Aaron Breakspeare, grandson of the founder, and Enoch, son of Christopher Gib, being of the same age, inheriting parallel estates in a town realized from a joint impulse of their forbears, grew up together. They were never friends. They were rivals, unable to conceal or control their rivalry, the essence of which was antagonism. But they were inseparable. They could not let each other alone. Enoch was the stronger physically. In their earliest games and contests his object was to make Aaron say, "I quit." And Aaron would sooner die than say it. In this strife Enoch had always the advantage of a definite, aggressive purpose. He created the occasions. Instinctively he knew that the way to save oneself in a trial of endurance is to keep one's mind not on one's own discomfort but on the agony of one's adversary.

Aaron's power was of pride and spirit. He would never say quit, no matter how much it hurt to go on, and when he was beaten he did not complain. Once Enoch invented a way of locking their arms so as to exert a mutual and very painful torsional leverage, perhaps enough to break the bones. The game was that each should go as far as the other could stand it. All the other had to do was to say enough. It was fairly played. But the word was never uttered and Aaron went home with a broken arm.

The imponderable values of life, —admiration, sympathy, sudden friendships, understanding, liking and being liked, —belonged to Aaron as by right. He was that kind of being toward whom the heart yearns for no reason but its own. Men and women loved him without knowing why. The people of New Damascus spoke of him with possessive affection and worldly misgiving; he would do himself no good, they said. That means whatever you make of it.

Enoch, pretending to be contemptuous, was secretly torn with envy. People looked at him and said: "The spit image of his father." He had many of old Christopher's facial expressions, especially one that was unnatural and very disconcerting. Anger or any strong adverse emotion caused the face to appear to be smiling. It wasn't; nor was the expression assumed as a mask. The effect was accidental, produced by some peculiarity in the action of the retractor muscles. He was by nature more saturnine than his father, or perhaps it was only that he more indulged the impulse to cruelty. At fifteen he was already feared by his elders for what he might say.

His character developed in a true line. The traits of his youth became only more pronounced as he grew up. To take the pride out of Aaron became almost a passion. He delighted to expose his frailities and limitations. Aaron bought a fast horse. Enoch hating horses bought a faster one and drove it to death. Aaron on a dare swam the river at flood, which was thought a fine feat. Enoch swam it with his legs tied.

Aaron apparently did not mind. If he suspected the envious motive in Enoch's conduct he never spoke of it, but generously applauded the other's trimphs. Whatever else happened their intimacy remained unbroken. This seemed to be no more of one's seeking than the other's. Those of their own generation wondered, but the elders, hearing it spoken of, said it was no more strange than the way General Woolwine held with Christopher to the end of his days, though it more than half ruined him.

They went to the same school at Philadelphia. Enoch worked just hard enough to beat Aaron in everything except mathematics and popularity, and spent a great deal of his leisure prowling about the iron foundries. They fascinated him. There was iron in the blood of his family. His grandfather and great-grandfather had been smiths in England. And his father had laid upon him one injunction, which was never to part with an acre of ore or coal land, for some day these undeveloped possessions would make him rich. Then secretly he took up the study of metallurgy.

Yet it was Aaron who proposed to Enoch that they should pool their interests in ore and coal and found an iron industry at New Damascus. This fatal thing happened sometime between midnight and dawn after a disastrous twin celebration of their twenty-first birthday with a party of friends at Fingerboard Inn.

Aaron's mood was sentimental. He felt a great twinge for Enoch, because of what occured at the party. He himself was the one to blame. First he had demanded of his friends, when he heard what they were doing, that they should invite Enoch, too, as an equal guest; then with great difficulty, he had persuaded Enoch to come. It was bound to be dismal. Only one of Aaron's reckless spontaneity could have imagined otherwise.

An archaic, mystical man rite survives in the panegyric supper. The root is hero worship. The impulse is exacting, jealous and sacrificial. Its chosen object, according to the rules, must submit to be clothed in the colors of perfection, set upon a pedestal and gorged with praise until he is purple. As the hero's embarrassment rises his makers become more solemn and egregious, until suddenly with rough hands they drag their colossal effigy down and embrace it and everything, itself included, dissolves in maudlin ectasy.

Obviously two human objects cannot be equally inflated in this manner at once. The impulse cannot divide itself. If it tried, no matter with what pains of tact, the effort would fall.

Having invited Enoch, whom they all disliked, Aaron's friends felt acquitted toward him, and then, knowing how he hated to see Aaron preferred, they carried praise of Aaron to a point grotesque. As the wine flowed they became heedless and took delight in Enoch's chagrin. No toast was drunk to him; his name was not mentioned. It was cruel but not premeditated. He ought not to have come. Aaron was ashamed to look at him.

Enoch, from having been at first merely bored, turned hot with anger, thinking the situation had been purposely created to humiliate him. He did not suspect Aaron of conscious part in that design; he blamed him, however, for having lent himself to it unwittingly. Hitherto convivialities had depressed and disgusted him. Now in the bitterness of his heart he made a judgment concerning them, that they were utterly beneath him; and made also a resolution which endured to the end of his life. That was to accept once for all the fact of people's dislike and turn it against them.

Was he not stronger than any of these who presumed to belittle him? One by one he passed them through a test. There was not one he could not break in any trial of mind or body. Perhaps it was for that reason they disliked him. No matter why. He did not return the feeling in kind. They were not important enough to call forth from him either dislike or hatred. They merited only his indifference. That put them in their right place. He would be indifferent to them so long as they stood out of his way. If they came in his path he would break them indifferently. His mind became cold and glittering. He no longer cared whether anyone liked him or not. But they should never be indifferent toward him. He would attend to that. They should fear him. That was it. He would rather be feared than liked.

With these self-saving thoughts he had become absent and oblivious when suddenly on both sides he was nudged to rise, join hands, and sing to the hero. He rose, but instead of joining hands he rapped heavily on the table for attention. There was much surprise at this. Everyone stared at him in silence.

"Gentlemen," he said, with the astonishing effect of a cold, sober voice, "I call your attention to an unfortunate omission. I propose that we shall drink to Aaron Breakspeare's ancestors, — to the man but for whom there would be no New Damascus nor any one of us here present, and to the woman without whose assistance even that great pioneer would be now entirely forgotten. We shall drink, I say, to Aaron Breakspeare's distinguished ancestors, —to Adam and Eve, if you please."

There was a sound of embarrassed laughter. It immediately broke down. Gib was holding up his glass. His expression was sneering. He had paid them off, going just far enough to do so cleanly, yet not so far as to give actionable offence. For a long awkward moment they could not think either how to turn it back on him or redeem their own conduct from the ludicrous light in which he had placed it. Then Gearheart, who was taking law, he who afterward became a great jurist in the state, lifted his glass and spoke in a calm, judicial manner.

"Mr. Gib is right," he said. "We regret the omission. Let us drink to Adam and Eve."

So they did and that ended the party. Nobody disliked Gib less; everyone respected him more.

Aaron, who by this time was feeling very miserable, made a point of walking off with him. He wished to speak of what had happened. Yet what could he say that would not recognize the fact of Enoch's humiliation? There was no way to speak tactfully of it. Still he could not let it alone.

"I'm sorry," he said, blurting it out.

"For what?" Enoch inquired dryly.

"I'm afraid you had a wretched time. I'm to blame for getting you into it."

"Not at all," said Enoch. "To the contrary, I'm indebted to you for the most profitable evening of my life."

He meant this. Those emotions of anger and mortification from which he had suffered so bitterly seemed now remote and insignificant. They had been swallowed up in a sense of deliverance. He had delivered himself from the torment of being disliked. The fact was unchanged, but he no longer cared. Therefore it had lost its right to oppress him. From this sudden birth of indifference he derived a feeling of solitary power. His mind was disenthralled. His whole outlook upon life was altered. For the first time he did not wonder whether Aaron really liked him or not, or how much, since it did not matter in the least. And also for the first time he did not dislike Aaron. His indifference included everyone, and it was sweet.

Aaron misunderstood the nature of Enoch's placidity. He thought it a kind of sublime generosity and felt deep remorse. He would not have believed it was in him to take a hurt to his pride so magnanimously. He was wrenched with a sudden desire to offer some sign or token of durable amity. So it was that as in one the well of friendship dried up in the other it overflowed.

They walked for some time in silence. On the first eminence east of the town their ways parted. There Christopher Gib had built the dark iron-stone house which was still Enoch's home. The Woolwine mansion where Aaron lived was higher up. Enoch would have turned his way, leaving it as usual for Aaron to say goodnight; Aaron detained him by the arm.

They stood for several minutes with their faces averted, gazing alternately at the stars that were God's, at the mountains that were theirs, and at the town beneath them, showing in silhouette against the moon-lacquered river, a dream of their forebears realized. It was a beautiful night. Their thoughts ran together. Both were stirred by a vague sense of freedom, knowledge and responsibility. Each had that day come into the possession of his estate. It was Enoch who spoke.

"What will you do with yours?" he asked.

Until this moment Aaron had never once thought what he should do with it. But at the sound of Enoch's voice asking the question so bluntly a complete idea crystallized in his mind. It had clarity and perspective, like a vision, and sudden as it was he felt very familiar with it.

"Look, Enoch," he said. "There is the New Damascus we grew up with. How still it lies in the moonlight! How permanent it looks I Yet when we were born it was not here. Before we die it will have disappeared. In its place will be a city that shall walk out of those mountains, —a city of furnaces, full of roaring and the clangor of metal, flaming and smoking to heaven. Your father and my grandfather imagined it. They could not themselves bring it to pass. It was not for their time. They left it for us to do. We have a destiny here. Let's take it together. Let's form a partnership and found an iron industry."

"That's what I am intending to do," said Enoch. "Not the partnership. I was not thinking of that. But the iron business, —I've had that in mind all the time. I've made a study of it." After a pause he added: "I didn't know your thoughts turned that way. You never spoke of it before."

"You never mentioned it, either," said Aaron. "You would prefer to go alone?"

"The idea of a partnership is new to me," said Enoch.

"But wouldn't it be advantageous to develop our ore and coal holdings jointly? They lie together."

"Yes," said Enoch, "I can see that."

"Is it only the newness of the idea that bothers you?"

"I would not have entertained the thought as my own," he said. "Since it comes from you I do not reject it. I merely do not wish to be responsible for it. You are not a man for business. Your father was not.

Your grandfather distinctly was not. You would do better in law or politics. Still, as you say, there's an obvious advantage in bringing all the properties together. We'll talk about it to-morrow if you like. It's on your initiative, remember."

"Let's agree on the main point now and leave the details," said Aaron. "I'll take my chances with business."

He held out his hand. Enoch took it slowly. They looked at each other steadily in the moonlight.

"Is it agreed?"

"Yes," said Enoch.

Then they said goodnight.

V

Enoch's misgivings notwithstanding, the partnership of Gib & Breakspeare was very successful. This was owing partly to the ripeness of the opportunity and perhaps even more to the sagacity with which Enoch allotted to Aaron the tasks that were suited to his temperament. They put in equal amounts of capital and pooled their ore and coal lands on a royalty basis. Enoch was the dominant partner by right of knowledge and force of doggedness. He had studied the business. He took the manufacturing end and spent the whole of his time in New Damascus. Aaron took the selling end and made all the outside contacts.

It was easy to open the mines. That kind of work was already well understood in Pennsylvania.

Building a blast furnace was much more of an undertaking. It was in fact a daring adventure. Older and wiser heads had left it to the foolhardiness of youth.

Hitherto iron had been produced in this country, as elsewhere in the world, by primitive methods. Ore was wastefully smelted in rude charcoal furnaces unimproved in design since the Middle Ages. The process was of great antiquity. It was uniform in India at the time of Alexander's invasion. Its origin even then was lost in myth. Tubal Cain, "an instructor of every artificer in brass and iron," was master of it in the city of his distinguished ancestor, Cain, which was in the land of Nod.

Between the old iron master of the Himalayas, 1,500 years before Christ, with his little clay oven resembling an overturned pot, urging the fire with a bellows clasped in his arms —(a bellows made from the skin of a goat stripped from the animal without ripping the belly part, then tied at the leg holes, fitted with a wooden nozzle at the neck and stopped with an air valve in the tail orifice) —the difference between him and the iron master if the early 19th century was only that the latter had learned to build his forge of rude masonry and to make nature blow his fire.

The prize in both cases was a nugget of glowing iron, the most useful non-digestible substance yet discovered by man. It is tenacious, ductile, easily tempered, malleable at red heat, marriageable at white heat and possesses one miraculous quality. It is magnetic. It calls electricity out of the void, snares it, delivers it helpless into the hands of man. Without this blackhearted substance, fallen from the sun, natively pure only in form of a meteorite, lightning could not have been captured and enslaved on earth.

The glowing nugget on the forge hearth, called the loup or bloom, is in a crystalline condition. It is removed and further refined by hammering, drawing and rolling at red heat. It may be hammered by hand on an anvil, or beaten under a trip-hammer, or rolled between rollers. The effect of this treatment is to elongate the crystals into tough fibres.

A blast furnace differs from a forge not in principle so much as in audacity, method and degree. The forge pricks nature and extracts iron one molten drop at a time. The blast furnace cuts a gash in her side and extracts iron in a blazing stream.

There were blast furnaces before those of Gib and Breakspeare, in England, Germany and France, but they were few and still in the stage of wonder. They were very costly to build, many failed for unknown reasons, and the conservative old iron masters stuck to the forge. Nowhere had a blast furnace been worked with anthracite or stone coal. All that had so far succeeded used wood, charcoal, bituminous coal and Coke. The fuel at New Damascus was anthracite.

So it was in all respects a rash experiment and in one respect unique. The partners were sure of the theory. The thing was scientifically feasible. Yet in practice it might fail for want of handiness with a strange process or because of some malicious chemical enemy lurking in the elements to be acted upon. And failures in iron experiments are ruinous. Nothing ever can be saved and the capital outlay will have been enormous.

The skill to build such a blast furnace as they required was not only dear and hard to find: when found it was pessimistic and disbelieving and disclaimed all responsibility for the outcome because it was something that had never been done before. Expert iron workers to man the process were of the same grey mindedness about it.

These iron workers had to be imported from England under guarantees and inveiglements. Nearly all the new iron working methods of that time originated in England and were as jealously guarded as military secrets. The rise of American industry against European competition was greatly hampered by lack of industrial knowledge. Europe would not part with it, or share it, since to possess it exclusively gave her manufacturers a world-wide advantage. So it had to be obtained surreptitiously. Much of it was smuggled out in the heads of English, Scotch and Welsh artisans who could be bribed to evade the embargo upon the emigration of skilled workmen and try their luck in the United States.

While Enoch worked indefatigibly at New Damascus, tapping the mountains and preparing the mule roads by which to drain away their coal and ore and limestone, Aaron was abroad impressing the skill that should convert those raw materials into iron.

Two years from the time they started, one evening, the first miniature volcano went into action.

That precisely is what a blast furnace is. The hollow, cylindrical furnace is the mountain cone, charged from the top with fuel, iron ore and limestone flux. The mass is fired at the bottom. The gases go off at the top in flame and smoke, an upside-down cataract of lost affinities, giddy, voluptuous, hungry and free. An odd circumstance has released them from the cold inert embrace in which they have lain for ages of years. Cinders and gross matter flow away below as lava. The iron, seeking itself, falls like rain into the hearth at the bottom and runs out on the sand, forming there a molten lake. Around the edges of this lake, taking off from it, is a series of moulded depressions. The lake drains into these depressions. They suck it dry. Ironworkers call the lake the sow. The forms that appear in the depressions, having devoured the sow completely, are called the pigs. The product is pig iron, —a lump of rough metal the size of a man's thigh.

After the fire is lighted at the bottom there is nothing to do for several hours but wait. In this interval the partners went to supper at Enoch's house. They ate in silence. Aaron made several ineffectual attempts at conversation. Their thoughts were far apart. One was thinking of details, of faults to be remedied, of errors in the next instance to be avoided; the other dwelt upon the achievement as a dramatic whole. Enoch was anxious to get back.

At a point from which the blast furnace was visible as a complete spectacle Aaron stopped and seized him by the arm.

"Take a look at it, man. There's plenty of time for that."

A blast furnace even then was what a blast furnace is, —the most audacious affront man has yet put upon nature. He decoys the elemental forces and gives them handy nicknames. Though he cannot tame them, he may control them through knowledge of their weaknesses. He learns their immutable habits. From the Omnipotent Craftsman he steals the true process. In the scale of his own strength he reproduces in a furnace the conditions under which the earth was made, and extracts from the uproar a lump of iron.

By the very majesty of the effects he conjures up he is himself absurdly diminished, to the point of becoming incredible. As you look at him he is neither impressive nor august. Perhaps if one had witnessed the creation the appalling effects in the same way would have seemed much more wonderful than the Creator. In His old clothes, anxious, preoccupied, intent upon results, He probably had been very disappointing to the eye.

From where he stood, detaining Enoch against his mood, Aaron could see the workers moving about the furnace hearth, —tiny, impish figures, grotesquely insignificant, scornfully manipulating the elemental intensities. The surrounding slopes were lined with people, their faces reflecting a dull, lurid glow; and there was an ominous, swooning vibration in the air.

"Admit it, Enoch," he said, "You get a thrill from that."

"I want to get back," said Enoch.

They remained at the furnace the whole of that night and handled the first cold pig iron.

"It's good," said Enoch.

It was a fine quality of pig iron. The demand for it was immediate and profitable. Furnaces were added one or two at a time until there were eight. Pig iron was for some time the sole product. The mill to draw and roll the iron came later.

In five years the population of New Damascus trebled. The mines, the blast furnaces and later the drawing mill, —the first in this country to pass iron through rollers, —employed thousands of workers. Their wants made business. The town was rebuilt. That made more business. Enoch on his own venture built houses for the iron workers and opened a large company store.

There was a third reason why the partnership, to everyone's surprise, was successful as a relationship between two antagonistic natures.

Aaron had all the popularity still. The social life of New Damascus centered upon him. The Woolwine mansion where he lived in bachelor eminence was full of entertainment and gaiety. His hospitality was memorable. Guests came from afar, from Pittsburgh, Philadelphia and New York, to attend his parties.

Enoch continued to live morosely in the old ironstone house below. The contrast was notable, even painful, but if Enoch minded at all there were compensations. Within the partnership and outside of it his power increased. There was never any doubt as to which of them exercised ultimate authority in matters of business. When it came to borrowing capital, as they did to build the mill, it was Enoch's word that persuaded the lenders. He made a sound they understood, —a crunching, horizontal sound that was not in Aaron at all. The instinct that preferred Aaron in friendship and the instinct that preferred Enoch in business could exist, and did, in the same people. Enoch was preferred where his vanity was. People feared and trusted him. That kept the scales even.

VI

Having heard of New Damascus that it was marked to become the seat of the American iron industry, there appeared at this time one Bruno Mitchell, a capitalist, thinking to open a bank if the repute of the place should prove to be well founded. He had prospered in New England, where the practice of banking was already well advanced; but he believed in the star of iron and it led him hither. In his active character he was hard and avaricious, yet there was a quaintness about him that first contradicted that fact and then mitigated one's opinion of it. He had never filled his skin, or perhaps it was a size too large in the taking. Instead of hanging loosely, as an over-size skin does on wavering natures, it had shrunk to measure, so that he was prematurely wrinkled and had a leathery look. His face wore a quizzical expression. His eyes were blue and restless. He walked softly.

Enoch Gib impressed him deeply. They understood each other at sight.

Persuaded by omens and discoveries that New Damascus was the place, Mitchell moved himself there, together with all his means and chattels and a daughter named Esther. He was an important addition to the community. He gave it the prestige of having one of the first banks west of Philadelphia. To Gib and

Breakspeare he was very helpful. Not only did he discount their bills and effect payments on their account at distant points in a manner then new and miraculous; he also advanced them considerable sums of credit and capital. He was anxious to make a permanent investment in the business, and Enoch was willing that he should. Aaron objected, as he had a right to do, and although both Enoch and Mitchell were disappointed,' there was no open feeling about it.

Esther Mitchell was twenty-four. Since the death of her mother five years before she had lived alone with her father, who took it each day for granted that she should be content to manage his household until whatever it is that happens to women happened to her. They never spoke of it and nothing happened. So time wore on. Once in a while he said to himself, "I wonder why Esther never has a beau," and then put it out of his mind. They behaved toward each other like two married people who run in parallel grooves and never touch.

When at the death of his wife the daughter returned to him from a convent school he hardly knew her. She was still, after five years, as much a stranger to him as on the day she voluntarily assumed the responsibilities of her mother. He never had been able to penetrate her reserve. When he tried, as he did at first, he had a sense of trespassing and guiltily retired. She had a way of looking at things, at people, at him, with steady, wide-open eyes that never betrayed what she was thinking. Sometimes a troubled expression would appear in them, like the shadow of a cloud on the surface of a still blue pool. They talked very little. What there was of it was friendly. He had no idea what she did with her own time, if she had any, and never asked.

As a housekeeper she was faultless. As the female adjunct of an elderly, selfish engrossed man she had all the merits and none of the liabilities of a perfect wife; besides she was in youth and sweet to the eye. As a fellow human being she was a riddle. In that light he knew hardly more than her name. Her castle! was invisible. There was no straight way to it. The outermost signs were all misleading.

The partners were frequent visitors in the Mitchell household. The atmosphere was social. The subject was business. They seldom talked of anything else. Business of course has many facets. It was not merely the affairs of Gib and Breakspeare they discussed. They debated the future of iron, metallurgical processes, the blundering stupidity of Congress.

The feud between politics and business was never new. An economic truth more obvious than daylight to the industrial founders was even then a tangle of obscurities to Congress. What statesmen could not see clearly, once for all, was that without high tariff protection the American iron industry would live at the mercy of foreign competitors. On that text Enoch said always the last word, which was his own, and became a famous slogan among the ironmongers of that generation. It was this:

"War or tariff."

That now sounds cryptic. Then it was clear enough. Everybody knew or could remember that there was no iron working in this land before the war of Independence. The mother country forbade it. What she wanted from the American colonists was the raw material to be worked up in her own iron mills with her own skilled labor, for if the colonists produced iron manufactures for themselves English exports to the New World would suffer. An act of the British Crown decreed that "no mill or other engine for slitting or rolling of iron, no plating forge to work with a tilt-hammer and no furnace for making steel" should be erected "in any of His Majesty's Colonies in America." Mills already existing were declared a public nuisance and abated as such.

So the colonists, forbidden to work their own iron, were obliged to sell their raw materials to England and buy it back from British merchants in the form of manufactures. The war cut the colonies off from these British manufactures. They were thereupon obliged by necessity to found a native iron working industry. After the war the British sent their products to the United States at prices with which the new American industrialists could not successfully compete, hence the demand that British iron be excluded, or at least that the importation of it be penalized by high tariff. This was the historic experience that caused the prosperity, in fact the life of the early American iron industry to be associated with war and tariff. They were in results the same. War had all the effects of a high tariff. It kept the foreign stuff out.

"And nobody wants war," Enoch would add.

Another topic endlessly debated was the railroad. It had just come within range of practical vision. What were its possibilities? Would it supplement or supersede canals? Enoch could not imagine that the railroad would ever take the place of canals. Aaron thought it would. Mitchell thought with Aaron and Enoch for that reason was more rigid in his opinion.

Once Aaron broke all precedent in this private chamber of commerce by saying suddenly to Esther:

"What do you think?"

He had been observing her for some time. Through all their interminable repetitious dinner table talk she maintained an air of rapt attention, with her gaze on the one who was speaking, and never uttered a word. He wondered if she were listening or merely watching them. Both her father and Enoch were surprised that anyone should address her with that kind of question. She was not startled.

"I wonder which will make the world happier," she said.

In the way she said it there was a kind of disbelieving that referred neither to canals nor railroads but to something represented by the discussion. The effect was strange. All three men were disturbed in their sense of importance. They attacked her in concert, with a condescending manner, Enoch leading. How like a woman to think that way! What had happiness got to do with it? The question was economic. Which would be the more efficient means of transportation? But anyhow-this was Enoch-anyhow, was it not obvious that whatever increased the wealth of the world increased also the sum of human happiness?

"Is it?" said Esther.

They could get nothing more out of her. She declined to be argued with and smiled at them from a great distance. Her smile was impassable.

Several times after that Aaron tried to involve her in their conversations, at dinner, or in the drawing room where she sat apart with her needlework, but never again with any success. She would look at him with a bothered expression, and either recognize his effort by no other sign or slowly shake her head. This he took for disapproval and thereafter ignored her, as the others did, except now and then to scrutinize her in a surreptitious manner. When she surprised him at that she returned his gaze with distant, impersonal curiosity, until he was the first to turn away.

A change took place gradually in the partners' relations with the Mitchell menage. Aaron's visits were no less recurring, but Enoch's became more frequent and regular. It was the only household in New Damascus in which he felt wholly at ease with himself and properly esteemed. He seldom went anywhere else. Very soon the women people were saying they knew what the attraction was. A certain expectation began to crystallize. Enoch became aware of it, not knowing how. Mitchell cultivated it adroitly. Since his offer to invest capital in the business of Gib and Breakspeare had been declined the idea of marrying Esther to one of the firm took possession of his thoughts. His preference was for Enoch because more securely through him than through Aaron would the Mitchell chariot be hitched to the star of iron. He talked of both of them to Esther, with an air of being impartial, as if giving her his intimate, unguarded impressions. As he understood women, their minds worked on these matters in a contrary manner. To disparage Aaron might be prejudicial to his ends. He never did that. Nevertheless, Enoch came off by every comparison as much the superior person. Esther listened attentively and said nothing.

"Do you ever think of getting married?" he asked her. "I sometimes wonder."

"No," she said. "I never have. Why do you ask it?"

"But you may," he said.

"Have you some one in view for me?" In her voice was a certain elusive tone, unresolved between doubt and irony, that he knew and hated. It made him uneasy. Sometimes it made him feel small.

"Seriously, I have," he replied. "That is to say, I have hoped you might become interested that way in Enoch Gib. You know what I think of him. He will be a great man in this country if nothing happens."

"Does it much concern your happiness?" she asked. There was that tone again.

"I wouldn't put it that way," he said. "I am thinking of your future. It would give me a sense of great comfort."

This was at dinner's end one evening when they were alone. As he talked, with his eyes down, he traced a figure on the table cloth with a spoon, making it deeper and deeper as his unease increased. He felt all the time that she was regarding him with a wide, impenetrable expression.

"Oh," she said, after an interval of silence.

He started and looked at her furtively. She was regarding him freely. There was in her expression the the trace of an ambigious, amused smile. He blushed and rose from the table.

Expectations increased. More marriages take place under the tyranny of expectation than Heaven imagines. New Damascus society became tensely expectant.

Enoch proposed, as Esther expected, with an air of bestowing himself where he was sure to be appreciated. She took some time about it and then accepted him.

Aaron was apparently the only person in New Damascus who had not foreseen it. He was deeply astonished. Why? It was not an improbable consummation. Yet it seemed to him strange and unnatural.

He first heard of it at dinner with the Mitchells. Enoch was present. Mitchell announced it as if Aaron were a large party of friends. He responded as such. There was a false note in his felicitations. He was aware of it; so was Esther. But in trying to cancel the impression he made it worse. Enoch was protected as by wool with a sense of proprietorship and self-satisfaction. Mitchell was insensitive.

Esther kept looking at Aaron. There was a troubled, startled expression in her eyes. He misread it for distaste. He had long imagined she disliked him. Several times that evening she was brief with him, almost curt, and this had never happened before.

His visits to the Mitchell house thereafter were formal and less frequent. Enoch's manner of making himself paramount affected him disagreeably. And Esther's behaviour perplexed him. She was at one time much more friendly than he expected and at another so deliberately indifferent that he could only conclude that she meant to estrange him.

Yet now a fatality began to operate. By a law of coincidence that we do not understand, and may not exist, they began to meet outside the household, purely, as it seemed in each case, by accident, —in unexpected places, on the street again and again, once at night in a crowd at an open air Punch and Judy show in which neither of them was at all interested, once in Philadelphia where he was transacting business and she was shopping with her maid, and once in a memorable way on a path through the woods to Throne Rock, a natural seat on the mountain summit from which the view of the valley was exciting.

It was a Sunday afternoon in early May. He was going; she was returning. They were at first surprised, then embarrassed, and became absurdly self-conscious. She wore a wide-brim hat, pulled down on both sides and tied under her chin. She was hot and tired; her color was high. Her dress was torn. He noticed it.

"I was after these," she said, catching his glance. She held out a bunch of dogwood blossoms, with a gesture to share them. He admired them and there was nothing else to say. So they stood, she looking at him and holding out the dogwood flowers. he looking fixedly at them, until her arm dropped and she turned to go on. He let her go and went his way up the path. But he looked back. She had stopped and was seated on a fallen tree trunk. He returned. She did not look up.

"I'd like to give you a farewell party," he said. "Will you come?"

"A farewell party?"

"There ought to be a better name for it," he said. "A sour grape party, then. I've always wanted to give you a dinner at the mansion. Will you come?"

"Yes," she said.

And again there was nothing else to say. She rose and he walked with her toward the town.

"If Enoch won't mind," he said.

"Why should he mind?" she asked.

"Perhaps he won't," said Aaron.

This thought, as to whether Enoch should mind, had far and separate projections in each of their minds and kept them silent until at the natural parting of their ways she turned to face him and held out her hand. It was a gesture of dismissal. He bowed and left her.

The dinner party took place just two weeks before her wedding day. It was perhaps too elaborate. It contained every preparable element of success. Aaron did his best to save it, and yet nobody enjoyed it. Esther was visibly depressed. Enoch sulked. The guests rallied them until it was seen to be hopeless and then let them alone. They simply could not react with gaiety.

Aaron as host had special rights in the guest of honor and took them. Enoch grew steadily worse. Opinion upon him was divided. Some thought it was the natural gloom of his nature and were full of foreboding for Esther. Others said they did believe the man was jealous.

After a dance Esther and Aaron walked on the terrace.

"Forgive me," she said. "I have spoiled the party."

"No," he said. "It's my fault. I knew better. Yet I couldn't resist it. And it is in a sense a farewell party."

"What does that mean?"

"After your wedding I may not see you again for a long time. I'm only waiting on Enoch's account. Then I shall be going to Europe for a year, perhaps more."

"On business?"

"Y-e-s," he answered slowly.

They took several more turns without speaking.

"What are your plans?" he asked.

"None that I know of," she said.

She had stopped. He saw that her gaze was directed at Enoch's ancestral iron-stone house below. The fitful glare of the blast furnaces, lower down, lighted its sombre nakedness and gave it a relentless, sinister aspect. The windows, which were small and unsoftened by copings, were like cruel, ferocious eyes in a powerful, short-haired, suspicious animal.

"Shall you live there?" he asked.

"Yes," she said, giving him a frowning, startled look, as if he had surprised her at a disadvantage. She added: "Enoch took me through it yesterday. The room where he was born, —that will be mine. The room where his father died is just as it was then. He thinks we shouldn't touch it."

She shivered. He asked her if she was cold. She wasn't, but on the next turn past the door she turned and they went in.

Enoch's idea of marriage was inherited. You take a wife from the church to the ancestral abode and become jointly responsible with God for her past, present, future and hereafter, for her body, her mind, her way with the neighbors, for everything about her save the separate flame of her individuality. That is vanity. The house is yours, therefore she must accept it. It was yours before she had any rights in it, therefore she must get used to it, as she must get used to you. And why not? If Aaron married would he not take his wife to the Woolwine Mansion just as it was? Well, what was Aaron's was like Aaron and what was Enoch's was like Enoch, and what a woman married was what she got.

Enoch rode home with Esther that night in her father's carriage. Mitchell had gone home earlier and sent the carriage back. As they were passing the ironstone house-fatally then-Enoch asked:

"What do you and Aaron find to talk about?"

"Nothing," she said.

That was literally the truth. It was with extreme difficulty that they found anything to say to each other. Never had they carried on an intimate, self-revealing conversation. There was too much constraint on both sides. But Enoch could hardly believe that Aaron was under any circumstances inarticulate, like himself. Or was it that he knew instinctively if what Esther said was true there lay in that very truth a deep significance?

Her answer made him seethingly angry. An ungovernable feeling rose up in him spirally. It was as an adder stinging him in the dark. He could not seize it, for he knew not what or where it was. He could not escape from it. The pain was horrible.

Esther knew nothing of these violent emotions. She had no more intuition of him than he had of her. That sense by which natures attuned exchange thoughts without words was impossible between them. Between Esther and Aaron it already existed: it always had. But it was unacknowledged.

Enoch passed three days without seeing Esther, hoping she might send for him. On the fourth day he went to dinner and she treated him as if nothing were the matter. She hardly knew there was. That made it much worse. Then he flourished the wound by pretending heroically to conceal it. That method will work only provided the woman cares and loves the child in her man. Esther did not care. She refused to discover the hurt. The man's last recourse is to injure the woman, to ease himself by hurting her. Enoch became oppressive. He began to mention the things that should be rendered unto Cassar, categorically, gratuitously; he revealed the laws of Gib; he appointed how the concavities of her life should correspond to the convexities of his; he spoke of penalties, forfeits and consequences, and of the ancient legal principle that ignorance of the statutes is no defence provided the statutes have been duly published. She listened with wide-open eyes. He believed he inspired her with admiration for the stern stuff he was made of, and thus blindly sought his fate.

So his hurt was revenged but in no wise healed.

On the eve of their wedding day, at dinner, Aaron's name was pronounced. The invisible circumstances were tragic. Enoch happened at that instant to be regarding Esther with a sensation that was new to him and very disturbing. He knew not what to do with it. Suddenly he had been seized with a great longing for her, a yearning of the heart toward the fact of her being that was savage, tender and desolate. He wondered that Esther and her father both were not aware of this singular and dramatic occurrence. It shock him like an earth tremor. An impulse to speak, to shout, to cry out words of fantastic meaning, to rise and touch her, became almost uncontrollable, —almost. It occurred to him for the first time, like a blow, that he had never discovered her nature, her true self. He had not tried. The importance of doing so, the possibility of it, had not been thought of. But he would. He would begin all over again to get acquainted with her.

In that moment he loved her.

And it was then, —just then, —that he heard the sound of Aaron's name. He could not say which one of them uttered it. The sound was all he knew. Instantly the hideous, stinging adder upraised from his depths and began striking at the walls of his breast. Vividly, steroptically, as a series of pictures, there flashed across his mental vision every situation in which he had seen Aaron and Esther together.

He had been able to control the impulse of love to vent its untimely ecstasy; his rage he could not govern.

To Esther's and her father's amazement he began, with no apparent provocation whatever, to utter against Aaron defamations of an extreme and irrevocable character. His manner contradicted the violence of his feelings. It was self-possessed, one would almost say restrained; that was his way under stress of emotional excitement. At no point did he become incoherent. His words were chilled and came to him easily. One might have thought he was thinking out loud, very earnestly, in solitude. On his face was that singular Gib expression, never witnessed before in the Mitchell household, —the mouth contortion one mistook for a smile. So far as Esther and Mitchell could see the performance was gratuitous and premeditated. It had gone far before they realized that his state was one of passion. But that discovery had no mitigating value. They made no effort to stop him. He spoke of things that are supposed to be unmentionable, and of his private intentions, and closed abruptly with the declaration that Aaron should never be received in his house as a guest.

"Let that be understood," he said to Esther. Then he rose from the table and departed.

Mitchell was stupefied. He looked slowly at Esther. Her face was a perfect mask.

"Do you know what it means?" he asked.

"Yes," she said.

"What? What?"

"It's the only way Mr. Gib has of paying your daughter a compliment," she said.

And now Bruno Mitchell suffered another shock. For the first time in her life Esther rose from the table and left him there.

She went to her room, sent her maid to bed, and sat for a long time perfectly still, at the core of a maelstrom, her emotions whirling and seething around her. They were her emotions. She recognized them as such. Only, they were outside of her. This had always been true. Even before she understood what it meant her mother, a stoic, began to say: "Don't give way to your feelings. They will swallow you up. Watch them. If you can see them they cannot hurt you." So she had watched them fearfully. To do that she had to put them outside. She had seen them grow, change and rise until they engulfed her, and then the only way she could save herself was to give them that whirling motion, which caused them to incline from her, as the waters of the whirlpool incline from the center. But it was harder and harder to keep them whirling and she dared not stop, for if she did they would swallow her up.

The spectacle became awesome and fascinating, as a maelstrom is, and there were moments when the perverse impulse to stop, surrender, cast herself headlong away, was almost irresistible. She thought of this as equivalent to suicide. And she had for a long time secretly supposed it would ultimately happen. Now she was terrified and thrilled by a premonition that it was imminent. Never had the waters been so mad, so giddy, so nearly ungovernable, so excitingly desirable.

That is all she was thinking of, —if it may be called thinking, —as she started up, drew on walking boots, took a shawl and descended the stairs. In the hallway she met her father. He looked at her with surprise.

"Are you going out?"

"For a walk," she said.

"But Esther!... at this hour... alone. I —"

"Yes," she said, waiting. "Do you forbid it?"

There was a note in her voice he had never heard before. She wished him to say yes, he forbade it. That was why she asked the question. And if he had said that the whirling flood would have collapsed at once. That again was all she was thinking. It was a wild, liberating thought. But instead he took a step toward her and scrutinized her face.

"Esther, what has happened to you?"

"On the eve of my wedding, for the first and last time, for an hour perhaps, I shall be Esther herself, alone," she said.

Since the unprecedented uproar of the inclined waters had begun an hour before she had not once thought of her wedding. The word of it, as now it came to her lips, seemed strange and fantastic, and yet she had made no resolve against it.

Her father stood aside and she passed out.

Half an hour later the knocker sounded and Mitchell himself went to the door, expecting to receive Esther. There was Enoch. He asked to see her.

"She has gone for a walk," said Mitchell. "Won't you come in and wait? She can't be long returning."

Enoch hesitated and turned away, saying he might have the good luck to meet her.

He had come to mend the impression he was conscious of having left behind him. At least that was the ostensible reason. That was what he would have said. The fact was that the adder had suddenly slunk away, and once more came that feeling for Esther which was so new and ir-rational and caused his heart to stagger back and forth. It was stronger than before, —stronger than pride. He could scarcely breathe for the ache of wanting to see her again that night....

Esther turned first toward the river path, changed her direction aimlessly, walked for some distance toward the limestone quarry, then suddenly swung around, passed the blast furnaces, and presently, only her feet aware of how they came there, she was high on the mountain path to Throne Rock. She had been walking too fast. Her breath began to fail. She sat on a log to rest. The moon came up. The log was the same fallen tree trunk on which she sat with her dogwood flowers the day Aaron turned round, came back, and invited her to a farewell dinner party. She knew it all the time. The scene restored itself, with all the feelings it had evoked, and she did not push them back. They detached themselves from the whirling mass and touched her. There was a moment in which she could not remember anything that had happened since; and in that moment, as an integral part of it, the figure of Aaron appeared, walking toward her from above, exactly as before.

She sat so still he might almost have passed her. He did not start. For a long time he stood looking at her. She did not move. He could not see her face. Then without speaking he sat beside her, at a little distance, on the log. The tree frogs informed on one another —*peep-ing* —*peep-ing*. A dry twig falling made a crashing sound. Far away below, at regular intervals, shrill whistle blasts denoted stages in the ring of smelting alchemies.

Aaron spoke.

"What day is tomorrow?"

"I don't know," said Esther.

They were silent until the whistle blew again.

"At ten o'clock," said Aaron.

"At ten o'clock," said Esther.

The exchange of wordless thoughts went on and on, and Aaron was expecting what she said.

"I do not love him."

"He loves you," said Aaron.

"Does that so much oblige the woman?" Esther asked.

"The woman is obliged," he said, "she is... unless — —" He stopped.

"Aaron," she said, "tell me this. How do friends regard each other's wives and sweethearts?"

"Sweethearts almost the same as wives," he said.

"So that if one loved the sweetheart of a friend he could not tell her that?"

"No, he could not."

"Not even if he knew the sweetheart did not love the friend?"

"No," said Aaron.

"Then should the woman tell?"

"Tell whom?" asked Aaron, trembling.

"The friend... the other man," said Esther.

Aaron slowly dropped his head between his hands. She could feel his body shake. A roaring blackness filled her eyes. She rose and would have gone, but he enfolded her, with arms that touched her lightly, almost not at all at first, then tightened, tightened, tightened, until her life was crushed to his, and all the waters fell.

He put her off at arm's length to see her better.

"Through all consequences... forever... to finality," he said.

And she was satisfied.

How long they stood so, either thus or as it was, gazing one upon the other, with no words to say, —how long they never knew. A sound of footsteps very near broke their ecstasy, and there stood Enoch.

They had no sense of guilt. They were shy and startled from the shock of coming back to earth.

Enoch stood there looking at them. Aaron moved, drawing Esther's form behind him.

At that Enoch turned away and laughed.

Twenty paces on his way he laughed again.

When he was out of sight he laughed.

At intervals all the way down the mountain he stopped to laugh.

The sound of his laughter reverberated, echoed, swirled, went and returned, filled the whole valley, blasting the night. Then when he was far off he uttered a piercing scream. It rose on the air like a rocket, hissed, burst with a soft splash and pitched off into space, and the world for a moment was deathly still. The tree frogs were the first to recover and began frantically to fill up the void.

Aaron touched Esther. They descended. She inquired of him nothing; he informed her of nothing. They did not speak again for hours. They walked to the Woolwine mansion. He called for horses, a light vehicle, and wraps. And all that night they drove, past the setting moon, into the darkness, through the dawn, toward Wilkes-Barre.

Next day at noon they were married.

VII

The partnership of Gib and Breakspeare was sundered.

Two weeks later, when Aaron returned to the little red office building across the road from the mill, he found on his desk a paper marked "Articles of Dissolution." Attached was a note of two lines from Enoch, saying: "Let any changes proposed to be made herein appear in the form of writing, or through an attorney at law."

They never spoke again.

The articles prepared by Enoch provided that the ore and coal lands, which had been pooled on a royalty basis, should release from that agreement and revert to their respective owners; that the eight blast furnaces should be divided equally, four and four; that Gib should buy from Breakspeare, for cash, his interest in the rolling mill, because it could not be divided, the price to be one-half the original cost, according to the books, and that all the money in the firm's treasury, less current liabilities, should be halved on the date of signature.

Aaron read the paper once through, put it down and signed it. The terms were unfair. Yet he had no impulse to change them. They were unfair because nothing was made of those two intangible assets which sometimes in business are worth more than the physical properties-namely, spirit of organization and good will of trade-all of which would automatically belong to the one who bought out the other's interest in the mill. This was so because the mill was now the crown of the business. What the firm sold was no longer pig iron, as at first, but wrought iron in standard bars manufactured from the pig by remelting, kneading, hammering and rolling it. The product of the blast furnaces, instead of going to market, only fed the mill.

What would Aaron do?

He could not sell the product of his blast furnaces to Enoch. Business transactions between them were unimaginable; besides, no sooner were the articles of dissolution signed than Enoch went about building four more blast furnaces of his own. That was to make himself independent of Aaron's product. Aaron, therefore, might choose between seeking a market outside for his pig iron or building a mill to work it. To build a mill would require, first, a large outlay of capital, then an organization of expert workers and superintendents, and thirdly a market for his wrought iron in competition with the product of the established mill, now Enoch's. For of course Enoch's iron would continue to be called Damascus Iron, which was its trade name, and it was already famous in the country for its fine texture and purity. Aaron's might be just as good, but it would have to take a new name and earn its own good will.

Well, but what he did was unexpected. He drew the fires from his blast furnaces and went to Europe with Esther.

It was more than a honeymoon, or less, as you may happen to think. In Aaron's case romance and work were easily combined, for as love is an adventure of the spirit, so to a man of his temperament work is a romantic enterprise of the mind and creative in a manner less wonderful than the mysterious life process only because we take it for granted. What is an engine? a steamship? a blast furnace? a tower? It is the materialization in form and function of an idea itself imponderable. It is the psychic power of man exteriorized in substance and there is no accounting for such phenomena save that it happens. Who knows but the Gods are as much puzzled by that form of glow worm full of parasites that we call a railroad train as we are by the things of cosmic origin?

Specifically Aaron was in quest of a secret that had eluded and baffled iron masters always. They were sure it existed. That certainty was deducible from the data of knowledge. Many times they had almost touched it; then it was lost again, like a coy, tantalizing vision of loveliness, and the pursuers were discouraged. Still, they never gave up. Whoever found it would be made exceedingly rich and the iron industry at the same time would be revolutionized.

It is to be explained.

Everybody probably knows that in the first place all the iron was trapped in the blazing heart of the earth. It forms no part anywhere of the earth's true granite crust. But it was rebellious and indigestible and had to be spewed up from the inflamed Plutonic belly through the tops of volcanoes. At that time volcanoes were near or under water generally, and when the molten iron came jetting forth in red lava streams a spectacular melodrama was enacted. Water was its adverse element. At the lava's touch the oceans boiled, hissed, upheaved and draped themselves in steam. They were not hurt really; they were outraged.

What happened to the lava?

The water shivered it to atoms and cast it high upon the wind as dust and ashes.

In that free and irresponsible condition iron travelled far, made his bed in many places, took up with new and strange affinities, —the flapper sisters Chlorine, the Sulphur Gerties, the lazy Nitrate Susans, the harmless Silicates, a score of others known and unknown, and most of all with a comfortable, indispensable element called Oxygen. The extent and variety of his embracings may be imagined from the fact that he is never found in a state of unattached purity save now and then when he falls from the heavens as a meteorite. In these haphazard, bigamous earthly alliances he is of no avail to man. The problem is how to disentangle him, —how to divorce him from his undesirable affinities and wed him durably and in a lawful manner to those elements which supplement his power.

It becomes extremely complicated when you begin seriously to consider it. How shall one be divorced from many miscellaneous affinities? You have to have been regularly wedded in order to get divorced. Well, the only way is the long, pragmatic way. You wed him to the affinities that are to be legally got rid of and then divorce him from them.

Now take it: The iron ore is in the ore bed, embracing those other elements at random, particularly Oxygen. First you oxidize him by roasting. That is, you wed him to Oxygen; you give him Oxygen until he is sick of it. Then you melt him down with coal in a furnace to deoxidize him-to divorce him, that is to say, from his affinity Oxygen. It is the first fiery ordeal. But at the same time you wed him to Carbon. Thus deoxidized and carbonized, divorced and wedded by one stroke, he becomes pig iron.

The wedding with Carbon, however, is not permanent. It has been contracted so to speak under duress, a miserable makeshift, because his earthly nature is such that he must be wedded to something all the time. Besides, there is now too much Carbon 'for his own good. So you melt him again and divorce him from Carbon, by the unexpected method of blowing Oxygen through him. At the end of this second ordeal he is free of both Carbon and Oxygen, many other elements have disappeared also, and you have wrought iron, practically pure, limp and malleable.

Now suppose you want to make him hard. You want to convert him into steel. In that case you melt him a third time and wed him permanently to a small amount of Carbon, more or less, the amount to be governed by the degree of hardness required. That makes steel. But to make it has required one roasting and three meltings.

The dream of the iron masters, beginning with the

19th century, was to make it all one continuous, fluid process, and bring the complete result to pass at one melting. If that could be done the cost of production would be enormously reduced.

The discovery of such a method now seemed imminent in either England or Germany. Many experts were pressing on the door. Suddenly it would fly open and whoever was there at the moment would be able to seize the secret. Rumors of success had been heard, disbelieved, denied, scoffed at and repeated. Aaron believed them, or believed at least that if the secret had not already been captured it was about to be. That was his quest in Europe.

After a year he returned with a steel making patent, enormous quantities of queer looking material, a crew of expert English erectors, and proceeded to build what the curious Damascenes called a concern. That word was in lieu of a proper name for an object which, without being supernatural, was unique on earth. In shape it somewhat resembled a gigantic snail shell, in a vertical position, open end up, thirty feet high, made of iron plates bolted together, lined with fire clay and so mounted at its axis that it could be tipped to spill its contents. On the same foundation was mounted a blowing engine to force air at high pressure through perforations in the bottom of the shell; and there was also a great ladle in chains for hoisting molten metal to its mouth.

The work of construction was slow and tedious; it came several times to a full stop for want of something that had not been provided beforehand and could not be made on the spot. Nearly another year passed.

Then one day smoke appeared at the top of one of Aaron's four blast furnaces and people by this sign were notified that the great experiment was about to begin. In a general way the population knew, from what the workers said, that the intention was to produce steel and to produce it direct from the ore, and also that if such a thing were possible the iron industry would undergo a basic transformation.

All of that was exciting and very important, especially to a town like New Damascus, whose living was in iron. Yet it was no technical interest in a metallurgical process that moved people to gather in large numbers to witness the experiment. What they sensed was its human meaning. It symbolized a struggle between the former partners. The outcome might deeply affect the economic position of New Damascus in the course of time. Immediately it had tense dramatic value. It would prove which was the greater man and which was right, —Aaron who believed steel cheaply produced in large quantities by a continuous one-melt process would supersede iron and bring a new age to pass, or Enoch who scoffed, who was known privately to have predicted Aaron's ruin, and who held that to think of getting steel direct from ore in that manner, skipping the iron stage, was as absurd as to think of getting a grandson from a grandfather, skipping the father. It was contrary to the way of nature.

All the iron wisdom of the community was with Enoch. All the inert scepticism with which people behold the trial of a new thing was on his side. But the heart was for Aaron. Everybody liked him still, as in the old days, and ardently wished him success. Besides, if he brought it off, Enoch Gib would be humbled. His tyrannical ways were increasingly complained of. New Damascus would rather be a steel town under Aaron than an iron town under Enoch.

With the outcome in suspense, the experiment itself was worth seeing as a spectacle. Nothing like it could have been imagined.

First, that strange, enormous tilting vessel, resembling a snail shell, was filled with fuel and fired under blast from the blowing engine until its clay-lined interior was white hot. Then it was tilted on its axis, emptied and tilted back again. Next the molten iron from the blast furnace, instead of being run off in the sand to make the sow the pigs devour, was tapped into that great ladle in chains, hoisted on high, and poured into the white hot gullet of the tilting vessel. At the same time the blowing engine to force air through the perforations in the bottom was set in fast motion with a terrible roar. A blast of air at high pressure began now to pass upward through the fluid metal.

A series of awesome pyrotechnics ensued.

In the belly of the tilting vessel occurred a dry, chortling sound, followed by a dull, regular clapping, as of Plutonic amusement and applause. From the mouth of the vessel issued millions of sparks, particles burning brilliantly in the air. This went on for seven or eight minutes. Suddenly the sparks went out and a dull, sluggish red flame appeared, turning bright and yellowish, then becoming high, brilliant and dart-like. After several minutes terrific detonations began to take place in the vessel. With each detonation the flame shot higher. This uproar was succeeded by a period of calm. The yellowish, dart-like flame rising from the throat of the vessel was replaced by a long, white flame, which stood for several seconds proudly, then trembled, tore at the edges and abruptly collapsed. Dense black smoke issued from the mouth of the crater and the scene was dark. This was the moment at which the metal itself began to burn. The workers, uttering shrill cries of anxiety, readiness, encouragement and damnation, seized the levers controlling the vessel and tilted it over to a spilling position. Through the black smoke that corked its throat burst the fluid, blazing metal, hissing like a tortured serpent, alive in every incandescent crystal, yet doomed quickly to cool and blacken, every element touching it being fatally adverse. Men in waiting caught it headfirst neatly into a trundle pot and wheeled it off to be decanted into sand molds, like pig iron molds, but smaller.

The experiment was finished. The test was yet to come. That waited on the cooling. What was in those molds? Those squarish lumps blackening in the sand, —what would they turn out to be? No one knew.

Aaron waited until one was cool enough to handle. Then placing it like a stick of kindling against the chopping block, he hit it one blow in the middle with a sledge hammer. It broke with an ironic, ringing sound and lay in two pieces apart. He never stooped to pick them up. Without a word he dropped the hammer and walked away.

Esther received him on the terrace. She had been there for hours, anxiously watching the spectacle from afar, then waiting for him to come and tell her what the outcome was. But he did not have to tell her. She knew by his look, by his walk, by the way he took her arm. They sat for some time in silence.

"It beats me," he said. "I can't explain it. I don't know what happened."

"What was it like?" she asked. "The product I mean-was it iron or steel?"

"Pot metal," he said contemptuously.

For a long time they stood there on the terrace looking their thoughts into space. Hers were personal. His were not. This she knew. There is probably no sense of loneliness so poignant as that which a woman feels when the idol of her being disembodies his soul and departs with it, leaving in her hands the fact of his empty presence. Lacking in herself his power of abstraction she cannot understand this phenomenon. But she verifies it and it fills her with terror. The form is there at her side, even in her arms, as it was a moment before. The man is gone. She has no idea where he is or what he is doing.

"Aaron!"

Esther whispered his name as one who dreads to wake the sleeper and yet cannot forbear to do so. Impulsively she buried her face beneath his arm as if she would enter the vacant premises. He laid his arm around her shoulder. It was an absent gesture. She had not waked him quite.

"Aaron!" she called again. "What does it matter? Come back to me."

At that he started slightly and began to talk in a slow, far-away manner, very much as he had talked to Enoch that moonlight night after the birthday party when the idea of making New Damascus an iron town had suddenly crystallized in his mind. Esther, loving the mere sound of his voice, did not at first get the sense of his speech. He was saying:

"Out there in unlimited space are the unborn...."

These were the first words she understood. They thrilled her. She was almost faint with an ecstasy that ran through her fibre up and down. "So," she thought, "it was that." And she had been thinking he was far away. Now she listened tensely. He went on:

"...Millions, infinite millions, clamoring to get born, perhaps dying because they cannot cross. Here is life on this side. There, out there, is but the hope of it."

"Cross what?" asked Esther, awesomely. "You speak as if you were gazing at it."

"Between life that is and life unborn I see the primal chasm," he said. "We who live have crossed. We do not remember how. The number that can cross is small. You cannot imagine how small it is. Only one in millions has the luck to get across. The rest are crowded on the edge, weeping, reaching out their hands, silently imploring us to get them over.

They struggle, overwhelm themselves and fall into the void like a cataract."

"Why is that?" asked Esther.

"Because the number that can cross is limited by the preparations of the living," Aaron answered. "The living are selfish and forgetful. All this I see as it has been for ages, as now it is, and as it shall be. Always it has been as it is on the other side-that infinite, voiceless, despairing multitude pressing down to the brink of the void. Here in the world of the living there has been some change. We have the power of preparation. How pitiably we have exercised it! I'll tell you all that has ever happened. Long ago, before he began by imagination to extend his faculties, man was like the other animals. He had only his hands and legs, his sheer brute strength, to work with. He housed himself in holes and caves and ate what the untilled earth set forth. You must imagine then across that primal chasm a chain of human bodies, a living monkey bridge, by which the unborn came to life most dangerously. How few they were! And yet, if more had come just then they would have starved, —died here instead of there, —because the means did not exist to house and clothe and feed them. It is man's business not only to bridge the chasm; he must also beforehand prepare the world for those who cross. Come ten thousand years through time this way. Now see him beginning to till the soil. See him building huts. More life may be sustained. Above the void a swaying bridge of sticks. More may safely get across. And yet so very few I Another thousand years. Enter historic man. He builds him cities and fine temples and there is a narrow stone arch to span the void. The bridge, as you will note, is at any time of that material in which mankind is working. This is better. The unborn begin to rush across. But, alas! the case is worse than ever. Many now are born that never will be fed. Why?

"Imagine the world at this time in panorama. There are cities, noble cities walled about; but they are few and very far apart, and the world at large is still an untilled waste. Tillage is in small adjacent areas, and when the produce of those areas is not enough the people in the cities starve. Further away are vast fertile plains uncultivated. They are of no use because food cannot be transported thousands of miles in great quantities. The art of transportation is undiscovered. Hence frightful famines on the bounteous earth. Then in his imagination man finds a ship. That makes it possible to transport food long distances, and yet the world is hardly touched. Life is increaseable only on the rim of the sea and in the valleys of rivers. An inland city is impossible.

"At length the iron age. It is our time. By mechanical means man has enormously increased his power to prepare the world for that infinite multitude unborn. It is tremendously excited-the voiceless, spectral multitude. It presses more wildly toward the void. An iron bridge has replaced the stone arch. It is a sign that many more may come. Now with railroads it is possible to bring food quickly from afar. No fertile area of the earth is inaccessible. Inland cities may begin to rise. More life in more ways can be sustained than ever before. Nevertheless, the iron bridge is a premature sign. The material is defective. It is not hard enough to bear the strain of that host pressing upon life. Besides, by no process yet discovered can it be made fast enough.

"And I see what has not yet happened. I see whole cities built higher than the tower of Babel. Those are steel buildings, sheathed with brick and stone. Brick and stone upon mortar would not stand so high. To serve but one of these cities, —to bring its food and take away its manufactures, —I see a thousand railroad trains, —trains of steel running on rails of steel. Compared with these the iron shod trains we know and think so marvellous are merely toys. I see ships of steel so vast in size that on the side of one the little vessel in which Columbus found a new world would swing like a silly skiff. I see steel in all its power-towers, tunnels, aqueducts, fantastic structures I cannot sense the meaning of. I see miles of smoking chimneys where steel is made for all these uses in unimaginable quantities. And spanning the prismal chasm I see a series of great steel bridges, multiplying as I look, seeming to cast themselves in air across the void like cobwebs. But reflect! We have not yet discovered the way to make this steel. Unless we find it quickly we shall fail that unborn host. It cannot get across; if it did it could not live. The iron bridge cannot bear its weight. Nor can the world be prepared with iron. These things of iron are premature, too soft, too slowly made, not big enough. Now do you know what it is we seek?"

"Forgive me. I did not mean to speak lightly of it," Esther said. "None of this had been revealed to me."

"Nor to me," said Aaron. "Not clearly until this instant. Man works mostly in the dark, without knowing what he seeks or why...."

They repeated the experiment many times, never with precisely the same technical result, though always with the same disappointment. The metal they got was worthless. It was neither iron nor steel. The process was true. It remarkably foreshadowed the Bessemer process which some years later did achieve the result, revolutionize the industry and cause steel to overlap iron. It failed in Aaron's hands for want of skill and chemical knowledge. The elements are not passive. They are wilful and rebellious. In their efforts to thwart man's designs upon them they become cunning and clannish. One helps the other to escape. With this same mechanical equipment steel workers of a later time would have been able to make a perfect steel. They would have known how at a certain stage of the process to cast into the fiery, detonating mass a handful of some tame, cajoling substance, and then the exact instant at which to stop the air blast and tilt the vessel to a spilling position.

Aaron was discouraged but not despairing. Half his fortune was gone. Still, it was not an irretrievable disaster.

To hold his organization together he built a small rolling mill. He called it the Blue Jay. The site on which it stood may still be seen in New Damascus after all these years. Nothing else has ever occupied it. The mill was large enough to keep two blast furnaces going, —that is, it absorbed their output of pig iron. This was merely to fill a gap. He was bent upon steel. Having opened the mill and having found a market for all the Blue Jay iron it could make, again he took Esther and went to Europe on the same quest as before.

While they were abroad a son was born. They named him John.

On the homeward voyage Esther died and was buried at sea. The waters at last did swallow her up.

Aaron returned to New Damascus with a new steel making patent, an infant and an empty heart.

What there was in the patent nobody ever knew. He did nothing with it. The whole steel adventure was too intimately associated with memories of Esther. To succeed without her would be worse than to fail. He could not think of it. There was very little in this world he could think of. He could not bear living in the mansion without her. He closed it and went to live at the inn with his child and nurse. Then presently he could not bear living in New Damascus without her. People said it was the state of his fortunes that made him morose. He had meant to retrieve his fortunes with Esther standing by. Now he neglected business, caring nothing about it, until one day he came awake to the fact that even so little business as it takes to support a lone man and child will not attend to itself. He had to do something. But he could not do it there.

One day he dismantled the mill, loaded it in a canal boat, abandoned the irremovable blast furnaces, took his child in his arms and disappeared.

The Blue Jay Rolling Mill became famous not for its output but for its migrations. He set it up in Scranton, then moved it to Pittsburgh. It was next reported in Texas and after that in Colorado. Then he ceased to be heard of, except once, when the old Woolwine Mansion was sold to a Roman Catholic order.

So he vanished from the light of New Damascus, with his steel patent, his grief and the fourth generation in swaddling cloths, —vanished away on a flying iron mill.

VIII

Meanwhile what of Enoch? He prospered in power and wealth and his soul turned black. From his birth he had been cruel, legal, injurious. The tragedy of Esther's elopement left a horrible sting in his face for everyone to see. After that he became, as the Damascenes said, unnatural. In that word they characterized and judged his conduct; they never understood it. They could not say in what his unnaturalness consisted. His acts were not unnatural as acts in themselves, nor in contrast, sum or degree. They were unnatural because they were his. He disbelieved in friendship; he knew it not and doubted its existence. He disbelieved in love, too, though not for the same reason.

Esther he had loved.

A man mortally hurt in love may do almost anything naturally. He is sick prey for the cuckoo woman willing to lay her egg in another's nest. She has only to touch him with her fingers softly and hold her tongue, but to make a soothing, mothering sound, and he will impale himself without looking.

But Jonet, daughter of Gearhard the blacksmith, was not that kind of woman. She could not have made that sound. And it seemed somehow unnatural that Enoch should marry her. No sound that was in him could imaginably vibrate in her. According to the local notion the girl was queer. Men let her alone because she made them vaguely uneasy. Her phantasies were of the primeval outdoors. She was sometimes seen in the deep woods by herself, dancing and singing as if she were not alone. She named the trees and conversed with non-existent objects. Her hair was black. Her eyes were brown and glistened. Her face was the color of iron at cherry-red heat and she had the odor of a wild thing. Enoch married her out of hand. There was no courtship. Then he proceeded to build a mansion on the west hill larger and more ostentatiously ugly than the Woolwine Mansion on the east hill. Some said, "Ah-ha! He has learned his lesson. No woman would live in that gloomy iron stone house." Others said he did it neither in wisdom nor in love of Jonet, but to spite Bruno Mitchell, who, though he was blameless of anything that had happened, was yet Esther's father.

A peculiarity of the Gib mansion was much talked of at the time. It was built on a twin principle, —that is, in halves, separated only by an imaginary bisecting line. Each half was as like the other as the right hand is like the left. There were two portals exactly alike, two halls, two parlons, two grand stairways, two kitchens, everything in parallel duplication until it came to the enormous solarium, which was a glass court between the two parts, the imaginary line cutting through the fountain in the center. The Philadelphia architect supposed there were two families. When he discovered it was all for one man and one wife not yet long enough married to have children he could not conceal his wonder.

"Well, why not?" said Enoch. "Haven't you two lungs, two kidneys, two ears? One of each would do."

The idea may have been thus derived from a principle of insurance through pairing which nature has evolved. It may have been. Nevertheless in time the imaginary dividing line became real. It was painted through the middle of the solarium. Jonet lived on one side and he on the other and there was no going to and fro, —not for Jonet. Agnes, their daughter, was brought to his side by the nurses until she was big enough to walk. She could cross the line as she pleased. But generally she had to be coaxed or bribed to cross to Enoch's side and was always anxious to cross back.

Between Enoch and Mitchell the subject of Esther was never mentioned, not even at first. For a while they went on as if nothing had happened. Gradually Mitchell became aware that Enoch was putting pressure upon him, silently, deliberately. He made harder and harder terms for the banker's services, until Mitchell's profit in the relationship was destroyed, and when this fact was pointed out to Enoch he suggested a simple remedy, which was that the relationship should discontinue. As Mitchell seemed disinclined to act on this suggestion Enoch at length invited a

Wilkes-Barre man to come and open a bank in New Damascus. Enoch himself provided most of the capital. The town's business went to the new bank naturally. It was

Gib's bank and Gib was a man to be propitiated in the community. Moreover, his turning from Mitchell caused Mitchell's bank to be regarded with a tinge of doubt. Thus Mitchell's hope in the star of iron miserably perished. His bank withered up. His years becoming heavy he returned to New England to die.

The saying was that Enoch broke him. It would have been quite as easy to say that Mitchell broke himself upon Enoch. Yet in putting it the other way people implied a certain subtle truth wherein lay the difference between Enoch Gib and other men, —the fact of his being unnatural. His feeling toward Mitchell was natural. Anyone could understand that. It was a feeling transferred from Esther to her father. Because he loved Esther he could not hate her as much as his hurt required; therefore he hated her father more. But where another man would have manifested this feeling in some overt, unmistakable manner, Enoch so concealed it that for a long time Mitchell did not suspect its existence. And when he was aware of it, then it was too late. If Enoch had committed upon him some definite act of unreason that would have seemed natural. Instead, he exerted against him a kind of slow, deadly hydraulic pressure. Nor was that all. Revenge may require the infliction of a protracted remorseless torture. Even that one may understand. But Gib, while exerting this killing pressure, apparently had no more feeling about it than one would have about an automatic, self-recording test for torsonial strength applied to a piece of iron, knowing that ultimately it was bound to break. If he had enjoyed it, if he had seemed to derive malicious satisfaction from the sequel, that would have made it human.

Yet here was a man but bearing witness for the child. The trait of character which appeared in his locked arm game with Aaron, in their boyhood, when it was Aaron's arm that broke, now fulfilled itself. There was in him a strange passion for trying the strength of materials. He invented various mechanical devices for that purpose. He knew to an ounce what iron would stand under every kind of strain. He knew what it took to crush a brick. Apparently his first thought on looking at anything was, "What is its breaking point?" The only way to find out was to break it. And people to him were like any other kind of material. He had the same curiosity about them. What could they stand without breaking? As in human material the utmost point of resistance is a variable factor he had to find it over and over. It is by no means certain that the mood in which he exercised this passion was deliberately destructive. That the final point of resistance is coincident with the point of destruction probably never once occurred to him as a tragic fact.

He might have said of people that in any case they were free to decline the test. They were not obliged to measure their strength with his. Yet they did it and they did it as if they could not help doing it. Here was a strange matter.

For example, how did he hold his iron workers? They hated him. They cursed him. Their injuries were as open sores that would not heal. Take the case of McAntee. It was typical. Tom McAntee was one of the best puddlers in the world. On a very hot day at the puddling furnace, in the midst of a heat, with six hundred weight of good iron bubbling like gravy, turning waxy and almost ready to be drawn, Tom dropped the beater he was working it with, wobbled a bit, put his hand to his head, and said he guessed he'd have to knock off and go home. Enoch, who watched every heat, was standing there. He called Tom's assistant to take up the beater and then without a word he handed Tom a blue ticket. The significance of the blue ticket was this: A man in Gib's mill had three chances with failure, —that is, he was entitled to three dismissals. The first was a yellow ticket. That was a rebuke. After three days he could come back to his job. The second dismissal was with a red ticket. That was a warning. It meant two weeks off. Then he might try again. But the third time it was a blue ticket, and that was final. He could never come back. So McAntee was fired for good, and this was without precedent under the rules because that was the first ticket he had ever got. The next day Enoch sent a clerk to McAntee's house with Tom's wages. A widow received them. Tom was dead.

The man who picked up Tom's beater and went on with the heat that day, all the men of the puddling and heating crews, every man in the mill, even the miners back in the mountains, — they were all white with rage and horror, yet not one of them fumbled a stroke of labor, or quit, or thought of quitting. The effect of this incident, in fact, was to lift the breaking point through the whole organization. Those who had already had yellow and red tickets went on for years and died without ever getting a blue one. Many were dismissed. Almost never did a man quit. Why? Because, more than anything else in the world they feared Enoch Gib's contempt for the man who broke. They could stand his cruelty; they could not bear his scorn. Also, in a strange way, the men themselves shared his contempt for the one who broke. They would not acknowledge it; they tried hard to conceal it. Yet a man could not quit without feeling inferior, not only in the sight of the tyrant but in the eyes of his fellow workers.

The demon who ruled them had no breaking point. Continuously day and night he walked among them like a principle of evil, calling to a spirit of demonry within them, —a spirit that racked their bodies, scared their souls, and responded in spite of their reason. A maddened hand would sometimes be raised against him. He never flinched. He was derisive. The hand would drop. He never gave a man a ticket for that.

Brains were another problem. He treated it separately, though in the same way and with the same consequences. Any inquisitive young man wishing to learn the iron business could begin at the bottom. He might begin in the mill and work toward the office or begin in the office and work toward the mill. He was sure to move fast in either direction. If he survived the ruthless selection that took place on the lower rungs of the ladder he could count on gaining a small partnership in a few years. An interest of two or three per cent. in the business was more stimulating than wages. As the business grew the number of junior partners increased. There might be six or eight at a time, all trying to keep pace with Enoch. They emerged from the flux like a procession of sparks, burned brightly for a little while and fell in darkness. He used them up and bought them out.

In time the town of New Damascus, like the yard of his mill, was littered with things Enoch Gib had strained to the breaking point. Some, like Tom Mc-Antee, were decently covered up in the cemetery. Others were aimlessly walking about. Conspicuous among these were the used up partners. They all had nice houses and plenty to live on. The business was profitable. But they were withered and rickety, older than old Enoch in the midst of their years, and had a baffled look in their eyes.

The town became rich and famous. The mill was the source of its greatness. There the first American rails were rolled. For twenty years they were the best iron rails in the world. There iron nails were first cut from a sheet, like cookies out of dough. Then the Civil War came and iron that cost ten dollars a ton to make could be sold for fifty and sixty.

IX

One August evening in 1869 a number of Damascenes were gathered as usual at the railroad station to witness and audit the arrival and departure of the seven o'clock train. This was an event still miraculous and unbelievable, requiring verification of the senses. A young man swung off before the train had quite stopped, walked forward, and stood watching the small freight unload. When the last of it was off one of the heavers, leaning from the car door, called to the station agent, Andy Weir:

"Give us an extra hand here. There's a flat passenger."

Weir came and looked in.

"Them's rawkis words you use," he said admonishingly. "Suppose it was somebody we knew."

"Come on," said the heaver. "Give us a hand. This ain't a hearse. It's a railroad train."

Weir beckoned. Several men stepped out of the crowd to help. With a hollow grating sound the end of a long pine box was pushed into view. It came out slowly. Weir felt for handles. There weren't any. It was a plain coffin case.

"Shoulder it," he said to his volunteers.

They walked with it to the far end of the platform and stopped.

"Might rain," said Weir, changing his mind. "Over there," he added, after looking around. "Under the overhang."

They turned back. Awkwardly, with scraping feet and gruntings, they put it down against the station wall under the projecting eave, and then stood looking at it, all a little red from the exertion and stooping.

"Tain't yours, is it?" said Weir, turning suddenly on the young man who had followed the box to and fro.

"Yes," he said.

"Who are you?"

"John Breakspeare."

The station agent bent down and read the card tacked to the top of the box. The name was Aaron Breakspeare.

"I knew him," he said, now gazing at the young man. "Knew him well, I might say. Everybody around here did. You ain't his boy?"

"He was my father," said the young man. "Will it be all right to — —"

"And he's sent himself home," said Weir. "Sent himself home to be buried. You all alone?"

"I'm the whole family," said the young man with a smile that made Weir look away. "Will it be all right," he began to ask again, and hesitated before the pronoun. For nearly a week he had been travelling with this freight and the dilemma was new each time. How should one refer to one's father in a pine box? Corpse was a sodden, gruesome word. Body was too cold and distant. Remains, —no. There were left only the pronouns —*it, this, that* —and they were disrespectful.

"It's all right there," said the station agent, seeing what the young man meant. "But if you want to leave it all night we'll take it in."

"Only for a few minutes," said the young man. "I'm coming right back."

The idlers about the station waited until he was out of sight and then gathered around the box, staring at it, reading the card, looking away, commenting —

"So that's poor old Aaron... As the fellow said, we're all alike at the end of the lane.... He wasn't so oldan, I ought t'know because wasn't I born —?... The young one brought him back... Where'd he come from, does it say?.... Likely looking boy... What's his name?... Wonder what old Gib'l say... This here one stole his sweetheart away back there in...."

To John Breakspeare, son of Esther, great grandson of the founder, now turning his twentieth year, New Damascus was a legend. He had never been there. Yet without asking his way he walked straight to the inn that was his grandfather's, since named Lycoming House, and wrote two names in the register thus:

$$\left\{ \begin{array}{l} \text{John Breakspeare.} \\ \\ \text{Aaron \quad ditto} \end{array} \right\} \text{Denver, Colo.}$$

They meant nothing to the clerk, who was new in the place. He blotted the writing, looked at it, and asked:

"Is your party all here?"

"Not yet," said the young man. "We want two parlor rooms on the ground floor."

"Connecting rooms?"

"Yes."

"You are John Breakspeare?" the clerk guessed.

"Yes."

"The other member of your party will be coming tonight?"

"He is waiting at the station," said the young man. "We shall want the rooms only for tonight and tomorrow. I'll pay now, please."

"We can send a rig to the station," said the clerk.

"No, thank you," said the young man.

He looked at the rooms. In the large one he set two chairs six feet apart, facing. Then lighting all the gas, he went out, locked the door, and carried the key away in his pocket.

One hour later an undertaker's wagon, followed by a hack, pulled up in front of Lycoming House. The young man got out of the hack and stood in the main doorway waiting. Four men drew the pine box out of the wagon, shouldered it, and started in.

There was a crash from end to end of the long front veranda overhanging the street, as twenty men sitting there in tilted chairs, their feet on the railing, smoking, all with one impulse dropped their legs and sat up straight to look. A rigid hotel custom forbids hospitality to Mr. Death. There is only one way for a corpse to pass through a hotel door. That is out. If you die inside that can't be helped. You must go out. But if you die outside you can't come in.

The clerk ran out to defend the threshhold.

"What's this?" he shouted. "You can't do this. You can't rent a mortuary chapel in a hotel."

His words were futile. The young man turned his back, beckoned the undertaker to follow, and led the way through the door and down the hall to the big parlor room, the door of which he unlocked and threw open. They put the pine box on the floor, opened it, raised the coffin to rest on the chairs. The young man followed the empty box to the street and returned with two high candlesticks and candles. These he set at the head of the coffin and lighted. Then, locking the door behind him, he joined the undertaker outside and drove away with him.

The clerk, outraged in both his authority and his traditions, meanwhile had fallen downstairs and was shaking a red, tissue-logged hulk that dozed in a hickory chair at the end of the bar. This was Thaddeus Crawford, the proprietor. He never opened his eyes but to eat and speak and look at the books. The sign he gave of listening, or of waking when addressed, was to open his mouth, —a small, cherubic orifice, —and roll the tip of his tongue round and round it. When he closed his mouth that was a sign he was no longer interested. When he opened his eyes and spoke it was a shock to discover that he could speak distinctly, that his senses were alert, that the triumph of matter was incomplete.

During the clerk's recital of what was taking place upstairs he rolled his tongue excitedly without opening his eyes. Then he heaved himself, achieved locomotion, and went up to look at the names on the register. He looked at them hard and long, dozed a bit, looked at them again, then returned inarticulate to the hickory chair downstairs and fell into it panting.

"What shall we do?" asked the clerk, who had followed him up and down again.

"Do the dishes," said Thaddeus. "Wouldn't, anyhow... Won't hurt the house... Care a damn if it does... Time we had a funeral here." He dozed off for a minute, chortled in his depths, and spoke again with his eyes closed.

"Put it on you, didn't he? Guess he did. Guess yes. Damn smart... Want to see him when he comes back... Knew his father."

When John Breakspeare returned, the clerk, now very civil, took him down to Thaddeus.

They talked until long after the bar closed. Thaddeus was surprised to discover how little the young man knew of his pre-natal history and proceeded to restore him to his background. The picture was somewhat blurred in the romantic passages, from a feeling of delicacy. That loss was more than compensated by high lights elsewhere. He told him in turgid, topical, verbless sentences what the old Woolwine Mansion was like in that other time, how Enoch and Aaron founded the iron industry together, how they prospered, how strange it was that they got along so well, how they parted suddenly when Esther, the banker's daughter, who was engaged to Enoch, changed her mind suddenly and married Aaron instead, and finally of Aaron's failure with steel and how he changed all over after Esther's death.

The narrative had form and drama and a proper ending, very unexpected to the young man. The parlor room in which the body of his father then lay and the one adjoining in which he himself would spend the night were rooms he had lived in once before. They were the rooms his father took when he closed the Woolwine Mansion, unable to live there without Esther, and came to this inn with nurse and infant. That infant was himself.

It came two o'clock. With no premonitory sign Thaddeus heaved himself out of the hickory chair and called for the porter to put out the lights.

"What are you going to do?" he asked.

"I haven't thought of it," said the young man.

"Stay with us," said Thaddeus. "Long as you like."

On his way to bed Thaddeus said to the clerk: "Give him anything he wants. Don't send him a bill till he asks for it. Don't send him a bill at all."

A spiritual adventure awaited John Breakspeare to complete his day. As he re-entered the room where his father's body was and closed and locked the door behind him he got suddenly a sense of reality beyond any perception of things. It was a reality to which he himself merely pertained. This was a sense of existence. The story he had just heard in the bar room, as he was hearing it, seemed to concern only his father; and his father was a separate being who had lived and was dead and about to be buried. But no. That was not so. Vividly, yet with no way of saying it, no way of thinking it, with only a way of feeling it, he became in one instant aware that the story no less concerned himself. Everything that had happened to his father had happened also to him. His father was dead, for there he lay. That was the evidence of things. Beyond was the truth that his father was not dead. The same life thread continued in him. That naïve delusion of youth in which oneself is perceived as a separate miracle, beginning at the toes and ending at the top of the head, was shattered. Back of his father and mother were others, numberless. Their history was his history. He was but a link in a continuous scheme, as his father was, and his father's father, and so on and on, back through an eternity of moments. The past surrounded him. It was intangible, enormous, indivisible.

One of the candles, dying with a splutter, startled him. The other one also was low. He replaced them, lighted the fresh ones, then slid back the panel of the coffin cover and gazed at the face of his father with strange, uneasy interest.

How little he knew of him! Always he had thought of him as a man of sorrow. Yet once he had been gay and spontaneous, full of the enthusiasms and compulsions of life. Never before had he sensed anything of that. The first recollection of his father was sad. It was of going with him, hand in hand, to an open air show, trembling with excitement. It was a special occasion. His father had come a long distance to see him. How he knew that he could not remember. There were animals in the show and men and women who made them perform, and noise and music and peanuts and wonderful smells and much going on. He was delirious with happiness until he noticed that his father was weeping. That almost spoiled the day. After that he could not remember him again until somebody took him a long journey, lasting many days, for aught he knew many years, and at last they found his father, who was in bed, in a little white bed, and very strange, and he had not liked kissing him. Then was a time, rather dim, when they were together and became great and equal friends. This could not last. He was sent to school in Philadelphia and saw his father only at long intervals; and each time they had to get acquainted all over again. They both looked forward eagerly to these meetings and always they were disappointed, especially in the beginnings of new acquaintanceship, until the strangeness wore off and they had reconstructed their memories of each other. At least, it had been so with him. He remembered it as a fact. And now he realized that it had been so also with his father. Intuition multiplied his recollections and made them new. He remembered something he had never once thought of before. They were together, waiting for the train that was to take him back to school. He was restless with childish impatience and counted the minutes that delayed their parting. The train was late. When it came he clamored to get aboard, lest he should be left, and almost forgot to look back and wave. The wistful sadness in his father's face meant nothing to him at the time. Now he understood it.

Suddenly, as he stood there gazing at his father's face, his spirit of itself achieved a form of mystical experience such as may occur naturally and surprisingly at a certain time of youth and is seldom if ever repeated save in the lives of ascetics. He felt himself flooded with understanding, though he knew not in the least what it was he so lucidly understood. There was a sense of new friendship then beginning with his father, —a friendship that should be perfect, wordless, indestructible, beyond peril. Never had he felt so near to his father, so alive to him, so communicative. Death at the same time changed its aspect. It was a castrophic event, but inconclusive. It was not the final enigma. It had nothing to do with life, for life was a prior transaction and bound to go on. It had nothing to do with love, for love was parallel to life and reached beyond death. Life and love, —they were truly mysterious. For death there must be some simple explanation, like the explanation of night, without which every sunset would fill mankind with the terror of extinction. It was…death was…death itself was only…*what?* He had almost seen it, what it was, and then suddenly it disappeared. He had looked the wrong way. For an instant it was there. He tried to reconstruct the point of view. But when he began to think of what he was thinking the dazzling, jewel-like space he had been staring into collapsed with an inaudible crash. All that was left of it was the dead face, reflecting the light of the candles. That experience was closed. Never in his life was it repeated. He had no idea what it meant, then or afterward. Yet the memory of it became his chief spiritual asset. One thought thereafter controlled his life. He was his father continued.

X

He was yet to see his father in another light. That was the light of universal human affection. For a day there were two kinds of people in New Damascus, —those who knew Aaron and others. Nobody was asked. It was meant to be a private ceremony. But that was impossible. All who knew him came to assist at the obsequies. They came from Quality Street and they came from the company houses beyond the canal. There were hundreds of old iron workers and miners, who, at John's suggestion, walked in a body behind the hearse. He was amazed and deeply moved by all this demonstration of feeling; and saddened by it at the same time, for here were people strange to him whose knowledge of his father was older and greater than his own.

Enoch Gib neither came nor stayed away. As the funeral procession departed from the inn he was observed sitting on the veranda, his feet on the railing, his hat on his head, smoking a cigar, gazing vacantly into space.

Somebody said: "Tonight he will give a blue ticket to every man in the mill who took time off for this. That's why he came."

That was not true. Then why did he come? There is no answer. He himself probably did not know. The mourners returning saw him sitting there still. He sat there for hours, until evening, utterly oblivious. Then he rose, crossed the town and disappeared up the path to Throne Rock.

Late that night the furnace men at No. 4, deaf as furnace men by habit are to the uproar of the smelting process, looked at one another saying, "What was that?"

It was a sound of ribald laughter off the mountain, borne downward by the wind.

An old man spoke, one who stood in an open shirt, grey hair on his chest, stray grey curls below the edge of his skull cap, alight in the furnace glow.

"That's Enoch," he said, "crowing over Aaron."

They listened. The laugh was not repeated. But as they turned away, letting down their breath, another sound much worse came down the wind and caused their skins to creep.

That was Enoch screaming.

XI

John Breakspeare sat on the veranda of Lycoming House thinking of this situation and of what he should do. His father's old friends had pursued him with offers of hospitality, and as he had to choose, he chose that of Thaddeus, for two reasons. One was that he liked Thaddeus extravagantly; the other was that living at the inn entailed no social amenities. He was by no means a solitary person. Naturally he was gregarious. But for the first time in his life he wished to be let alone, and that great friendly hulk dozing in the hickory chair at the end of the bar was the only person who had no meddling curiosity and tactfully ignored his existence.

Well, first, there was no available estate, save only a few thousand dollars in money. The wandering Blue Jay mill wore out at last. Aaron's final act of business was to sell its good-will to a corporation. That was where the few thousand dollars came from. The plant itself was scrapped for junk. The day after that had happened Aaron lay him down with a fever and never got up again. John, in his junior year at college, was summoned at once, at Aaron's request, as if he knew he were going to die. Yet he could not wait. He died the night before the boy arrived.

His will, written by himself on a sheet of foolscap, was very simple:

"All I have whatsoever I leave to my son, John. There is no one else."

Pinned to this was a personal note as follows:

"Boy of Esther, I am leaving you. Go straight and God bless you. Bury me at New Damascus."

The writing, though clear, was evidently an achievement of great effort. He was dying then and was gone in less than an hour.

The old Woolwine holdings of ore and coal, though still intact, were in a state of suspended development and not very valuable, perhaps quite unsaleable. As for the ore, it would not pay to develop that any further. The whole iron region was now beginning to be flooded with cheap Mesaba ore from the head of the Great Lakes. Gib, in fact, was already buying this ore for his blast furnaces. He could buy it for less than the cost of producing his own. As for the coal, the only market there had ever been for that was at the New Damascus blast furnaces. Gib owned all the furnaces and had all the coal he needed. Coal is coal, of course; it may be sold anywhere. But the Woolwine holdings, which John Breakspeare inherited, were probably not large enough to bear the capital that would be necessary to put New Damascus coal into commercial competition with the output of the big established collieries up the river.

These thoughts all wound up together in the young man's meditations led nowhere. They merely revolved. They fell into a kind of rhythm. The same ideas kept repeating themselves in an obsessed, uncontrollable manner. "I'm stupid," he said, and got up to walk. Of a sudden he became aware of what it was that had been making his thoughts go round like that.

There was a throbbing in the air, a rythmic punctuation, a ceaseless hollow murmur. He had heard this voice before, continuously in fact, without attending to it. Now he listened. It came from the chest of the great driving engine in the rolling mill, at the other side of town. It said:

Wrought iron

Wrought iron

Wrought iron

Iron, iron.

The mill!

The mill his father founded!

Volcanic fires, incandescent difficulties, quick, elemental fluids, —in these his father wrought and failed. Had not the son some pressing business with that same Plutonic stuff? He moved as if he had. With no shape of an idea in his mind he walked purposefully, stalking the voice of the engine, and came to the rear of the mill.

It was evening.

He had never seen an iron mill before. For some time he stood outside the gate, viewing it at large, smelling and tasting its fumes, acquainting his senses with its moody roar. There was at first no sign of human agency. Then he made out figures passing back and forth through bolts of sudden light. They seemed solitary, silent, bored. The notion crossed his fancy that man had tapped the earth of forces which turned genii on his hands, enslaved him, commanded weary obedience and in the end consumed him.

Now a shift was taking place. Night crews were coming on; day crews were going out. Those arriving walked erect; their faces, white and clean, showed vividly against the murky texture. Those going out were limp and bent; their faces did not show at all. Twice a day they passed like that, bodies healed by sleep and food relieving those all fagged and bruised from a twelve-hour struggle with the genii. Puddlers, heaters, hammermen and rollers were marked apart from common, unskilled labor by leather aprons on their feet, tied round the ankles, flapping as they walked.

Curious glances fell upon the young man idling there in the dusk. Nobody spoke to him. On the gate was a painted sign: "Positively no admittance." The rule was rigid, even more so in Gib's mill than at any other in the country, and all iron working plants in those days were guarded very jealously because spies went to and fro stealing methods, formulas and ideas. The weakness of a rigid rule is that everyone supposes it will be observed. No doubt the men who saw Breakspeare enter took him to be a young man from the office. No common trespasser would be so cool about it; a spy would make his entrance surreptitiously. Whatwise, nobody stopped him. He went all the way in and was swallowed up in the gloomy, swirling, glare-punctured commotion. And once inside he could move freely from place to place. No one paid him the slightest heed.

The air was torn, shattered, upheaved, compressed, pierced through, by sounds of shock, strain, impact, clangor, cannonade and shrill whistle blasts, occurring in any order of sequence, and then all at one time dissolving in a moment of vast silence even more amazing to the ear. Conversation would be possible only by shrieks close up. The men seemed never to speak at their work. They did not communicate ideas by signs either. Each man had his place, his part, his own pattern of action, and did what he did with a kind of mechanical inevitability, as if it were something he had never learned. They were related not to each other but to the process, kept their eyes fixedly on it for obvious reasons, and stepped warily. A false gesture might have immediate consequences.

The process just then was that of rolling iron bars. From where Breakspeare stood he saw the latter end of it. He saw the finished bars spurt like dull red serpents from between the rolls. Two men standing with their gaze on the running hole from which the reptile darted forth snared it by the neck with tongs, walked slowly backward with it as the rolls released the glowing body, until its tail came free; then dragged it off, a tame, limp thing, turning black, and put it straight along with others to cool.

The whole process could not be seen at once. It took place in a train of events covering many acres of area. It could be followed backward, —that is by going from the finished bars to the source of the iron, or in the other direction downstream, from the puddling furnaces where the iron is cooked, to the hammermen who mauled it into rough shape and thence to the rolls. Breakspeare, having started that way, traced it backward, from the finished bar to the source of its becoming.

He moved to a position from which he could see all that happened at the rolls.

The rolls were merely enormous cylinders revolving together in gears, with grooves through which to pass the malleable iron. The first groove through which it passed was very large, the next one smaller, the next one smaller still, until the last, out of which the final form appeared. The iron had to be passed back and forth through each of these grooves in turn.

On each side of the rolls stood men in pairs with tongs, —silent, foreboding men, with masks on their faces and leather aprons on their feet, singularly impassive and still, save in moments of action. At intervals of two or three minutes a man came running with two hundred weight of incandescent iron in the shape of a rough log five or six feet long, held in tongs swung by a chain to an overhead rail, and dropped it at the feet of the rollers. Becoming that instant alive, the rollers picked it up with tongs, passed it through the first groove of the rolls, giving it a handful of sand if it stuck, and then stood again in that attitude of brooding immobility, leaning on their tongs, looking at nothing, bathed in sparks as the tail of the iron disappeared. On the other side of the rolls similar men with similar tongs seized it as you would take a reptile by the neck in a cleft stick, controlled and guided its wrigglings, turned and thrust its head into the next smaller groove. Thus they passed and repassed it through the rolls, catching it each time by the neck and returning it through a smaller groove. Each time it was longer, more sinuous, less dangerous, until at last, with the final pass, it became what Breakspeare had first seen, namely, a finished wrought iron bar, ready to cool.

From the rolls he moved to the tilthammers. At corresponding intervals the hammermen received on tongs from the puddling furnace two hundred weight of iron in the form of a flaming dough ball, laid it on a block, turned it under the blows of the tilthammer falling like a pile driver from above, until it was the shape of a log, fit to be passed through the rolls. Then helpers, lifting it in tongs, ran with it to the rollers.

Beyond the tilthammers were the puddling furnaces. There the process began.

A puddling furnace is a long, narrow, maw-like chamber of brick and fire clay with a depressed floor for the molten iron to lie in and a small square door at the end. It is heated to inferno by a cataract of flame rising from a fire pit at one side and sucked by draught across the roof of its mouth. When the whole interior is like a dragon's gullet, white hot, wicked and devouring, cold pigs of iron are cast in, the door is banged to, the chinks are stopped and the puddler gathers up his strength.

In the door is a small round hole. Through that hole the puddler watches. When the iron is fluid his work begins. The thing he represents is Satan raking hell. With his beater and working only through that little round hole, he must stir, whip, knead and skim the iron. The impurities drain away in a lava stream beneath the door. He may not pause. The beater gets too hot to hold, or begins itself to melt. He casts it into a vat of water and continues with another.

The puddler is the baker, the pastry cook, the mighty chef. All that follows, the whole pudding, the quality of the iron to the end of its life, will be the test of his skill and daemonic impatience.

Presently the iron begins to bubble gravely, turning viscous. Now the art begins. The puddler, still working through that small hole with a long, round bar, must ball the iron. That is, he must divide the molten mass into equal parts and make each part a ball of two hundred weight just. Having made the balls he must keep them rolling round without touching. If they do not roll they will cool a little on the under side and burn on top; and if they touch they will fuse together and his work is lost. One by one he draws them near the door. They must not all come done at once. Therefore this one takes the hottest place; that one stays a little back. Then one is ready. The door jerks open. A helper, working tongs swung by a chain to a monorail overhead, reaches in, plucks out the indicated flaming pill, rushes it headlong to the hammermen and comes running back to get another.

The puddling process fascinated Breakspeare. He watched it for a long time. He particularly enjoyed watching the work of a certain young puddler, tall and lithe, in whose movements there was an extraordinary fulness of power, skill and unconscious grace. He was bare to his middle, wore a skull cap and gloves, and in his outline, turning always in three dimensions, a quality was realized that belongs to pure sculpture. He moved in space as if it were a buoyant element, like water. Never did he make a sudden start or stop. No gesture was angular. One action flowed into another in a continuous pattern. When with the furnace freshly loaded, the door closed, the chinks all stopped and the draught roaring, the moment came to rest he flung himself headlong but lightly on a plank bench and lay there on his side, his head in his hand, propped from the elbow. And when he rose it was all at once without effort.

Standing in deep shadow, outside the area of action, Breakspeare was not aware that the puddler had once looked at him or knew of his presence there; and he was startled when without any warning at all that person departed from his orbit, came close to him, and shouted in a friendly voice:

"Well, how about it?"

"Bully," Breakspeare shouted back at him.

They looked at each other, smiling.

"Don't let the old man catch you," said the puddler. "He's about due."

"All right," said Breakspeare.

The puddler went back to his work and never looked at him again.

Breakspeare liked the encounter. He liked the puddler, whose friendliness was in character with his movements, swift and unerring. He was at the same time in a curious way disappointed. When the puddler spoke he was a man, like any other, who made the same sounds and had the same difficulty in overriding the uproar. Speaking was the single act that visibly required effort of him. But as a puddler, with the glare in his face, an ironic twist on his lips, his body glistening with perspiration, his left leg advanced and bent at the knee and his other far extended, every muscle in him running like quicksilver under satin, —then he was a demon, colossal, superb, unique. When he spoke that impression was ruined; when he returned to his work it was restored.

These were not Breakspeare's reflections. They were his feelings, and so engrossed him that he was unaware of being no longer alone in the shadow. Enoch Gib stood close beside him watching the puddlers. The puddlers knew the old man was there. One sensed their knowing it from an increase in the tension of the work. But they did not look at him. Breakspeare turned as if to move away.

"Stay where you are," said Gib, in a voice that pierced the uproar. He seemed to do this with no effort. It was in the pitch of his voice. When he had seen the end of the heat and the iron was out he added: "Come with me."

They walked out side by side through the front gate, across the road to the little brick office building, into the front room. The old man took off his coat, hung it on the back of his chair, spread a towel over it, and sat down at a double walnut desk the top of which was littered with ragged books, unopened letters, scraps of metals, sections of railroad iron, scientific journals, cigar ashes and little models of machinery, in the utmost confusion. Breakspeare, unasked, sat himself down at the other side of the desk and waited. He had a feeling that all the time Gib had been expecting him to break and run and was prepared to detain him forcibly. Why, he could not imagine. He knew nothing about the sacredness of iron working premises nor of the suspicion with which intruders were regarded.

"What were you doing in the mill?" Gib asked, brutally.

"Looking at it," said the young man.

"Who sent you?"

"Nobody."

"How did you get in?"

"Walked in."

"At what gate?"

"On the other side."

Gib made mental note of that statement. Then he asked:

"Who are you?"

"John Breakspeare."

Gib had been regarding the young man in a malevolent manner. That expression seemed to freeze. Then slowly he averted his face. His gaze fixed itself on a burnt cigar hanging over the edge of the desk. He sat perfectly still, as if rigid, and Breakspeare could hear the ticking of a watch in his waistcoat pocket.

"What do you want?" he asked in a loud voice, as if they were in the mill.

Until that instant Breakspeare had no definite thought of wanting anything in this place. First had been that reaction to the throb of the engine. Then came the impulse to visit the mill. That impulse was unexamined. It had not occurred to him to think that anything might come of it; he had not thought of meeting Gib. Nevertheless the question as it was asked started a purpose in his mind.

"I want to learn the iron business," he said.

"Here?" said Gib, quickly.

"Isn't this a good place to learn it?" the young man retorted.

For a long time the old man sat in meditation.

"The iron business," he said. "Mind now, you said the iron business."

"Yes."

"Not the steel business... Iron! Iron!"

"I don't know the difference," said Breakspeare, adding: "Anyhow, you don't teach the steel business here, do you?"

The old man looked at him heavily. Then he got up to pace the floor. Once, with his face to the wall, he laughed in a mirthless way. That seemed to clear his mind.

"Come Thursday at eight." he said.

XII

When John told his friend Thaddeus he was going to work in the mill Thaddeus rolled his tongue in a very droll way.

"You seem surprised."

"Ain't," said Thaddeus. "Ain't. Can't tell when I'm surprised."

That was all he would say.

Everybody who knew the past was astonished. It was supposed that the young man did not know what he was doing. A very old citizen of Quality Street, with a glass eye that gave him a furtive, untrustworthy appearance, came to visit Aaron's son on the hotel veranda and approached the subject by stalking it. He was not a presumptuous person. Never had he meddled in the affairs of others, though he would say that if he had it would have been more often to their advantage than prejudice. This matter of which he was making at his time of life an exception, a precedent in a sense, was nobody's business of course. Still, in another way it was. There had been a great deal of talk about it. Nobody wished to take it upon himself to speak out. That could be understood. There were so many things to think of. Feelings of great delicacy were involved. Still what a pity, he said-what a pity for any of these reasons to withhold from

Aaron's son information he would not come by for himself until it was perhaps too late.

"I must be very stupid," said John at one of the significant pauses. "You are evidently trying to tell me something."

"You are going to work in the mill?" said the old citizen.

"Yes."

"Do you know what happens to Enoch Gib's young men?"

He did not know. The old citizen told him. When he was through Aaron's son thanked him and made no comment. After that people said he knew what he was doing. Some said he had a subtle design.

That was not the case. He had an inherited feeling for iron. Here was an opportunity to learn the business. There was of course a romantic touch in learning it on the ancestral scene. But that was an after-thought. It never occurred to him that he had a feud to keep with Enoch Gib. So far as he could see there was more reason for Gib to hate him as his father's son than for him to hate Gib as a man who might have been his father if his mother had not changed her mind. His father had never spoken ill of Gib-had never spoken of him at all in fact. It was not in the Breakspeare character to bequeath a quarrel. And since Gib had been willing in this strange way to receive the son of a man whom he hated indelibly why should the son be loath? As for what happened to Enoch Gib's young men, —and of this

John heard more and more, —that was a matter he lightly dismissed.

A curious fact was that from the first Aaron's son liked Enoch Gib. Perhaps like is too strong a word. His feeling for him was one of irrational sympathy, which, though he did not know it, had been Aaron's feeling for Enoch to the end.

When John presented himself at eight o'clock Thursday morning Gib's way with him was impersonal and energetic.

"Did you ever sell anything?" he asked.

"No," said John.

"You will," said Gib, "I see it in you."

He removed the towel from over his coat on the back of the chair, folded the towel, laid it on the desk, and drew on his coat, saying: "I'll show you now the difference between steel and iron. The first thing to be learned. The last thing to be forgotten."

They went to the mill yard. Laborers were piling up rails that looked all alike to John except that they varied in length and weight. Gib led the way straight to an isolate pile and pointed John's attention to the name of an English firm embossed on the web of each rail.

"That's a steel rail," he said. "It's imported into this country from England. Now look."

He beckoned. Four men who knew what he wanted lifted one of those rails and dropped it across a block of pig iron on the ground. It snapped with a clean, crisp break in the middle.

"That's steel," said Gib with a gesture of scorn.

The men then laid half of the broken rail with one end on the ground, the other resting on the pig iron block, and hit it a blow with a spike maul. Again it snapped.

"That's a steel rail," said Gib, "to run locomotives and cars over. It breaks as you see, —like glass. When they unload steel rails for track laying they let them over the side of the car in ropes for fear they will break if they fall on the ground."

The same four men, evidently trained in this demonstration, went directly to another pile of rails, carelessly picked up the one nearest to hand, laid it on the ground against a stout iron post and attached to each end of it a chain working to a windlass some distance off. Then they started the windlass. As it wound in the chains, pulling at both ends of the rail, the rail began to bend at the middle around the post. As the windlass continued to wind the rail continued to bend until it became the shape of a hairpin, without breaking, without the slightest sound or sign of fracture.

"That is one of our iron rails," said Gib. "You can't break it. Look at the bend, inside and out."

John looked. The bent part was smooth on the outside and a little wrinkled on the inside. There was no break in the fibre.

"Do it for yourself as often as you like," said Gib. "That's what the men are here for. We buy steel rails to break. Bring anyone who wants to see it. Devise any other test you can think of. I want you to sell iron rails." Suddenly he became strange from suppressed emotion. "Steel is a crime," he said, in a tone of judgment. "The only excuse for it is that it's cheaper than iron. The public doesn't know. Congress doesn't care. It lets these foreign steel rails come in to compete with American iron rails. The gamblers who build railroads are without conscience. They buy them. Yet a man who lays steel rails in a railway track is a common murderer! He will come to be so regarded."

John was embarrassed. Gib's exhibition of feeling seemed to him inadequately explained by the technical facts. The possibility that personal facts were primarily involved made him suddenly hot and uncomfortable. Steel, he knew, had been the symbol of his father's defeat in New Damascus. Correspondingly, iron had been the symbol of Enoch's triumph. Was it that Enoch hated steel as he hated Aaron? That his feeling for steel *was* his feeling for Aaron?

It partly was. That day, twenty-five years gone, when Aaron made his spectacular steel experiment, with Esther watching from the Woolwine Mansion terrace, was a day of agony for Enoch. To Aaron and Esther a victorious outcome meant power, fortune, the thrill of achievement. For Enoch it meant extinction. He could not have survived it in mind or body. Simply, he would have died.

The failure of the experiment saved him. It plucked him back from the edge of the void. It saved him in the sight and respect of New Damascus. And he had a feeling that it saved him even in the eyes of Esther, though from what or for what he could not have said. Forever after the word steel had a non-metallurgical meaning. It associated in the depths of his emotional nature with black, ungovernable ideas, including the idea of death.

And now this rare, this altogether improbable irony of teaching Aaron's son the iron trade! of demonstrating to him the fallibility of steel! of sending him forth from New Damascus to sell iron rails against steel!

Did Gib relish the irony? gloat on it, perhaps? That may not be answered clearly. There was at any rate a strong rational motive in his behavior.

Hitherto New Damascus rails had sold themselves. Therefore Gib had no sales department in his organization. Now steel rails were coming in and steel rails were being *sold*. There was a powerful selling campaign behind them. The competition was not yet alarming, but it was serious and likely to increase, and the way to meet it was to *sell* iron rails. Gib had business foresight. It revealed to him the use of salesmanship to meet a new condition. What he had been seeking was not then so quickly to be found. That was a selling genius. John Breakspeare was not the first young man he had personally conducted through the testing yard. Three had already failed him and he was wondering where he should look for another prospect when Aaron's son appeared. Gib perceived or felt in him the latency of what he wanted. If the same young man had been anyone else he would have taken hold of him in precisely the same way. The fact of his being Aaron's son-no Esther's —was one to be set aside. The relationship was experimental, on the plane of business, and what might come of it-well, that would appear.

On John's part a personal sensibility at the beginning gradually wore away as he discovered the drift of events, which was this:

The star of iron was threatened in the first phase of its glory.

The day of steel was breaking.

It was not a brilliant event. It was like a cloudy dawn, unable to make a clean stroke between the light and the dark. Yet everyone had a sense of what was passing in this dimness.

Gib, whose disbelief in steel rested as much upon pain memories and hatred as upon reason, was a fanatic; but at the same time great numbers of men with no such romantic bias of mind were violently excited on one side or the other of a fighting dispute. Fate decided the issue. The consequences were such as become fate. They were tremendous, uncontrollable, unimaginable. They changed the face of civilization. Vertical cities, suburbs, subways, industrialism, the rise of a wilderness in two generations to be the paramount nation in the world, victory in the World War, —those were consequences.

It is to be explained.

Less than ten years after Aaron's failure the great

Bessemer process, a way of producing steel direct from ore, was successfully evolved in England, and the British now were producing steel, especially steel rails, in considerable quantities. Americans as usual were procrastinating, digressive, self-obstructing. The Bessemer patents were bought and brought to this country. A Kentucky iron master filed an interference on the ground that although he hadn't developed it in practice he had had that same idea himself, and had had it first, and his contention was sustained. Several years were lost in wrangling over rights. Meanwhile, England entered the American market with steel rails. These now were competing with iron rails. When at last the Bessemer process began to be tried in this country the principle of perversity that animates the untamed elements bewitched it. Disappointments were so continuous, so humiliating, so extremely disastrous, that a period was when one would have thought the whole thing much more likely to be abandoned than persevered with. And when at length there was a useable product at all it was a poor and very uncertain product, comparing unfavorably with English steel, and how the English steel rails compared with good American iron rails has already been witnessed in Gib's mill yard.

Man is the only animal that whistles in the dark. Being so long in a dogged minority, so much discouraged, so sore in their hope, the protagonists of steel were boastful. They could not boast of their product. It was bad. Nor of their success. It was worse. They had to boast of things which one could believe without proof. The Bessemer steel process, they said, was the enemy of privilege. It was for the many against the few. It would transform and liberate society and cast down all barriers to progress.

They were the radicals, the visionaries, the theorists, the yes-sayers of their time. Many a sound, conservative, no-saying iron man was seduced by their faith to exchange his money for experience.

And all the time, bad as it was, steel kept coming more and more into use, especially, —that is to say, almost exclusively in the form of rails. And the reason the steel rail kept coming into use was that an amazing human society yet unborn, one that should have shapes, aspects, wants, powers and pastimes then undreamed of, was calling for it, —calling especially for the steel rail.

The steel men heard it. That was what kept them in hope. The iron men heard it and were struck with fear.

Why was it calling for steel rails instead of iron rails? —steel rails that broke like clay pipes against iron rails that could be tied in knots? Did it care nothing for its unborn life and limb? It cared only a little for life and limb. Much more it cared about bringing its existence to pass, and that was impossible with iron rails, with anything but steel rails, for reasons that we already know, having passed them. They require only to be focused at this point.

It was true of the iron rail that it was unbreakable and therefore safe and superior to the steel rail for all uses of human society in the sixties and seventies of the nineteenth century. That was still the iron age. But human society as it would be in the twentieth century was calling for a rail that would meet the needs of a steel age. This was a society that was going to require a ton of freight to be moved 2,500 miles annually for each man, woman and child in the country! Transportation on that scale of waste and grandeur had never been imagined in the world. Iron rails simply could not stand the strain. They would not break under it. They would be smashed flat. They would wear out almost as fast as they could be spiked down.

It was true of the steel rail, as the iron people said, that it was very breakable, of tricky temper, dangerous to life and limb. Society in 1870 ran much more safely on iron rails. But the unborn society of the steel age was making rail specifications beforehand. It was a society for which a quarter of a million miles of railway would have to be laid in one generation. That simply could not be done with iron rails. There would not be enough fuel, labor and time by the old wrought iron process to make or replace iron rails on any such scale. Shoeing that society with iron rails would be like shoeing an army with eiderdown slippers.

The iron people of course could make a steel in their own way from wrought iron, melted again and carbonized, —fine, cutlery steel, very hard and trustworthy, —but you could not dream of making rails by the millions of tons from that kind of steel. The making of it was too slow and the cost prohibitive.

The three primary desiderata in the oncoming society's rail problem were *hardness, cheapness, quantity.*

The new process produced a rail within these three requirements. It was hard because it was steel. It was cheap because the steel was got direct from the ore at an enormous saving of time and fuel. And it could be made in practically unlimited quantities.

The Bessemer method made possible at once an increase of one hundred fold in metallic production. That was miraculous.

The iron age took three thousand years.

The steel age developed in thirty.

Enoch Gib stood with his face to it. He fought it with his eyes closed. His strength crystallized against it. When it passed him by with a rush and uproar it passed New Damascus. Never was a pound of steel fabricated at New Damascus. It was an iron town. Steel towns grew up around it. That made no difference so long as he lived, and when he was gone, then it was too late. Opportunity had forsaken that spot.

The meaning of events is swift. Yet events are spaced with days and days are of equal length, lived one at a time. Historically you see that the iron rail was suddenly and hopelessly doomed. But from a contemporary point of view one might have been for a long time in doubt. It was not until 1883, thirteen years after John's arrival in New Damascus, that the steel rail definitely superseded the iron rail.

XIII

Enoch Gib's knowledge of human nature in the uses of business was deep and exact. He was not mistaken in Aaron's son. John Breakspeare could sell iron rails. He could sell anything.

Selling ability in its highest development is a strange gift. There is no accounting for it. One has it or one has it not. He had it in that all-plus-X degree, which is the indefinite part of genius. The final irony was that Gib should have discovered it, for it belonged to the steel age and was destined to be turned against him. In this young man who could sell iron rails he prepared a weapon for his invincible adversary.

The steel age always knew in advance what it needed. Salesmanship was its very breath. Why? Because when it came suddenly, like a natural event, men found themselves in command of means for producing wealth, —that is to say, goods, enormously beyond any scale of human wants previously imaginable. Production attended to itself. It ran utterly wild. There was a chronic excess of producing capacity because the supply of steel had been magically increased one hundred fold and steel was the basis of an endless profusion of new goods.

The dilemma that presented itself was unique. Its name was over-production. It occurred simultaneously in Great Britain, Germany, France and the United States. They all had the same goods to sell, the very same goods, rising from steel, and they sold them to each other in mad competition. Prices fell steadily for many years, continuously, until goods were preposterously cheap, and always there was a surplus still. Rails fell from $125 to $18 a ton, and the face of two continents was netted with railways. Yet there was a surplus of rails.

Never before in the history of mankind did goods increase faster than wants. It is not likely ever to happen again.

In a way that becomes clear with a little reflection, a surplus of steel caused a surplus of nearly everything else-food to begin with. There was a great surplus of food because steel rails opened suddenly to the world the virgin lands of the American west. The iron age had foreshortened time and distance. The steel age annihilated them.

It made no difference how far a thing was hauled. Transportation was cheap because steel was cheap. Kansas wheat was sold in Minneapolis, Chicago and in Liverpool. Minneapolis made flour and sent it to New York, Europe and back to Kansas.

The great availability of food released people from agriculture. They went to the industrial centers to make more steel and things rising of steel, so that there were more of such goods to sell.

More, more, more of everything.

Sell! Sell! Sell!

That was the voice of the steel age.

But we overrun the thread of the story. It lies still in the iron age.

How did John Breakspeare sell iron rails for Enoch?

It is to be mentioned that he founded the art of Messianic advertising. He took the message of iron rails to the people. He dramatized the subject.

After four weeks of study and reflection, going to and fro in the mill, absorbing all the technical literature there was, acquainting himself with the way of the trade, —Gib watching and letting him alone, —he outlined a plan of campaign. It involved a considerable outlay of money. Gib approved it nevertheless and the young evangel set forth.

At Philadelphia he arranged an exhibit the first feature of which was a pair of New Damascus iron rails that had bridged a perilous gap twelve feet wide and twelve feet deep washed out under a railway track at night. A locomotive and six passenger cars passed safely over those rails in the dark. The miracle was discovered the next morning. Steel rails under that strain would have snapped. This was very effective. He reproduced in public the breaking tests applied to steel and iron rails alternately in the New Damascus mill yard. He collected data on railway accidents, which were then numerous and terrifying, and published regularly in the newspapers a cumulative record of those that were caused by the failure of imported steel rails, at the same time offering $10,000 for proof of the failure of a New Damascus iron rail under any conditions. He handled his facts in a sensational manner. Public sentiment was aroused. In several state legislatures bills were introduced requiring all new railway mileage to be laid with iron rails and all steel rails in use to be replaced with iron. None of these bills was passed. Still, they were useful for purposes of propaganda. A Committee of Congress made an extensive inquiry at which the young Elias from New Damascus appeared and made a worthy impression. This was the beginning of his familiarity with the lawmaking mentality. Without asking for it directly he got what the iron people had prayed for in vain. That was a punitive tariff against foreign steel rails. He had moved public opinion; the rest was automatic.

Thus he sold first the idea of iron rails. Next he proceeded to sell the rails.

Railway building at that time was the enchanted field of creative speculation. Railways were made in hope, rejoicing and sheer abandon of wilful energy. Once they were made they served economic ends, as a navigable waterway will, no matter where or how it goes, but for one that was intelligently planned for the greatest good of the greatest need four or five others derived their existence fantastically from motives of emulation, spite, greed, combat and civic vaingloriousness. When in the course of events all these separate translations of the ungoverned imagination were linked up the result was that incomprehensible crazy quilt which the great American railway system was and is in the geographical sense. It was more exciting and more profitable to build railways than wagon roads. That is how we came to have the finest railways and the worst highways of any country in the civilized world.

Into this field of sunshine and quicksand marched the young man from New Damascus. He could scent a new railway project from afar, up or down wind, and then he stalked it day and night. He sold it the rails. Without fail he furnished the rails. He sold them for cash when he could, and when he couldn't get cash he took promissory notes, I O U's, post-dated checks, bonds and stocks. He took all he could get of what he could find, but whatever it was he sold the rails.

Enoch Gib, greatly startled at first, was willing to see how merchandising by this principle would work out. But as he was unused to excursions in finance and as the notes and stocks and bonds of railways in the gristle piled up in his safe he called in his banker for consultation. John was present.

"It's not so much of a gamble if you go far enough," said John. "There's a principle of insurance in it. It would be risky to sell insurance on one ship. Nobody does that. It is perfectly safe to sell insurance on a thousand ships. This is the same thing. Some of these railways will

bust of course. But if we sell rails to all of them we can afford to lose on the few that go down.
The whole question is: do you believe in railways?"

The two old men looked at their youthful instructor with anxious wonder.

"Is that your own idea?" the banker asked.

"It's pretty obvious, isn't it?" John answered.

"When you mention it, yes," said the banker. "I should never have thought of it that way."

Later the banker spoke privately with Gib.

"That's a very dangerous young man."

"Very," said Gib.

Yet it worked out rather well, owing partly to the principle and partly to John's uncanny
instinct for making a safe leap. He could smell bankruptcy before it happened. Moving about
as he did continually in the surge of the railway excitement he had access to much private information. He knew pretty well how it fared with the companies that owed the mill for rails.
If one were verging toward trouble he knew how and where to get rid of its paper at a discount.
There were losses; but the losses were balanced by profits in those cases where a company that
had been charged a very high price for rails because it was short of cash and nobody else would
take its notes was able at length to redeem its paper in full.

In John's mind was no thought of either loyalty to iron or disloyalty to steel. It was a question
of American rails against foreign rails. Steel rails were entirely of foreign origin. The steel age
had not crossed the ocean. His work justified itself. It was immediately creative and greatly
assisted railway building. It was speculative also, and this is to be remembered. A collateral
and very important result was that it hastened the advent of the American steel rail, since the
punitive tariff against foreign rails gave the American steel people the incentive of greater profit.
That presently changed the problem.

Meanwhile, never had the New Damascus mill been so active. Never had its profits been
greater. Yet Enoch Gib was uneasy. He had offered the young man a partnership. John had
flatly declined it.

What did that mean?

XIV

For twenty years the social life of New Damascus had been as an untended orchard, —shapeless,
perfunctory and reminiscent. Its estate was a memory running back to the old Woolwine Mansion and the days of Aaron. It had no rallying point. There was youth as a biological fact
without gaiety, sparkle or sweet daring. Quality Street lived on its income. Young men succeeded their fathers in business. The girls, after music and finishing at Philadelphia, returned
to New Damascus and married them.

The Gib Mansion might as well have been a mausoleum. Life was never entertained there.
It did not expect to be. Jonet was nobody until Gib married her. After that she was the community's commiseration. She died when Agnes, their only child, was ten. The obsequies were
private. At the grave, besides the sexton and the minister, and Gib holding Agnes by the hand,
there was one other person. That was Gearhard, the father of Jonet, who stood with his feet
crossed and his left forearm resting on the sexton's shoulder as on the bellows-sweep, in a contemplative attitude. People spoke of it literally. There, they said, was another thing Enoch had
broken and cast away. No wonder he wished to bury it privately. Agnes was sent off to school.
She had lately returned and was now living at the Gib Mansion alone with her father. Nobody
knew her. There was some mystery about her. A story of unknown origin, and unverified,
was that she had been found out at school in an unchaperoned escapade, which so enraged old
Enoch that he brought her home and deprived her of liberty. It would be like him to do that.
Moreover, in the iron age such discipline was feasible. Youth had not yet delivered itself from

parental tyranny. That was reserved to be one of the marvels of the steel age.;! In 1870 any girl of seventeen was dependent, and one in the situation of Agnes Gib was helpless.

John's advent on this iron grey scene produced a magical change. He was rightful heir to all the social tradition there was in New Damascus. This would have meant nothing in itself. But he liked it. He was not then nor did he ever become the kind of man who must renounce life to reach success. That is a matter partly of temperament and partly of capacity. Knowledge necessary to his ends he acquired easily, seemingly without effort, even technical knowledge. His imagination worked with the ease of fancy and knew no fatigue. Business was a game at which he played. Therefore it could not devour him. Without a moment's notice he could turn from one kind of play to another and back again. He would dance all night and come with a crystal mind to the day's work. Frivolity seemed to stimulate or recharge his mind.

The youth of New Damascus adored him. A group spontaneously formed around him. He kept large rooms at the inn, where he entertained. More than half his time was spent away from New Damascus, but the new social order adjusted itself to his movements. When he was at home there were parties, dances, suppers, excursions, flirtings and episodes. All this took place on the plane of Quality Street. But his liking for people neither began nor ended there. It knew no petty distinctions. There were two kinds of people in the world, —his kind and others. And his kind were all the same to him no matter where he found them. He had friends among the mill workers-big, roystering fellows with whom he often went revelling to fill out a night. One of these was Alexander Thane, the splendid puddler who had spoken to him that first night in the mill. They became fast friends.

He scandalized people without offending them. Whatever he did, that was John. He did anything he liked and it was forgiven beforehand. His errancies were extravagant and alarming, such as had been almost certain to involve a superficial nature in disaster. They were never wicked or immoral, never hurtful to others and seemed but to innocently enhance the romantic aspect of his personality. This may be true only of one whose character is superior to his follies. As his character came more and more to be realized people began to say, "Well, that's one young man Enoch Gib won't break."

Enoch regarded him with wonder and misgiving. John's impact on the business had been phenomenal.

Perhaps no one else could have done it; certainly no one else wasting so much of himself in ways for which Gib felt the utmost contempt could at the same time have attended to business at all. Yet his way with it grew steadily stronger and more remarkable, no matter what else he did.

Gradually there grew up in Gib a vague baffled sense of recurrence. As New Damascus had idolized Aaron in the old time so now it idolized John. Was that because he was Aaron's son? For a while it had that aspect. Then it could no longer be so explained. Something that had been was taking place again. What was it? The old man came to this question again and again. It tormented him for a year of nights. Then suddenly he had the answer.

New Damascus idolized this person not because he was Aaron's son but *because he was Aaron!*

Once this wild thought had occurred to Enoch it expanded rapidly, filling his whole mind, and became an obsession. Aaron lived again! He had returned with youth and strength restored.

The physical resemblance was in fact very striking. Enoch began to study it surreptitiously. The sight tortured and fascinated him. He could not let it alone. He decided he had been mistaken about that look of Esther which at first he had seemed to see in the young man's eyes. It was not there. Thank God for that. This youth was Aaron himself.

From the moment of perceiving this thing with hallucinated clarity Enoch hated John and arranged his thoughts to dwell against him dangerously. How should he deal with the situation? It had no tangibility. If he spoke of it people would think he was crazy. Yet there was the fact. Aaron by foul strategy had entered the business again. The circumstances of his entering it in the guise of a son were extraordinary. As the old man reviewed the incident it assumed a flagrant, preposterous aspect. Aaron had outwitted him.

Yes. Aaron had always been able to do that. But this was an outrageous act! Nothing like it had ever happened before in the world. And now it behooved him to act cautiously, think cunningly, and above all to conceal the fact that he knew. Merely again to put Aaron out of the business, as he could easily do, would be neither quittance nor justice.

XV

There was much curiosity about Enoch's invisible daughter. Was she really imprisoned in that gloomy mansion on the west hill? Or was she. queer, like her mother? How did she live? What was she like? The mill workers, passing the house at all hours, were said to have seen her walking in the landscape at twilight. There was also a legend that she was beautiful.

The young Quality Street set with whom John played and danced talked itself into a state of romantic feeling about her. There was competition in fanciful suggestions. One was that twenty of them should become a committee and move in a body on the mansion. What could the ogre do then? Only of course nothing so overt could really be done. Besides, that would be too serious, not mad enough, and the prisoner might turn out badly. Nobody knew what kind of person she was. Whatever they did should be something to which she assented beforehand.

The suggestion that did at length unite all silly young heads was this. They would give her a party. That was a natural thing to do. She was a New Damascus girl, wasn't she? There was no reason in the world why they shouldn't give her a party. It was perfectly feasible in social principle. The difficulties, as an engineer would say, were merely technical. They were awkward nevertheless. How should they ask her? And if she were unable to bring herself, as would certainly be the case, how should they get her? They appealed to John. He was responsive. It appealed to his spirit of reckless frivolity. He undertook offhand to bring Agnes Gib to a party. It might take some time. He would tell them when and where.

First he made a reconnaissance of the enemy's position. It had its vulnerable points, one of which was an Irish gardener with a grouch on the place. Beginning with him and working in, John proceeded to corrupt the Gib menage. He learned that Agnes was confined to that part of the mansion in which her mother had been immured. She was not permitted to go out, except to walk in the grounds with a woman who was Gib's servant, not hers, and performed the office of a gaoler.

In time he succeeded in getting a note to the prisoner. In it he said simply that she was desired to come to a party. There was no answer.

He sent a second note. The party he had mentioned before was one proposed to be held in her honor. There would be introductions, then supper and dancing, informal but all very correct and duly chaperoned. Still no answer.

He sent a third note in which for the first time he recognized deterrent circumstances. However, all difficulties should be overcome. She had only to consent.

Then a way would be found. The young set of New Damascus was very anxious to get acquainted with her, hence this friendly gesture. To this was returned a note, unsigned, as follows:

> "Miss Gib thanks Mrs. Breakspeare and his friends and regrets to say she cannot come."

That was more or less what John by this time was expecting. He was not discouraged, but he needed light on the young person's character and it occurred to him in this need to explore Gearhard the blacksmith, her grandfather. He melted the hoary smith's ferocity of manner, which was but a rickety defence of the heart, by taking him headlong into the plot with an air of unlimited confidence. Gearhard at first worked his bellows furiously and stirred the fire in his forge, pretending to be angrily absent. But the strokes of the sweep-pole gradually diminished, the fire fell, the bellows collapsed with a rheumatic commotion, and he stood in his characteristic attitude of contemplation, listening. When he spoke his voice was remote and gentle.

"She won't," he said. "That's all there's into it. She's as proud as that bar of steel."

Youth understands its own. It knows the chemistries of impulse and how to challenge them. Curiosity overcomes pride, shyness and fear; and if it be touched through the arc of vanity all else is forgiven, for the desire of youth to be liked for itself alone, in the sign of its personableness, is a glowing passion.

What followed was absurd. Youth delights in high absurdities. It has a way with them that wisdom pretends to have forgotten. Away wisdom! You spoil the cosmic sorceries.

John sent another note.

It was to this effect. At the south boundary where the boxwood grew he would be waiting Thursday evening. She would have only to come straight on fifty paces more instead of turning in her walk at that point as her habit was, and the frolic would begin.

There was no answer. He expected none. But on Thursday evening he was there. From where he stood behind the boxwood he could see all that part of the grounds in which she walked. She appeared at the usual time, attended by a powerful looking woman who disliked exercise and made heavy work of it. Their relations were apparently hostile. They never spoke. The girl was supercilious; the woman grim. After a while the woman sat on an iron bench. The girl walked to and fro. Twice she came within a stone's throw of the boxwood and turned back. Once she stood for several minutes, looking slowly up and down the boundary line of hedge and stone, and at the sky, and all around, with a wilful blind spot in her eye. She did not for an instant look seeingly at the spot her mind was focussed on. Yet John, who watched her, knew she sensed his presence there. That was all that happened. She presently went in without notice to the woman, who saw her going toward the house and followed.

John sent another note. A second time he waited. This time she changed her walk in oblique relation to the boxwood and finished it without the slightest glance or impulse in that direction.

There was a third time. And that was different. On the first turn she came closer to the boxwood than ever before, closer still on the second turn, and then, when the gaoler woman had become inert on the bench, she came within speaking distance and sat on the grass.

"We are here," said John.

"Who are we?" she asked.

This was parley.

"I am their deputy," he said. "Constructively they are here. Naturally, all of us couldn't come at one time and —" He stopped. She wasn't the kind of girl he was expecting. She embarrassed his style.

"And hide in the hedge," she said, finishing his sentence. "Why not? It wouldn't be any less rude if twenty did it."

"That isn't fair," he said. "We don't mean to be rude. We only want to get you out."

"You think I couldn't get out by myself if I wanted to?"

"Yes," he said. "That's what we thought. It's so, isn't it?"

She framed a reply, but withheld it, or, rather, she bit it in two and threw it away, symbolically. It was a clover stem. She sat on her feet, bent over, plucking at the grass, with an occasional glance at the woman on the bench.

"Do you think it's nice to spy on a girl as you have been doing?" she asked.

"Very nice," he said, to tease her.

"And is this the way you get girls for your parties?"

"May we drive up to your door and ask for you there?"

"You may."

"Then will you come?"

"No, I won't be home."

"Why not?"

"I won't. That's why not."

"Do you dislike parties?"

"Yes."

"Do you hate people?"

"I hate people who feel sorry for me."

"Do you wish me to go away?"

"Not if you like what you are doing."

"I'm not doing this because I like doing it," he answered. "I'm doing it because I was asked."

"Oh," she said.

"They felt —I mean, they had this friendly impulse to give you a party. They didn't know how to get you and asked me to manage it. Now what shall I say to them? Shall I say you hate parties and wish them to mind their own business?"

"Tell them what you like," she said. "I can't talk to you any longer," she added. "It will be noticed."

"I won't tell them anything," he said. "But I'll be here a week from tonight at this time if it doesn't rain, and the week after that if it does, and every week for the rest of the summer until you say positively you will not come."

"Haven't I said that?" she asked.

"No."

She got up, shrugged her shoulders and walked away.

Silly!... Silly!... Silly!...

That was what John kept saying to himself without subject or predicate. It was the way he felt. The situation was absurd. His part in it was ludicrous. They were all a lot of sillies, —save one. What he really minded was the sense of having come off badly with her. She was not the wistful, longing prisoner people imagined her to be. He could not make out precisely what she was. She was under restraint. Not only had she not denied this; she had treated it as a fact. But her attitude seemed to be simply that it was nobody's business. Meddling was unwelcome. And such puerile interference as he represented had been treated as it deserved, with high disdain. Never had he met a girl with so much bite and tang. Well, however, it was not all to the bad. She might have cut him away clean. Instead, she had left it as it was.

"I think she will come," he said to his friends.

"Have you seen her?" they asked.

"Yes. I've talked to her."

"Oh, what is she like?"

"Like a grain of salt," he said, rather absently.

At this several girls looked at him anxiously, and although they pretended to be as keen as ever for the party, even more than before, still, misgivings assailed them and secretly their enthusiasm fell. John was an unenclosed infatuation on which everyone had rights of commonage. Numbers preserved him. And here he was keeping tryst with a girl they knew nothing about. It was not his fault. But it was too romantic.

Another thing youth knows is that there are sudden, leaping, dare-me-not moments, wild moments of yes, in which the most improbable events come naturally to pass. It did not rain Thursday. John waited in the boxwood. She came slowly, in the magnetized direction, went back, returned, loitered about for some time, then sat on the grass again.

"Aren't you ashamed to be standing there?" she asked.

"I feel a perfect fool," he said.

"Oh, do you?" she retorted, and with not another word she rose and walked away.

Whistling softly John departed. It became interesting. Thursday he was there again, and so was she.

"Then why do you do it?" she asked, resuming the conversation at the point where she broke it, as if a week had not elapsed.

"I've told you why," he said. "Can you see me?"

"No."

"How did you know I was here?"

"I didn't. Only that you said you would be," she answered.

"That meant last Thursday," he said.

"Do you mean to annoy me like this all summer?"

"As long as you will come to talk with me," he said.

"Or until I say positively I won't come to the party. That's what you said before."

"Will you come?" he asked.

So they went on in a spirit of banter, touching invisible strings, attending less and less to the meaning of words and more to the language of sound.

Scientists ask: Is there such a thing as biactinism? —vital animal magnetism, producing an effect apart from itself with no mechanical means of transmission? Is personality radio-active? Does the human organism possess the property of radiating an influence capable of acting at a distance upon another human organism? Ask youth.

The barrier gave way the next week.

John dwelt as usual in the boxwood. The girl was tardy. Portent one. She wore a pretty dress and high heeled French boots. Portent two. She was on terms of amiability with the gaoler woman. Portent three. It was a musky, August evening, coming twilight. For half an hour or more she walked in an aimless, listless way, stopping, starting, plucking here and there a flower until she had a handful, and then with steps unhurried, with still an air of sauntering, she came straight on.

"Oh, here you are," she said, in the cool, entrancing way youth has of doing an audacious thing.

"I'll have to hand you down," said John.

Below them in the road, twenty paces off, a horse and buggy waited.

XVI

The party took place in John's rooms. First there was a dainty supper; then dancing. It was a heart breaking failure. Everyone tried to save it. A party that needs to be saved is already hopeless. The more everyone tried the worse it was until the lovely, dark-eyed little matron who chaperoned it was on the verge of tears, the girls were divided between sulks and hysterics and the men wondered vaguely what was wrong. It was inevitable. The fluids were perverse.

In the first place, the guest of honor flatly declined the rôle of Cinderella. She was not in the least grateful. The little matron on receiving her said: "We've tried so long to get you."

What could be more innocent.

She replied, "Oh-h!" with ascending accent.

The wreck began there. The matron's tone and manner revealed to her the light in which she was regarded. She was an object of curiosity and a subject of commiseration. One figure she hated as much as the other. To be pitied-particularly that, —was intolerable. She was stung with chagrin and humiliation. It was nobody's fault, —at least, no more theirs than her own. She might have known it would be so; she had placed herself in this position. None the less, or perhaps all the more for that reason, she could not help behaving in that way which is meant when one says she took it out of them. She took it out of her own sex of course. Her power to do that was extraordinary.

The matron did not know what next to say. That was generally the trouble. None of the women knew how to talk to her. There was nothing in common to talk about, except the circumstances, and these could not be mentioned. At the slightest reference to them she coldly cut the conversation.

"If she couldn't get into the spirit of it why did she come at all?" one girl asked another.

"That's easy to see, I should think," the other said.

What was easy to see was that she was too good looking. No other girl was anywhere near so attractive to the male principle. That was why she could carry off a reckless part. She became more heedless and dangerous about it as the psychic tension increased. She did not care in the least what happened.

It was nothing she did, —nothing you could isolate as an example and criticise. Her behavior was basically naïve. It was what she was. It was what she had been for thousands of threaded years. It was life at a pitch of intensity, life of a certain quality, looking out of her eyes, seeking itself.

"Don't you see what she is doing?" asked a feline girl, speaking to John in the dance.

"No," he said. "I don't see what she is doing. I see only that you are treating her badly. I suppose it can't be helped."

"She's having a very good time, all the same," the girl retorted.

Most of the young men felt as John did and took pains to keep her supplied with attention. She received it not ungraciously, but lightly, with an amused and cynical smile. She seemed to be saying to herself: "All grapes are a little sour."

The party was rapidly approaching a state of distress when a call for Mr. Breakspeare was handed in from the office. He went out. A feeling of suspense went all around. It seemed only at that moment to have occurred to anyone that there might reasonably be some sort of sequel. John returned in ten minutes, claimed his partner and entered the dance as if nothing had happened. But there was an uneasy look on his face. When the dance was over he went about looking for someone. Then he began to ask.

No one had seen her go. She had taken no leave. She had simply vanished.

When the fact was definitely established John excused himself and went in pursuit. He hoped to overtake her on the road home, supposing, as was true, that she had scented trouble and wished to meet it alone. That much of her character he understood. His anxiety was real.

The man who had called for him at the inn was no other than his corrupted gardener. And what he had come to say was that whoever brought the young lady home had better be careful. He would do much better not to bring her at all. For Enoch Gib, in waiting with a blunderbuss, yearned to abate his existence.

"An' he is after findin' out who be takin' th' young laday away," the news bringer said at the end of his tidings.

All that had happened might have been foreseen if anyone had been thinking of consequences.

When the gaoler woman discovered that Agnes was gone the first thing she did was to go to her room and search it. She found John's notes-all of them. As the whole exhibit made too strong a case against her gaolership she destroyed all but the last two. These, which referred only to the surreptitious meetings at the boxwood, she took to Enoch, saying she was sure from certain other evidence that it was not an elopement but an escapade. Agnes would return before daylight.

The result upon Enoch may be imagined.

This was Aaron again, —the same Aaron who stole Esther away from him. The terrible wound fell wide open. The pain of it wrecked his mind. It would have killed him, perhaps, but for the solacing thought that revenge was near.

So John pursued Agnes, Agnes was lost, and Enoch waited with death in his heart.

XVII

Agnes expected to be followed.

Instead of going directly home she made a wide detour, skirting the town, and ascended the west hill obliquely by a path the mill workers used. Nobody would think to look for her there.

She meant to enter the grounds by the main gate, defiantly, but she would take her time. As for the consequences, —well, the worse the better. Any change would be welcome.

What made the feud with her father unendurable was its monotony. She had meant to fight it out with him alone to the end, with no outside help or interference. That was the true impulse of her nature. But it had begun to be like fighting it out with some colossal stone image. What terrified her was nothing he did, or could do, but the sheer glacial mass of his hostility. No, —not hostility. It was something else. It was a kind of malevolent indifference.

The feud was about nothing. It rested on their mutual obstinacy. A word would deliver her. That word she could not utter, or would not, which is all the same matter.

At school she had been one of ten girls suspected of having taken part in a frolic much more exciting than wicked yet deserving the extreme penalty. The nine denied it. When she was asked she said yes, she had done it. When they asked who the others were she refused to tell. They disciplined her. Still she refused. They offered her immunity if she would tell. She refused all the more. They sent for her father. He rashly said he would make her tell, and walked head-on into an impassable wall. After an hour alone with her in the reception room he marched her off, just as she was, saying as he crossed the threshhold that her things were to be sent after her. Defiance was something he knew little about. Disobedience he could not comprehend at all. All the way home he pondered it.

"I understand why you refuse to tell on the others," he said. "Now I waive that. You do not have to tell on them. But you shall tell me you are sorry."

She wouldn't. She would say she was wrong; she had broken rules. But she would not say she was sorry, for the reason that she wasn't. This she explained. That made no difference.

"You shall tell me you are sorry," he said.

She refused.

"You will," he said. "When you do you may have your liberty again."

With that he banished her beyond the white line that had divided the household in her infancy, set a woman to be her keeper, and then apparently forgot her. She sometimes saw him at a distance. He never looked at her.

The girls on whom she would not tell sent her a beautiful present. She sent it back. That was the last of her contacts with the outside world. Her mail was cut off. No one was permitted to see her. More than a year had passed in this way. Once she sent word she wished to see him. He answered: "If she is sorry she may come." That ended her overtures. Fighting it out with him apparently meant living it out, as her mother did, and that for her was grotesque. Besides, in that kind of contest he had the advantage of age. Age has all the time there is. Youth has neither past nor future, —only the present. The situation was impossible. It could not go on. Yet she had found no clear way out. She was too proud to seek refuge with anyone she knew. Moreover, she was a minor with no rights of her own. And as for casting herself free upon the wide world, —well, she had not yet come to that desperate thought.

As she ascended the hill a mood that had been rising in her for several days became suddenly intense and exulting. It made her short of breath. The excitement of breaking bounds, of going to the party, of what she did there, now a feeling of utter contempt for all the human values it represented, an emotion of trampling upon her adversaries among whom to her surprise was foremostly John, a sense of unknown power, particularly that voluptuous unconcern with consequences-all these different actions and reactions were as one effect. The cause was the mood. She recognized it. She knew about how long it should last. Never before had it been so tormenting. Never had she let it possess her entirely. Surrendering to it was like a physical experience, fearful and sweet.

She sat on a stone at the edge of the path, on the lower side, with a wide view of the valley and gave herself up to ecstasy. She was attuned to wonder and understood it. The hymn of night bewitched her. Becoming luminous, her thoughts touched objects and subjects alike and returned to her charged with sensation. In the vastness of space, in one's impulse toward it, in the thrust of the church spire through the black panoramic foliage, in the tearing way the moon sliced his path through the clouds, in the shapes of the clouds, in convexity, concavity, temptation, and selfness, in hereness and thereness, in all that one saw and felt there was one meaning, —and she almost knew what it was. But the thought that excited her to suffocation was the thought of all that had not yet happned to her, —in that same one meaning. The rest of her, most of her in fact, was out there in the void. It was everything that had not happened. It might be anything. Whatever it was she embraced it, accepted it unreservedly, consented to it beforehand for the thrill of consenting.

For the first time in her existence she felt knowingly the passion of youth to pierce itself with life.

XVIII

There came a sound of footsteps on the path, —that plunging sound of muffled resonance men make in iron-studded raw hide footgear, with also in this case a swishing minor note from the play of the ankle aprons worn by the mill workers. Agnes had never heard any sound like it. Not until two men met and passed in the path, so close that she could smell them, did she quite make out what it was; and by that time her heart was making more noise than the men's feet. They did not see her. They passed without speaking to each other, which was strange for mill workers; but when they had walked maybe twenty paces in opposite directions one cast a taunt backward over his shoulder. What it was Agnes could not tell. The other answered it. Both stopped. Then she heard them slowly returning.

They met again at the same spot where they had passed and stood there looking at each other warily, suspiciously, their eyes rolling in the moonlight. She could see them distinctly, for they were very close, yet as it happened she herself was so concealed that the men, though they might have touched her, did not see her.

One had a very pleasing aspect. He was tall and vibrant with a fine profile and no bristles. That was Alex Thane, the magnificent puddler.

The other was of lower stature, much heavier, massive, in the form of a wedge, with a width at the top across the shoulders that was almost a deformity. He was neckless. His head started from between his shoulders like a gargoyle. Coarse black hair grew all over him. His moustache was like a worn brush. His eyes were wide apart, set very high, denoting enormous animal vitality.

It was he who had cast back the taunt; and it was he with his chin thrust out who spoke first when they met again and stood facing each other in that singular way. He was a Cornishman. What he said Agnes could not understand. Thane answered him in words which, though she knew them as words, most of them, imported to her mind no sense whatever. Still she got the drift of what they were saying, for they said a good deal of it in a universal language more gleaming and subtle than the language of words. She got it from their tones and gestures and what radiated from their eyes. And it was the drift of what men have been saying to each other from the beginning.

First it was, "Which of us can kill the other?"

After a very long time, millions of years maybe, it became, "Which of us *could* kill the other?"

That was the leap that placed an abyss between man and animal. No creature but man exists on this side. The animals still say *can*. He says *could*. It was the beginning of civilization. And all that we have done since has been to elaborate the ways of could, ways to conquer without killing, and to evolve the sporting code in which the potentials of could are standardized. According to that code one may acknowledge that another could have killed him without losing one's life, one's self-esteem or one's social caste.

These two, Thane and the Cornishman, had been egged by their fellows into a state of intense rivalry. They were the most powerful men in the mill. Each in his daily work easily performed feats of strength beyond the power of others, but with this difference, that while Thane exerted himself only now and then for the mere feeling of it and the sooner when no one was watching, the Cornishman exhibited his superiority continuously because his vanity required it, and set a killing pace for the men of his crew. He was brutal and laughed exultingly if one of them dropped.

There was much debate as to which was the better man. A majority inclined to the Cornishman for that he was always and instantly ready to try it out, whereas Thane put every challenge aside, not as if he were afraid but with an air of distaste.

"I'm making no show of myself," he said.

"Show be damned," the eggers said. "The man is braggin' he can do yu. Ain't that a show?"

No use. He could not be goaded into a public match. Many misunderstood it. The Cornishman particularly was misled. He got the notion that Thane was afraid of him, and so he became arrogant and offensive.

This is what had been going on for some time. It was what was going on now in the path to the great wonder of a special, fascinated audience of one.

The Cornishman, jutting his chin piece further and further out, did the boasting. Thane answered him with contemptuous looks and now and then a derisive word. Suddenly they brought it to a head. As with one impulse they walked a little apart, put down their dinner baskets, threw off their caps and slipped out of their shirts. This seemed all one movement. Then, facing at the same instant, they drew slowly together. Their bodies, nude to the middle, were crouched in a manner that gave Agnes a new and terrific sensation of the human form, especially of its splendid, destructive power. Each had his left arm upraised and bent, as if to guard his face and head, and in their eyes the lust of combat glistened.

Agnes was transfixed with horror and at the same time thrilled as she had never been thrilled in her life before. No excitement she had ever imagined, waking or dreaming, was remotely comparable to this. She perhaps could not have run if she had tried; she would not have tried if she had thought of it. She thought of nothing. She sat perfectly still, her mouth hard set, her hands clenched, a look in her eyes she would not have believed in her own mirror.

The fighters seemed to pursue each other slowly in a small circle, eye to eye, sparring a little, and Agnes gasped with delight. They moved with the fluid ease and unconscious grace of leopards, and gave the same impression of tense coiled strength. She had not the faintest idea hitherto that the man thing could be like this.

Then, so swiftly that she did not see it, the first clean blow went in, with the sound of a butcher's cleaver falling on the block. The effect of that sound upon Agnes was tremendous. She felt a swooning of worlds in the pit of her stomach. Solids were fluid. Her moorings gave way. Nothing in her experience of men had prepared her for the possibility of this. She had seen below the surface. The surface would never be the same again. What an awful sound! She felt she could not bear to hear it again; yet she listened for it breathlessly, frantically.

She saw blood on the tall one's face. That did not make her sick. It made her violently partisan. She has been so all the time without knowing it. Thought of the heavy brute winning was intolerable. She could not see his face distinctly, for he crouched much lower than his antagonist and looked out from under his shaggy eyebrows, thus presenting the top of his head. When by accident, however, his face did come into full view she was relieved to see that he was bleeding freely. The tall one in fact was not bleeding at all. It was the other's blood transferred to him. And then, as she saw how it was really going, she beat her knees with her fists and could hardly restrain the impulse to cry out.

The Cornishman was Thane's equal in strength and vitality and forced the fighting at first with ferocious onsets. But he was as a bull against a tiger. His blows, falling short or going wild, landed always where his enemy precisely was not. Thane, doing it thoughtfully, planted his blows unerringly. He let the Cornishman come to him so long as he would and simply cut him to pieces, keeping some of himself all the time in reserve.

The end came in that instant when Thane really exerted himself. The Cornishman changed his tactics. He stopped lunging, stood on the defensive, and waited for Thane to come to him.

In this attitude it happened that the Cornishman's back was to Agnes, not squarely, but only slightly oblique. Therefore, she had a fair full view of Thane as he came toward the Cornishman.

The cool, easy purposefulness of him agitated her in a most extraordinary way. She knew he had won.

He walked straight into the Cornishman's guard and without any feint or pass he did two things at once with such amazing swiftness that the eye could not follow. With his left hand he put aside the Cornishman's defending arm and with his right he hit him, on the point of his offensive chin, a blow the sound of which was like the snapping of a great tree trunk on the knee of a windstorm.

For an instant nothing happened, except that Thane folded his arms and stood looking seriously at the Cornishman. Then the Cornishman's arms fell, his form swayed, and he began to go around in a circle faster and faster, as if one leg at each step became shorter and was letting him down in spite of his efforts to overtake his balance. He was going to fall. Where?

The battle had taken place all at one side of the path where a level space was. From the other side of the path, where Agnes was, the ground pitched off. The stone on which she sat was two feet below the level of the path. The grass concealed her head.

The spinning Cornishman was almost in the path, directly above her. It seemed probable that he would fall in a heap, pitching forward. It was incredible that he should catch himself up; yet he did it with a mighty effort, stopped spinning, stood upright for a moment, then unexpectedly toppled backard over the edge of the path and fell with all his weight upon Agnes.

She screamed and tried to parry the awful mass. It bore her under and she rolled with it a little distance down the hillside. Before she was free of it she saw above her the face of Thane, white and scared.

He picked herup, all of her, bodily, as if she were a doll, carried her back to the path, and stood her on end experimentally.

"Hurt?"

"No," she said, grimacing with pain.

"You are," he said. "Let's see you stand up."

He let go of her and she began to go over.

"My ankle," she said. "It got a little twist. Let me sit down."

Having lowered her gently to a sitting posture he got down on his knees and regarded her anxiously.

"That all? Just the ankle?"

"I'll be all right in a minute or two," she said. Pointing to the vanquished lump she asked: "What about him?"

"That?" he said. "Don't worry. It ain't dead. It'll come to after a bit."

Her breath was in her throat and her mind was filled with after images of the event. She was still outside of herself with excitement.

"I was on your side," she said naïvely. Some secret thought then touched her and she doubled up with a tickled sound. Her suppressed feelings were exploding.

Thane at that moment realized that she had witnessed the fight. Next he became painfully conscious of himself. He felt a burning sensation from his middle to the roots of his hair; and as he rose and went looking in the grass for his shirt his movements were awkward, almost clumsy. Having found his shirt he walked a long way off to put it on. When he returned he had the Cornishman's shirt. That hulk of vanity was beginning to stir as from a deep sleep. Thane helped him to his feet, set him in the path with his face averted, put the garment in his hands, and earnestly desired him to disappear.

Then he stood looking down at Agnes. A moment before they had been as free and natural as children. Now they were false, self-embarrassed.

"How is it now?" he asked.

"Better," she said.

Silence.

"Maybe you could rub it."

"It's getting all right," she said.

More silence.

"My name is Alexander."

"My name is Agnes," she replied.

Silence again.

"Agnes what?"

"Gib," she said.

"You old Enoch's girl?" he asked.

She did not answer.

"Was you cuttin' it?" he asked.

"Was I what?"

"Givin' 'im the slip?"

"I'm on my way home," she said. "Please don't bother any more about me. I'm quite all right now."

Her manner had changed. Her tone was formal and dismissive. Thane moved away from her, uncertain what to do, looked about in the grass for his lunch basket, found it, stood for some minutes twirling it in his hands, and slowly came back.

"Better 'd let me take you home."

"Thank you," she said. "I know my way home."

"It ain't no place for you out here. Them from the mill is all right, but these new miners, they go back 'n forwards singing and fighting. They'd scare you most to death... or worse."

She was looking off into the valley and made no reply.

"Better 'd let me take you home."

"Please," she said, "I don't wish to be taken home."

"Ain't you got to go home?"

To this her only answer was an exasperated shrug of the shoulders. All he could see of her was the expression of her back and it was so unfriendly that it took everything out of him but the doggedness. He waited until it was evident she did not mean to speak again. Then he walked about in a fumble of perplexity and at length threw himself on the grass and comfortably lighted his pipe.

After a while she spoke without turning her head.

"Are you there for the night?"

"Jus' standing by," he said. "Can't leave you here like you was a cripple bird."

Agnes was secretly entertained. She had also a feeling of being wonderfully safe. Yet the absurdity of her predicament filled her with chagrin. She hated to be helpless. "I can walk," she said to herself. "I will."

She got up, took one step bravely and came down again with an involuntary cry of pain.

At that Thane rose with a fixed intention, knocked his pipe clean on his heel, dropped it in his pocket, and came toward her, hitching at his belt. She knew intuitively what he meant to do and felt herself for an instant in the place of the Cornishman as he stood waiting for Thane to come and finish him.

He did not speak. Leaning over, he picked her off the ground and settled her high in his arms.

First she was furiously angry. Her thoughts were: "How dare you! Put me down instantly and be gone." The words did not come. She noticed how lightly he carried her, almost as if he were not touching her, and how easily he walked. She was helpless. If she resisted he would only hold her differently and go steadily on. She could scream or struggle. To scream would be childish. She had not the least inclination to scream. And to struggle would be futile. So she took refuge in passivity. Then sensations began to assail her. She was suddenly afraid. Fear was an emotion she seldom experienced. Never had she been afraid like this. What she was afraid of she did not know. She was not sure it was fear. It was more like the thrill one gets in a high swing from the thought, "What if the rope should break I" or in the phantasy of taking the place of the animal trainer, from the thought, "What if the lion should turn!" She remembered not the words but the sense of a line of Greek poetry about maidens swooning from fear of finding that which not to find would grieve them unto death.

She was still herself, Agnes, furiously angry at being carried without her consent. At the same time she was not Agnes. The Agnes she knew was but a name and a memory. She herself, now existing originally, was someone whose only desire was to be carried further, faster, higher, off the edge of the world. She breathed deeply, inhaling his odor.

Seeing that he should carry her more easily if her weight were somewhat distributed by her own effort she put an arm around his neck. It tightened there as she suspended her weight to relieve his arms. Then came an instant in which she was amazed at the impulse, which she restrained, to fasten the other arm about his neck. In the rough places he began to hold her a little closer each time and not to relax when it was smooth again. She was not aware of it. Her odor intoxicated Thane. Sometimes he lost the path and stumbled. That she did not notice. She listened to his breathing, counted it against her own, and felt the rythmic rise and fall of his powerful chest.

At a point where they turned out of the path through a piece of high grass to enter the highway both of them as it were came awake.

"Put me down, please," she said in a low voice, hardly above a whisper, —a voice she did not know.

He apparently did not hear her.

They came to the great iron gate.

"Put me down," she said again.

Still he seemed not to hear. With his foot he rattled the gate, calling in a loud, uncontrolled voice, —the voice of a man in danger —"Hey! Hey!" He was trembling all over.

Three times he rattled the gate and called. Twice he was answered only by the reverberations of his own clamor, which shocked the stillness of the night and left a vacant ringing in the ears. In the grass the crickets sang. Far away a dog barked once and a cock woke up. Each could hear the beating of the other's heart.

What happened the third time was apparitional. Suddenly, there was Enoch, behind the gate, looking at them. He had been there all the time in the shadow of the wall. He held a lighted lantern. That also had been concealed. Slowly he raised the latch-bar and swung the gate ajar. Then he held the lantern high and gazed unbelievingly at Thane, who was the first to speak.

"Found her up there in the grass. Was having a bit of a tiff, two of us, me 'n the Cornishman, 'n he fell on her when I knocked him out, 'n hurt her ankle, hiding there so as nobody could see her. She couldn't walk, so's I brought her home."

Agnes neither stirred nor spoke. In the light of the lantern her eyes gleamed with a trapped expression. Enoch did not look at her, not even on hearing that she was hurt, but continued to stare fixedly at his puddler, repeating after him: "In the grass."

"Don't you want her?" Thane asked.

At that Enoch lowered the lantern, swung the gate open and stood aside.

"Take her in," he said.

As the puddler passed, Enoch closed and barred the gate; he followed them up the driveway toward the mansion. The only sound was the crunching of the two men's feet on the gravel.

Then Enoch laughed. It was an abominable sound, denoting a cruel conclusion in his mind. Agnes shuddered. Her hold around the puddler's neck involuntarily tightened. So did his hold of her. Thus a subtle sign passed between them. Neither one spoke.

At the entrance Enoch overtook them, opened the door, and walked ahead. There were no servants in sight. In this household servants appeared when summoned and never otherwise.

"In here," said Enoch, opening the hall door into the back parlor on the ground floor. This was his side of the house. The room was dimly lighted. The puddler put his burden down on a couch and turned to look at Enoch, who stood in the doorway.

"Stay here, both of you, until I return," he said. With that he closed the door and turned the key from the outside.

Thane in his mill clothes, —iron studded shoes, ankle aprons, trousers, shirt open to the middle of his chest, and cap, —was bewildered and overcome with conscious awkwardness. He looked at things as if they might bark at him and stood with his weight on one leg, having no use for the other. It stuck out from him at a great distance, and terminated absurdly in a performing foot, rocking on its heel and wearing a place in the varnished surface of the floor.

Agnes, who had been straining her faculties to hear what might be taking place outside, became aware of his distress.

"Please sit down and listen," she said. "Over there," pointing to an arm chair.

They heard the jangling of bells, the opening and closing of doors, and presently a carriage went off in haste. It must have been waiting. There had not been time to harness a team. Then faintly they heard footsteps patrolling the hallway. They were Enoch's.

"I haven't any idea what I've got you into," said Agnes.

"Seem's it ain't ready yet," he said, and smiled at her.

His smile was a revelation, swift and unexpected, like an event in a starlit sky. Agnes had not seen it before. It gave her a start of joy. She smiled back at him and then blushed. That made her angry. She was always angry at herself for blushing because it gave her away. Her defense was to look at him steadily and; that made him self-conscious again. She had discovered that when his thoughts were dynamically engaged, or when his mind was intended to action, instantly all awkwardness left him. Then he was graceful unawares, as children and animals are, never thinking of themselves. She could not bear to see him fidget.

"You don't seem to care," she said.

"He bears down hard on you, don't he, Enoch?" he asked.

"His nature is hard," she said.

"Maybe you was cuttin' it an' here I brought you home. Ain't that so?"

"No," she said.

He came half way across the room and regarded her earnestly.

"If that's it, it ain't too late now. I'll take you anywhere you want." As she did not answer, he added: "Jus take 'n leave you there so's you need never see me again."

"Thank you," she said, gently. "That wouldn't be nice, would it, —never to see you again after that?

No. I'm —what was it you said? —I'm standing by."

He sat down again, disappointed.

"I must tell you what happened," she said. "I broke out and went to a party in town. That isn't allowed. I expected a scene when I got home. It might have been very disagreeable for the-for my escort, you know. So, having first run away to go to the party, I next ran away from the party and started home alone. You know the rest."

"Oh," said Thane, thoughtfully.

A sudden constraint fell upon them. Their eyes did not meet again.

They were sitting in silence, she in reverie, when a sound of commotion was heard in the hallway. The carriage had returned. Double footsteps approached.

The door opened, admitting Enoch, and with him the Presbyterian minister, a clean, tame, ox-like man with a very large bald head, no eyebrows and round blue eyes. Enoch closed the door. Thane stood up. The minister looked first at him and then at Agnes. Her eyes were full of wonder, tinged with premonition. Enoch spoke.

"We found her in the grass. That's the man. Marry them."

The minister, regarding both of them at once in an oblique manner, began to nod his head up and down as if saying to himself, "Oh-ho! So this is what we find?"

Thane was slow to understand Enoch's words. He had the look of a man in the act of doubting his familiar senses.

Agnes, very pale, lips slightly parted, nostrils distended, sitting very erect, turned her head slowly and gazed at her father. The muscles around her eyes were tense and drawn, her eyes were hard and partially closed as if the sun were in them, and she looked at him so until his countenance fell. But not his wickedness.

"Marry them," he said.

Thane reacted suddenly. He cleared his throat, swallowed, glanced right and left, and took a step forward, with a tug at his belt.

"You're supposing what ain't so," he shouted at Enoch. "What do you mean by that about finding her in the grass? What does that mean? Me 'n the Cornishman was racketing up there in the path like I told you at the gate. He ain't come to yet, so there's nobody can say as what happened but me 'n the girl. She oughten have seen it. That's correct. But there ain't no harm done-none as you could speak of. If you don't believe me ask her... You tell them," he said, turning to Agnes.

"My father is mad," she said.

Thane began to tell them what had passed on the path and became utterly incoherent. Despairing, he made a move toward Enoch. The minister raised his hand.

"What is your name?"

"Alexander Thane."

Enoch, who had been standing with his back to the door, opened it, reached around the jamb and drew it back holding a shot gun, the barrel of which he rested on his left arm.

"Marry them, I tell you." His voice was low. "Make it short."

Thane made another move toward him. The minister raised his hand again, —a fat, white hand. It fascinated Thane and calmed him.

"Thane," said the minister, "do you take this woman to be your lawful wife?"

"Not as he says it. Not for that shooting thing as he's got there in his hand," said Thane. "Not unless the girl wants it," he added, as a disastrous and extremely complicated afterthought.

If he had flatly said no, the shape of the climax might have been different. There was no lack of courage. What stopped him was a romantic seizure.

The minister turned to Agnes.

"Will you, Agnes, take this man Thane to be your husband?"

The die was then in her hands. Thane had not meant to pass it. Gladly would he have retaken it if only he had known how to do so. The situation was beyond his resources. Moreover, the question —"Will you, Agnes, take this man Thane to be your husband?" —was so momentous to him that it deprived him of his wits and senses, save only the sense of hearing.

Emotions more dissimilar could scarcely be allotted to three men in a single scene, one of them mad, yet for a moment they were united by a feeling of awe and regarded Agnes with one expression. The woman's courage surpasses the man's. This he afterward denies in his mind, saying the difference is that she lacks a sense of consequences.

Agnes was cool and contemplative, and in no haste to answer. She kept them waiting. They could not see her face. Her head was bent over. With one hand she plucked at the pattern of her dress and seemed to be counting. Then slowly she began to nod her head.

"Yes," she said, distinctly, though in a very far voice, "I will."

"Stand up, please," said the minister.

Thane made his responses as one in a dream. Hers were firm and clear, and all the time she was looking at her father as she had looked at him first, with those tight little wrinkles around her eyes.

So they were married.

"That's all," said Enoch, to the minister, curtly. "The carriage is at the door."

The minister bowed and vanished.

Enoch drew a piece of cardboard from his pocket and handed it to Thane. It was a blue ticket, —the token of dismissal.

"Now go," he said, "and let me never see you again."

Agnes looked up at Thane.

"I can walk," she said, taking him by the arm. It was so. She could, with a slight limp. Enoch, seeing it, sneered. He watched them walk into the night and closed the door behind them.

At the gate Thane said: "But you can't," and started to pick her up.

"Don't," she said.

They had changed places. She was no longer afraid of him. He was afraid of her.

XIX

All this time John had been seeking Agnes. First he went the high road to the mansion until he was sure she had not gone that way, for if she had he would have overtaken her. Turning back he began to make inquiries and presently heard of someone, undoubtedly she, who had been seen walking wide of the town, past the mill, toward the mountain. Knowing the path and divining her intention he walked in her footsteps.

The smell of Thane's pipe was still in the air when he arrived at the place where the fight had taken place. A thing of white in the grass drew his eye. He picked it up and got a bad start. It was a tiny handkerchief. By the light of a match he made out the initials A. G. embroidered in one corner. Looking further he found a scarf that he instantly recognized. He had particularly noticed it on their way to the party. Now in a panic he began to examine the ground closely and discovered extensive evidence of a human struggle. Running up and down the path a short distance each way he came on the Cornishman's shirt a little to one side where the groggy owner had tossed it away. To John's disgust it was slimy with something that came off in his hands; as this proved to be blood his disgust gave way to horror.

Without actually formulating the thought, because it was too dreadful to be true, he acted under the tyranny of a fixed idea, which was that Agnes had met with a foul disaster. The possibility was real. Lately there had come to New Damascus a group of mill hands whose ways and morals were alien to the community. They were bestial drinkers and had been making a great deal of trouble.

In a state of frenzy he explored the mountain side, calling her name. His panic rising, it occurred to him to ask at the mill among the men who continually used the path. He found several who had been over it within a hour or so. Someone was missing, he told them. Something unknown had happened. Had they seen or heard anything unusual. They became individually contemplative, made him say it all over again, repeated it after him, thought very hard and shook their heads. Nobody had seen or heard the least thing strange. But somebody did, by a freak of intelligent association, remember the Cornishman. He was out there under the water tank, speechless and weeping, not caring whether Enoch saw him or not. Maybe something had happened to him.

John found him as indicated, with his face in his hands, water dripping on his naked back.

"What happened to you?" John asked, shaking him.

"Gotten m'dam head knocked off," he groaned, without moving. It was a refrain running through him. John's attack had made it once audible.

"Up there in the path?"

He grunted.

"Who was it?"

Faintly, though very definitely, the Cornwall beauty expressed a passionate desire to be let alone.

"Was there a girl?" John asked.

"Huh!" said the hulk, instantly penetrated by the sound of that word.

John repeated the question.

The Cornishman stirred painfully, sat up, turned a stupidly grinning face and nodded-yes.

"Who took her away?" John asked, thumping the body to keep the mind afloat. "Tell me," he said, shaking him by the hair. "Where did they go?" he asked, kicking him in the shins.

But the Cornishman was either slyer or more stupefied than one could imagine. He relapsed. Nothing more could be got out of him.

There now was but one rational thing to do—report to Enoch and raise a general alarm.

From running hard with a load of dread John was almost spent when he arrived at the mansion gate. It was shut and barred; the house was dark and where he had expected to find alarm and commotion everything was strangely still. Foreboding assailed him. Thinking it might be quicker to open the gate than to climb the wall he put his hand through and began to fumble with the latch bar inside. He was so intent upon the effort that a certain indefinable sense one may have of another's invisible proximity failed to warn him of Enoch's presence.

There was a swift, noiseless movement in the darkness and a hand clutched him powerfully by the wrist. The physical disadvantage of his position made him helpless. Over the vertical bars of the gate ran a pattern of wrought iron ornamentation in the form of vine and leaves; the interstices were irregular, with sharp edges. It was impossible to use his free arm defensively because there was no other opening through which he could reach far enough in. Besides, if he resisted Enoch could instantly snap the bones of his trapped arm. He was utterly bewildered by the circumstances. Enoch's gesture was menacing, even terrifying in its sinister precision, and yet John could scarcely imagine that his intentions were destructive. So he submitted his arm passively to the old man's dangerous grip and spoke.

"It is I," he said. His voice betrayed his spirit, which was at the verge of panic. Enoch did not speak. His hold tightened. "I was trying to let myself in ta save time," said John. "Agnes is lost. That is, I can't find her. I was coming to tell you."

Enoch still did not speak.

"Perhaps she is home," said John. "Have you seen her? If you haven't I'm afraid something has happened to her."

The old man's continued silence was unnatural and ominous. Slowly, purposefully, he drew John's arm further in, to almost the elbow; it came to him unresistingly and bare, the cuffs of the coat and shirt having caught on the vine work outside. Then he began to explore it upward from the wrist, feeling through the flesh for the edges of the radius and ulna bones, passing them an inch at a time between his tumb and forefinger as if searching for something he was afraid to find. John's arm had once been broken in a football game at school. There was a perceptible ridge in the radius bone at the point of fracture. On this ridge Enoch's fingers stopped, lost their strength and began to tremble. At the same time the grip of his other hand around John's wrist began to relax in a slow_involuntary manner.

"*Aaron!*" he whispered, awesomely.

The next instant John's arm was free and there was the sound of a body falling on the gravel inside the gate.

Now John scaled the wall. He stopped to make sure Enoch was breathing and to ease his form on the ground; then he ran to the mansion. His furious alarm brought a stolid, dark woman to the door, holding a small oil light over her head.

"Is Miss Gib at home?" he asked.

The woman shook her head.

"Does anyone know where she is?"

In a dull manner the woman shook her head again.

"Mr. Gib has fallen at the front gate," said John. "Go to him at once and send someone for the doctor."

The woman put the lamp down on the floor where she stood and started alone down the driveway, running.

"Call the servants," said John. "You may have to carry him in."

But she went only faster. He followed her. Before he could overtake her she met Enoch. He could see them both clearly in the light streaming from the doorway. The woman looked at Enoch anxiously and made as if to touch him, solicitously. He did not exactly ignore her; he seemed not to see her at all and walked steadily on.

John turned out of the light and passed unobserved in the darkness. Then he ran headlong off the grounds, feeling at each step that his knees would let him down. His emotional state was almost unmanageable. The episode with Enoch at the gate had been not only very mysterious but fraught with some ghastly inner meaning to which he had no clue whatever. He knew nothing of Enoch's obsession that he, John, was Aaron reincarnated. He had never heard of that boyhood contest in which Enoch broke Aaron's arm. Therefore he could not know what it meant in Enoch's troubled brain to find in the arm of Aaron's son the scar of a similar fracture at almost precisely the corresponding place. To him it *was* the same scar in the same arm. It was the last thing needed to fix his hallucination and the discovery had momentarily overwhelmed his senses.

In that instant he had called John by his father's name, —Aaron!

What did it mean? Intuitively John knew that here was the key to the riddle. But he could not apply it. He could see that in taking Esther, his mother, away from Enoch his father had brought upon himself

Enoch's undying hatred. He could understand how such hatred might naturally be transferred to the son. Only, in that case, how could he explain the fact that until now Enoch's attitude toward him had been friendly or indifferent?

XX

So his thoughts were running in this perplexed and absent manner when suddenly a very urgent question burst through.

"What of Agnes?"

She was not at home. He could think of no way to find her unassisted. He knew not where to look next and time was pressing. It was necessary to raise a wide alarm and organize a search. But he had no authority to act. It was her father's business to take such steps. Now recalling what he had said to Enoch through the gate about Agnes he realized that it was absurdly inadequate. He had not at all communicated his fears concerning her. Therefore, though the thought of another encounter with Enoch made him shudder, he would have to go back. On this decision he came to a sudden stop and was surprised to see how far he had come unawares, and that he was not on the highway. When or how he had left it he did not remember. "I must have come fast," he thought. He was half way back to New Damascus, not far from the mill, in a road that further on became a street running into sooty locust trees, cinder sidewalks, rows of company houses and a stale, historic smell of fried food. Turning in his tracks he was making back when his name was called from the side of the road by a voice he instantly knew.

"Thane!" he said, going toward him. "I need you. Please go-oh! I'm sorry. I thought you were alone."

He veered off at seeing the figure of a woman behind Thane, leaning on the fence, her face averted; but Thane, coming forward, caught him by the arm, saying anxiously:

"I need your advice is why I called you."

"Hold it, whatever it is, Thane," John answered. "I can't stop now. I just can't." He was pulling away.

"Won't hold," said Thane.

"It must," said John. "I can't stop. I'm sorry." He liked Thane and was loath to leave him in a lurch. "Go to the hotel and wait for me there," he said, pushing him off. "I'll be back as soon as I can."

With that he was going when the woman spoke.

"Are you looking for me?"

"Agnes!" said John to himself, as a declaration of preposterous fact. He wheeled around and stood stone still.

One instant before he had been mad with anxiety to hear her voice. Yet to the sound of it, so collected and sure, his emotional reaction was one of fierce anger. There was also a desolate world-wide sense of loss. Why he was angry or what was lost he could not have said in words. These feelings referred to her. Toward Thane there was a thought that seemed to rise behind him with purpose and power of its own; and he braced his back against it.

"I've been looking everywhere for you," he said, approaching her. "I found these." He held out the handkerchief and scarf. She took them. "Then I went to the mansion...and..." There he stopped.

"Yes. What did you learn there?" she asked.

His anger kept rising. How could she be so suave and frontal about it? He had actually the impulse to set hands upon her roughly and demand to know what she had been doing, how she came to be here alone on a dark road with an iron puddler and how she could pretend to be so unembarrassed.

"Nothing," he said. "It had just this instant occurred to me to go back and try again. I was in a beastly fume about you."

"And seem to be still," she said, in a way to put him in mind of the high tone he had been using.

"For reasons to which you are pleased to be oblivious," he retorted. "It is to be imagined that I have some interest in seeing you safely home. May I take you on from here?"

"Another one," Agnes murmured in a tone of soliliquy. "How repetitious!"

The thought touched off her feelings. They exploded in a burst of shrill, irrelevant laughter. John was scandalized. His rage was boundless. Yet at the same time his sense of responsibility increased. Abominable thoughts assailed him. He wondered if perhaps her father had not been right to keep her under restraint. He fervently wished he had never tempted her to break out. A resolve to get her home by force if necessary was forming in his mind when Thane put in.

"They ain't no home," he said. "That's the trouble."

"What do you know about it?" John asked, blazing.

"Oughten I know somewhat about it seeing as she's my own wife?" said Thane, with dismal veracity.

John, for an instant appalled, turned fiercely on Agnes. "Now what have you done?" he asked. She was so startled by his manner that she couldn't speak. "What have you done?" he demanded, now shaking her and with such authority that for a moment her spirit quailed. "Is it true? Are you married?"

"Yes," she said.

"To a...." He caught the word just in time, slowly let go of her and stepped back.

"Say it," she dared him. "To a... to... a what? Go on. Say it."

John's anger was gone. Other emotions had swallowed it up, —sorrow, pity, remorse, that devastating sense of loss again, more poignant than before in some new way, and above all a great yearning toward both of them.

"Where?" he asked, in a changed voice.

"In my father's house," said Agnes, derisively. "What a pity you missed it!"

"But what happened?" asked John.

She answered weirdly, improvising silly words to a silly tune: —

> *"What hap-pen-ed*
>> *"What hap-pen-ed*
>> *"What hap-pen-ed*
>> *"Here Mildred?*
>> *"That hap-pen-ed*
>> *"That hap-pen-ed*
>> *"That hap-pen-ed*
>> *"Sir, she said."*

A horrified silence fell.

"Was it flat?" she asked. "I'm sorry. I know something to do. Let's each one tell the story of his life. Shall I begin?"

She began to sing again —

"What hap-pen-ed... "

"Please," said John. "Please don't. You make my blood run cold."

"She's that way ever since," said Thane, with an air of sharing his misery.

"Then you tell me," said John.

"I carried her home," said Thane, now weary of telling it, "from where she got hurt between me an' the Cornishman knocking ourselves around in the path, an' old Enoch he got a wicked notion as I don't know what an' sent for the preacher an' we was married. Then he handed me the blue ticket an' put us out of the house."

John turned to Agnes with a question on his tongue. She anticipated him and began to sing: —

"What hap-pen-ed..."

As he shuddered and turned away again she stopped.

"I was coming for my street clothes to where I live," continued Thane, "being as I was all that time in my puddling rig an' we got bogged here like you see us now. Nothing I say let's do will move her. And when I say all right, what does she want, she chanties about me, making them up out of nothing."

"When they get like that," said John, "you have to use force. You've got to pick them up."

"Can't work it," said Thane.

"Why not? Does she bite?"

"No."

"What then?"

"Can't work it,' said Thane. "Not since," he added.

"The subject of this clinic is conscious." said Agnes, pleasantly.

They paid no attention to her.

"You board, don't you? You were not intending to take her there?" said John.

"Only so as to get my clothes," said Thane.

"We can't do anything until you get your clothes," said John. "That's plain. I'll stay here with her while you go for them. But don't be long. Then maybe we can think of something to do."

Thane went off at once with a tremendous sigh of relief in the feeling of action. His feet made a cavernous *tlump, tlump, tlump-ing* on the hard dirt road. John, who stood regarding Agnes from the side of the road, was sure he saw her shudder. Then from the heedless tone with which she broke the silence he was sure he had been mistaken.

"It seems you know my husband," she said.

He was surprised that she had no difficulty with the word, though it must have been the first time she had ever used it in the possessive sense-and in such circumstances!

"Can't you think of anything feasible to do?" John asked.

"Do you like him?" she inquired.

"Because if you can't," said John, "I can. It's too much for Thane. That isn't fair."

He supposed she was thinking. To his disgust she began to sing, softly, tunefully:

> *"Lovely maiden, tell me truly,*
> *"Is the ocean very wet?*
> *"If I meet you on the bottom,*
> *"Will you never once — —"*

"Stop it!" He moved as if to menace her. She stopped and looked at him soberly.

"Is there nothing I can do to entertain you? I might recite. And you haven't answered my question."

"You give me the horrors," he blurted. "No, no I'm sorry. I'm unstrung, that's all. Please do be serious. We've got to think of what we shall do."

"Who are we?"

"I beg your pardon. You, then," he amended.

"Who are you?" she asked.

"Agnes, do for... "

"Mrs. Thane, please."

"I don't expect you to be amiable," he said, "but please for one moment be reasonable."

"When they are like that you can't do anything with them," she said. "Really you can't. You will have to see my husband."

She had seated herself on a grassy bench with her back to the fence, her feet in the dry ditch, and was viciously jabbing the earth with a limber stick. She threw the stick from her, leaned back, folded her arms and tilted her chin at the sky, with an air of casting John out of existence. He had given up trying to talk and stood observing her in an overt manner. It was thus he saw how she looked at the moon, first vacantly without seeing it, then with a start as of recognition or recollection, and at length with an expression of such twisted mocking wistfulness that he knew one shape of her heart and turned wretchedly away, almost wishing he had not seen.

For a long time she did not move. She seemed under a kind of spell. Thane found them so, in separate states of reverie. Neither heard his footsteps approaching.

"I was thinking why should I bother you like this," said Thane, "being though as we are friends in a way. If only it was so as I could touch something."

"Thane," said John, slowly, "listen to what I am thinking. The skeins of our three lives have run together in a hard knot. Mine and that of Agnes were already twisted together in a very strange history. Yours got entangled by chance, heaven knows why. Fate does it. Nobody is to blame. But I am responsible."

"For us being married?" asked Thane.

"For that, yes. But for a great deal more. I am only beginning to see the meaning of things. By inheritance I am responsible for something my father and mother did to Enoch before I was born, for the fact that Agnes is his daughter and he is not my father, for the fact that he is mad. He has had his revenge on Aaron's son, greater than he knows. What that means I cannot tell you. I shall never say it again. But what I want you to see is that I cannot leave you to face the consequences alone. It is not a matter of friendship. You are married to Agnes. In a foster sense I am married to both of you."

His face was lighted from within. He spoke in the absent, anonymous manner of one undergoing a mystical experience. Something of his mood entered Thane. With one impulse they had struck hands and now stood looking deeply into each other's eyes.

"I don't know as I see what you mean," said Thane.

"No," said John. "You wouldn't. I've confused you, trying to get it all said at once. There is first the fact that we are friends. My feeling for you in that way has increased suddenly, I don't quite know why. And now, above that, is my sense of responsibility for what has happened. You must accept my view of that. It shall be understood that I have a right to stand by and that I may be trusted... absolutely trusted... whatever comes...."

He groped and stopped and seemed to have gone to sleep with his eyes open.

Thane moved uneasily. John, returning to himself, started slightly and released Thane's hand. When he spoke his voice was altered.

"I can't make it come clear," he said. "I thought I could."

"I've looked my eyes out that way, too," said Thane. "Let's take it as it is."

What John at first had so clear a vision of was an act of heroic self-denial. It thrilled him with momentary ecstasy. That may be understood. Man is an emotional formation, subject to sudden passions, one of which is the passion of sacrifice. Blindly on the spot he rears an altar, lays the wood in order and looks to see what offering hath in a miraculous manner provided itself to be burnt. Lo! there stands the one thing most beloved in all the world. The Lord sometimes interferes, as for Isaac. Sometimes the victim saves itself. Then again the man draws back. He has not the heart to do it.

John drew back. To conclude the covenant with Thane meant forswearing Agnes in his heart forever. That was a vow he could neither bring himself to make nor trust himself to keep. And yet, any secret reservation seemed treachery to Thane. So there he stood before this truth of contradiction and "looked his eyes out" at it. How came Thane to have a thought like that?

Agnes was observing them intently with one elbow on her knee, her chin in her hand, eyes half closed. She was not thinking. She was verifying a kind of knowledge that underlies the mind. She knew why John faltered, why he lost his way toward what he meant to do, what that was, and why he dropped Thane's hand. She knew what it was of a sudden to become a woman and why a woman need never be afraid.

Far away in the sky of her immemorial self, so far that what she saw of it was but its heat's reflection, passed a flash of contempt for those tame, romantic vanities in which now man sublimates the reckless impulses of his savage egoism. At that instant, too, as it were in the light of this archaic intuition, there stood upon her memory the figure of the Cornishman, and she was horribly ashamed.

Nevertheless she continued to feel cynical about the emotional male principle. It bored her. There was one obvious thing to do. There was in fact only one thing possible to be done. But apparently neither Thane nor John was ever going to think of it, or give her a chance to suggest it without boldly naming it. One might have thought they had forgotten her existence. They stood in the middle of the road, John with his back to her, Thane with his eyes in the heavens, sharing a vast man-silence. She was at the core of that silence; she was all there was there. That did not interest her at all. She wished to be somewhere else.

She got up quietly and walked away from them, away from New Damascus, with a very bad list and limp. They overtook her in four or five steps, one on each side.

"What's this way now?" Thane asked.

No answer.

"She isn't fit to walk," said John. "Don't let her; do it."

She looked at Thane; the gesture he was making toward her froze in the air.

"Take her as you would a nettle, firmly," John recommended.

"'Tain't what's outside I'm afraid of," said Thane.

Stepping ahead and turning, John confronted her. Thane did the same. She made to go around them, right. They moved that way. She made to go around them, left. They moved that way. With a frustate gesture she gave it up, turned a tormented profile and made them feel how much she despised them.

"Mrs. Thane," said John, "do you wish to leave New Damascus-leave it now-tonight?"

Agnes turned on him in a sudden rage of exasperation.

"Fly, I suppose! Fly away with a —a —what is he? I forget."

"Oh, oh," John groaned.

"What are you?" she said to Thane.

"Puddler," he answered, with dignity, the look of a hurt animal in his face.

"It's very well known," she said, "puddlers don't fly. Besides it's too late. We've stopped to think. We had to take time to change his clothes. He's out of a job and has no money. He told me so. I wonder what the wives of puddlers do."

"Some would envy you your sting," said John, horrified at what she was doing to Thane. She understood him perfectly.

"But you are immune," she said. "I have not married you. Or have I? Are you this puddler's David? What are your rights in him? How come you to suppose that you have rights in me?"

"Tantrums, thank God, and not hysterics," said John.

"Shall we spend the rest of the night in this way?" she asked. "And what then?"

"I am leaving New Damascus tonight," said John, pursuing a flash of intuition.

Agnes gave him an incredulous glance.

"So far as I know, forever," he continued. "This decision is my own. You have nothing to do with it. But if you were also about to leave, perhaps taking the same direction, why shouldn't we go together, as far as it's parallel?"

"Who goes or stays, no matter what happens, I shall not be in sight of New Damascus at daybreak," said Agnes, her face averted from both John and her husband, and she spoke as one making a vow. "So, whatever you do," she added, "please hurry."

Thane would have asked her a question, *not* knowing how women consent; John restrained him with a sign.

"Then I'll pick you up here," he said, setting off abruptly. "And I won't be very long."

When he returned with a smart bay team and a light road wagon, his own rig, the moon was sinking. Agnes was asleep on the dewy grass in Thane's coat. He wrapped her in the rug John held out to him and lifted her to the seat. She was docile and limp, like a groggy child. John had to hold her erect until Thane got up on the other side. She sat between them.

Where the road turns abruptly out of the valley John pulled up and looked back. It was now quite dark. All that he could see was the mill, like a live malignant cinder in the eye of darkness, glowing faintly, going almost out, then spurting forth quick tongues of flame. He had the sensation of a great solitary weight rolling about in his stomach. Tears came to his eyes. Until that moment he had not known that he cared for New Damascus. His caring was like an inherited memory.

And though he knew it not, this night was the time and his exit the sign that sealed the fate of New Damascus. It was left in the hands of Enoch, who fanatically withheld it from the steel age.

"Where to?" Thane asked.

"Wilkes-Barre tonight," said John. "Then to Pittsburgh. I'm buying a mill at Pittsburgh that I want you to take hold of. We'll discuss it tomorrow."

"What shape of mill?" asked Thane.

John hesitated.

"Nothing like the mill behind us," he said.

The idea of buying a mill had only that instant come to him. So of course he did not know what kind of mill it was.

He looked at Agnes. She was sound asleep, leaning on Thane, who had his arm around her. Again he looked at her. She was in the same position, but her eyes were wide open, staring straight ahead.

XXI

The flying triangle reached Wilkes-Barre for breakfast.

While waiting for Agnes, John and Thane transacted an important piece of business.

"Look here," said John.

He sat at a desk in the office and wrote rapidly on a sheet of hotel paper as follows:

MEMORANDUM OF CONTRACT

In consideration of one month's wages paid in hand on the signing of this paper, Alexander Thane agrees to give his skill and services exclusively to the North American Manufacturing Company, Ltd., (John Breakspeare, agent), for a period of two years, and the North American Manufacturing Company, Ltd., agrees to pay Alexander Thane not less that five thousand dollars a year, plus a ten per cent, share in the profits.

<h1>Signed { John Breakspeare</h1>

"Put your name over mine," he said, handing the paper to Thane, who read it slowly.

"This the mill you meant last night?"

"Yes," said John.

"How did you come to know as I could run a mill?"

"I think you can," John said.

Thane signed his name in large, bold writing, blotted it hard, and handed the paper back to John.

"You're right," he said. "I can. And if it appears for any reason as I can't that thing ain't no good and you can tear it up."

It never occurred to him that the business had a fabulous aspect. He took what John said at its face value. He could imagine no other way of taking a friend's word. And if it were unusual for a young puddler to become a participating mill superintendent over night, so urgently wanted that he must sign up before breakfast, that might be easily explained. His friend, John Breakspeare, was an extravagant person, very impulsive, with unexpected flashes of insight. Who else would have known what Thane could do? Anyhow he had got the right man to run the mill. Thane was sure of that. He supposed John was sure of it, too.

John just then was sure of nothing. His one anxiety was to get Thane and Agnes into some kind of going order. He was aware that his motives were exceedingly complex and would not examine them. He let himself off with saying it was his moral responsibility; he was to blame for having got them into a dilemma that neither was able to cope with. Yet all the time he was thrilled by what he did because he was doing it for Agnes.

Thane's artlessness about the contract was an instant relief. A fatal difficulty might otherwise have arisen at that point. But it was also very surprising. Was he so extremely naïve? Or had he such a notion of his ability to conduct a mill as to think he would be worth five thousand a year and one-tenth of the profits? Yes, that was the explanation, John decided: and it gave him a bad twist in his conscience to think how hurt and unforgiving Thane would be if he knew the truth, —that he had signed a contract with a nonexistent company to superintend a mythical mill.

They ate a hearty breakfast, coming to it from a night in the open air with no sleep at all. Although they talked very little they were friendly under a truce without terms, all tingling with a sense of plastic adventure. There was no telling what would come of it; but it was exciting; and everything that happened was new.

Both Agnes and John had a surreptitious eye for the puddler's manners. They were not intrinsically bad or disgusting. They were only fundamentally wrong. He delivered with his knife, took his coffee from his saucer, modelled and arranged his food before attacking it, cut all his meat at once, did everything that cannot be done, and did it all with a certain finish. That is to say, he was a neat eater, very handy with his tools, and cleaned up. He took pride in the. performance; his confidence in it was impervious. He was not in the least embarrassed or uneasy. He did not wait to see what they did. He did it his way and minded his own business.

Once John caught Agnes eyeing Thane aslant, and she stared him down for it. He could not decide whether she was scandalized or fascinated.

When they had finished Thane called for the reckoning and paid, John politely protesting, Agnes looking somewhat surprised. After that in all cases Thane paid for two and John paid for himself.

Instead of resting for a day in Wilkes-Barre they chose to go on by train to Pittsburgh and arrived there in the middle of the afternoon. John recommended a hotel where he was sure they could be quite comfortable while deciding how they wished to live. He was acquainted there. He would introduce them. In fact, it was where he meant to lodge himself. So of course they all went together.

John managed the whole affair of settling them in their rooms, doing it so tactfully, however, as to leave Thane with the sense of having done it himself. When at last there was not another thing to be thought of John held out his hand to Agnes, saying:

"Congratulations."

This was subtle, wicked treachery, and in the act was a sting of shame, yet her coolness was so audacious he could not resist the temptation to try its depth. She took his hand and met his look with steady eyes.

"Thank you," she said. "May I share them with my husband?"

"No, don't," he said. "They are all his. I'm about to lose my wits. Well, no matter.... Thane," —turning to him, —"Mrs. Thane may want to do some shopping. The best places are three blocks east. I'll see you in the morning. Or later, perhaps? There's no hurry."

"Tomorrow morning," Thane answered.

They were standing in a group outside the Thanes' rooms, loath to break up, each for a different reason.

"I'm under the same roof, you know, if you should need me," said John.

"Thanks," said Thane.

Still they lingered in a group.

"Have a bit of supper with us," said Thane, suddenly.

"Not tonight," said John. "We shall be too sleepy."

Agnes was silent.

After a long pause, "Well," said Thane, "this is Pittsburgh."

John pensively nodded his head, and added, "Well."

Agnes might have yawned. That would have produced the necessary centrifugal impulse. Or she might have said something to have that effect. But she was apparently sunk in thought.

After another long pause the two men shook hands in a hasty manner and John walked rapidly down the hall. From the head of the staircase he looked back. They were still there, — Agnes, her hands behind her, leaning against the wall with her head thrown back, gazing from afar at Thane, who stood in an awkward twist, with one superfluous leg, looking away. His face was towards John, and John waved his hand, but there was no response. The puddler was staring at an invisible thing.

That last accidental glimpse of them left a vivid after-image in John's eyes. It stood there for hours like a transparent illusion. He walked the sun down on a country road and still it was there. Returning, he paced the streets until ten o'clock and it tortured him still. Coming presently to a fine brick house, not very large, with a marble fountain and small flower garden in front, he turned in. His feet knew their way up the narrow walk and he pulled the bell knob with the air of one to whom nothing unexpected is likely to happen. No light was anywhere visible. The windows were hermetically shuttered. Nor did his pull at the bell knob produce any audible sound. Yet almost at once the door opened, revealing a brilliantly lighted interior, and a servant in livery bowed him in. There was an air of vulgar elegance about the hall. The servant did not speak. Having offered to take the visitor's hat, to which the visitor shook his head, he opened a heavy door to the right and there came from beyond it intermittent sounds of small clatter. The room John entered was what had been the front drawing room. Back of it were two more rooms, in a train to the depth of the house, all thrown together by means of unfolded doors, so that the effect was of one very long apartment, about thirty feet wide, laid with rich, deep carpet on which the feet made not the slightest sound. The walls were full of pictures, some of them good. There were several art objects on pedestals, a great many nice chairs and some small tables, like tea tables, evidently used for serving refreshments. On one of these tables was a large humidor and on another a tray with a cut glass service of decanters, goblets and ice bowl. That was all, except down both sides of the first two rooms roulette wheels and in the last room at the end three faro layouts.

Twenty or thirty men were betting at roulette, in groups of three or four each. John passed them with a negligent, preoccupied air, walking straight back.

No faro play was just then going on. At one layout sat a dealer in that state of chilled ophidian tension characteristic of professional gamblers in the face of their prey, and by none so remarkably achieved as by the faro bank dealer, who drinks ice water without warming it, who sees without looking, who speaks only under great provocation and then softly, and whose slightest movement is pontifical until he reaches for the six-shooter. That movement is as a rattlesnake strikes.

On the players' side of a faro table are representations of the thirteen cards, —ace, deuce, trey, etc., to the king, in two rows of six each with the seven at one end. On the dealer's side, besides the rack containing the chips, the cash drawer and the invisible six-shooter, is a little metal box in which a pack of cards will snugly lie, face up. The dealer moves the cards off one at a time. They fall alternately into two piles. One pile wins; the other loses. The players bet which pile a card will fall in, indicating it by the way they place their money on the table. No vocal sound is necessary. It is a silent game. The expert might play for ever and never speak a word.

John dragged up a large chair, hung his coat on the back of it, settled himself to face the dealer and passed five hundred dollars across the table. The dealer put the money in the cash drawer and pushed out five stacks of yellow chips. John began to play. He did not make his bets at random. He played a slow, rhythmic, two-handed game, never hesitating, always thoughtful, precisely with the air of a man playing solitaire.

For an hour or more he lost steadily. Several times his hands made a bothered gesture, as of clearing the space in front of his face. The dealer, the cards, the yellow chips, all objects of common reality, were dim and uncertain, by reason of the image persisting in his eyes, —that etched impression of Agnes and Thane in the hallway, so twain, so improbable, yet so imminent, so —... so —....

He groaned aloud and held his head between clenched hands. The dealer stopped and waited. Players sometimes behave that way.

Recalling himself with a start, John looked up, cleared his play, gave the dealer a nod to proceed and doubled the scale of his bets. That made his game steep enough to attract attention. A little gallery gathered. No one else cut in. He kept the table to himself. Gradually the haunted mist broke up. The tormenting picture went away. If it threatened to return he raised his bets again. His health revived. He had some supper brought in and ate it as he played. He played all night.

At seven he rose, yawned, stretched, rubbed his eyes like a man coming out of a deep sleep, pushed his chips across the table to be cashed, and drew on his coat while the dealer counted them.

He had won over three thousand dollars. But it was neither the fact of his winning nor the amount of his gain that floated his spirits. It was getting that picture out of his eyes and the feeling that went with it out of his heart. Losing would have served him quite as well, psychically, though of course winning was only that much more to boot.

Always for him the excitement of chance was a perfect refuge from thought and reality, better than sleep, which may be troubled with dreams, and restful in the same way that dreamless sleep is.

Now as he walked toward the hotel, though the morning was wet and heavy, he felt fresh in his body and optimistic in his mind. He could think of seeing Agnes and Thane at breakfast without that ugly lurching of his heart.

They were in the dining room when he arrived there an hour later. His impulse was to let them alone, but Thane, seeing him, stood up and beckoned.

"We kept a place for you," he said.

It was so. The table was laid for three. John wondered whose wish that was.

"I've had word from New Damascus," he said to Agnes. "Your father is all right."

"Was there any reason to think he might not be all right?" she asked in surprise.

"No, no," he said. "It was merely mentioned, like the state of the weather."

She detected his confusion.

"You saw him last," she said. "Did anything unusual occur?" She was regarding him keenly.

"I thought he looked ill, or about to be," John said,

"And I asked the servants to call the doctor. Apparently it was nothing. Anyhow... I've had word that he's all right."

She did not pursue the subject, but became suddenly silent, and thereafter avoided John's eyes, for in the midst of his explanation his expression had changed. He had looked at her in a most extraordinary way and she suffered a deep psychic disturbance. It was as if he had blunderingly discovered a nameless secret. And that was precisely what had happened. As he was talking to her, —positively as he would swear with no wanton curiosity in his mind, —as he looked at her and as her eyes met his in open frankness there came an instant in which he saw how matters stood.

How can one tell? One cannot tell. It tells itself in the way the eyes look back, in what is missing from them, in something there that was not there before, in a certain hardness of the chin.

In no such way had Agnes changed.

That was what John saw. The discovery shook him. All his senses leaped exultingly. She was not Thane's, —not yet. Wild thoughts got loose. The dining room began to sway. Then he looked at Thane and enormously repented. His feeling for Thane was one of intense affection. He could no more help it than he could help his feeling for Agnes. They were separate chemistries, antagonistic. So he was torn between them, and when he could bear it no longer he began clumsily to excuse himself.

"We are delayed by legal formalities," he said to

Thane. "May be three or four days yet. Take it easy. The company can stand it."

So he left them abruptly.

All that day he fled from himself. All night he played. The next morning he looked at his haggard self in the mirror, —looked deeply into his own eyes, and said aloud:

"But she is his, not mine, and I will let her be, by God."

On that he slept for twenty-four hours and rose on the third day with a strong appetite, a clear mind and a great vow to the divinity with whom he kept now a time of feud, now a time of grace, whimsically alternating.

XXII

The divinity that made the pattern of John's life is infinitely mysterious. Some call it luck. Others call it chance. Both are begging names. Mathematicians call it probability-the theory of, and devote a branch of their science to it. Definition is impossible. It is whatever it is that causes, permits or brings one thing to happen in place of all the other things that might just as well have happened. Its commonest manifestations are profoundly obscure. On the first toss of a coin the chances are even between head and tail. On the second toss they change. Why they change nobody can tell; but everyone knows that the odds against the heads coming twice in succession are two to one. If you think of it, how preposterous I Rationally, how can the result of one throw create any probability as to the result of the next? Yet it does. Here evidently is some principle or rhythmic variation that we do not understand.

We speak of the law of chance. There is no such thing, for if chance could be reduced to law it would cease to be chance. It is outside any law we know. The mathematical odds are two to one against double heads, yet the head may happen to come ten times in succession, so that the actual predestined odds against the tail showing once in ten throws were ten to one. If the head may come ten times in succession, could it come a thousand times? No one will say it could not. But since it has never happened as a matter of record you can't imagine it, and the odds against it are what you will.

The fact of oneself is an amazing unlikelihood. The biological chances against one's getting born as one is, plus the chances against any particular organism getting born at all, must have been billions to one. Yet here one is, thinking it had been precisely inevitable since all eternity. Perhaps it was. There may be no such thing as chance. It may be only that we never know all the factors. It may be. Yet does not everyone believe from experience that survival is a continuous chance?

There are innumerable chances for and against one's living another day, another hour. These chances are estimated statistically and great companies are formed to bet on them. That is life insurance. The insurance company bets not on the life of an individual, for that would be gambling; it bets that the aggregate life of ten thousand people will correspond to the average duration of human life, and that works out, because those who fall short of the average are balanced by those who exceed it, and there is an average. But any single life is the sport of pure chance. And we know nothing about this fickle arbiter. Therefore we become superstitious. Belief in luck is the only universal religion. Luck is the happy chance. The right thing happens when it is needed. It strains a point to happen. Why it happens, in streaks, why it happens more to some than to others, why to a darling few it happens importunately, —these are questions one asks in a rhetorical sense. There is no answer. Luck and genius may be two aspects of the same thing. Luck happens and genius happens, and there is no accounting for it.

It came to be a notorious saying about John Breakspeare that he was lucky. But people at the same time said he was dangerous, which would mean that he sometimes failed. That was true. He often failed. When that happened he did not curse his luck. It only occurred to him that he had played the wrong chance, and he went on from there. Probably in a case like his there is a highly developed intuition of the winning chance corresponding to a musical composer's intuition of harmony. The principles of harmony have been partially discovered. But the rhythms of chance are still a mystery.

Certainly it was chance, not luck, that brought John this day to the edge of a small crowd in front of the county court house just as the auctioneer was saying:

"Three thousand-three thousand-three thousand —t-h-r-E-E thous-A-N-D! Three thousand dollars for a first class nail mill. Why, gentlemen, it would fetch more than that by the pound for junk. Three thousand do I hear one? Three thousand do I hear one? GOING, at three-One! Thank you, sir."

He bowed ironically to John.

"Thirty-one —thirty-one —thirty-one hund-r-e-d! Do-I-hear-two? Do-I-hear-two? Do-I-hear-two? Two over there! Now do I hear three? Do-I-hear-three? Two-do-I-hear-three?"

He was looking at John.

"Going at thirty-two. Are you all DONE? T-h-i-r-t-y-two, ONCE. T-h-i-r-t-y-two, TWICE. T-h-i-r-t-y-two for the third and —"

John nodded his head.

"Three! Three-I-have, three-I-have, three-I-have. Thirty-three-hundred dollars for an up-to-date iron mill in the great city of Pittsburgh. Thirty-three-hundred. Do I hear four? Four do I hear? Thirty-three, thirty-three, thirty-three. Going at thirty-three hundred. Going, ONCE. Going, TWICE. Going for the third and last time-SOLD! to that young man over there. Now, gentlemen, the next property to be sold by the decree of the court is a nail mill as is a mill. It has a capacity of —"

John, thrusting his way through the crowd, interrupted.

"Where shall I go to settle for this?"

The auctioneer eyed him suspiciously and relighted his cigar before speaking.

"If I were you," he squinted, "I'd try the clerk of the court."

"Where is he?"

"Haven't you seen him?"

"No."

"Why not?"

"There was no occasion."

The auctioneer could not stand anything so opaque. It made him sarcastic.

"If you have been playing booby horse with me and the court, —if you h-a-v-e! Does any-body around here know your figger to look at it?"

"This is a public auction, isn't it?" John asked.

"Yes-sir-ee."

"A certain property was put up here for sale?"

"Yes-sir-ee."

"Well, I bought it," said John. "Now I want to pay for it. Is that clear? I want to pay for it in cash. Does that make it any clearer? Whom shall I pay? That's all I want to know."

The auctioneer saved his ego with a gesture of being exceedingly bored. He turned to the bailiff at his side and wearily tore from his hands a large legal document. "I'll read this," he said. "Take him in to the clerk." Then he resumed —"A nail mill as is a mill, gentlemen, particularly described, if we may read without further interruption, in terms as follows: —"

Half an hour later John walked out of the courthouse with title to a mill he had never seen, guaranteed by the bankruptcy court to exist in Twenty-ninth Street and to contain tools, machines, devices, etc., pertaining to the manufacture of cut iron nails. It was one of four nail mills sold that day on the court house steps.

"Can't be much of a mill," mused John. "Still, it doesn't take much of a mill to be worth thirty-three hundred dollars."

Not until long afterward, and then not very hard, did the incongruity of this transaction strike his sense of humor. And in fact it was not as irrational as it might seem. He had to have a mill of some sort in which to place Thane. Nail mills were very cheap because they had increased too fast and were falling into bankruptcy. The other bidders undoubtedly were men who not only had examined the mill but who knew the state of the nail industry. It was not likely that they would over-value the property; and he paid only one hundred dollars more than they had been willing to give for it.

The next thing he did was to visit a lawyer whom he favorably remembered from slight acquaintance. That was Jubal Awns, —two small black eyes in a big round head and a pleasant way of saying yes.

John drew a slip of paper from his pocket. He wished to incorporate a company, to be styled the North American Manufacturing Company, Ltd., with an authorized capital of a quarter of a million dollars and three incorporators, —himself, the lawyer Awns and a man named Thane.

"What is the business?" Awns asked.

"Manufacturing," said John.

"Yes," said Awns, "but what do we manufacture? What is the property to be incorporated?"

"A nail mill to begin with," said John.

"Where is it?"

"Here in Pittsburgh. Thirty-ninth Street."

"That's got me," said Awns. "I can't think of any nail mill in Thirty-ninth Street."

John looked at the bill of sale and improved the address without the slightest change of expression.

"Twenty-ninth," he said.

The lawyer took the bill of sale, glanced at it, and gave John a curious look.

"Have you seen it?"

"No."

"Bought it sight unseen?"

"Yes."

"How much stock of this new company do you mean to issue?"

"Founders' shares, or whatever they are, and then stock to myself for what I put in, —the mill, the money to start with, and so on."

"Then why an authorized capital of a quarter of a million?"

"Because I'm going into the iron and steel business," said John.

Awns studied him in silence.

"You have quit with Gib at New Damascus?"

"I'm out for myself," said John.

"All right," said Awns. "Here's for the North American Manufacturing Company, Limited."

They drew up papers. At the end of the business John asked: "Will you take your fee in cash or stock?"

Jubal Awns was amazed, and somehow challenged, too. He was ten years older than John, successful and shrewd, with a delusion that he was romantic. He loved to dramatize a matter and make unexpected decisions. Putting down the papers he got up and walked three times across the floor with an air of meditation.

"I'll take it in stock," he said, "provided I may incorporate all of your companies and take my fees that way each time."

They shook hands on it.

It was late that afternoon when John and Thane together set out in a buggy from the hotel to inspect the mill. Thane was eager and communicative. He had not been taking it easy. He evidently had visited all the big mills in and around Pittsburgh. He had seen some new practice and much that was bad, and had got a lot of ideas. He had informed himself as to the conditions of labor. Here and there he had found a man he meant to pick up.

And all the time John's heart was sinking.

As they turned into Twenty-ninth Street the eight stacks of the Keystone Iron Works rose in their eyes. No other iron working plant was visible in the vicinity, and as John, looking for his nail mill, began to slow up, Thane leaped to the notion that the Keystone was their goal.

"She's a whale," he said, enthusiastically, but with no sound of awe. John gave him a squinting glance.

"Would you tackle that?" he asked.

"Oh," said Thane, "then that ain't it." In his tone was a sense of disappointment that answered John's question. Of course he would tackle it.

They drove slowly past the Keystone, past dump heaps, sand lots, a row of unpainted, upside down boxes called houses, and came at length to a group of rude sheds, one large one and four small ones. One of the small ones, open in front like a wood-shed, was filled with empty nail kegs in tiers.

The front door of the big central shed was propped shut with an iron bar. John kicked it away, pulled the door open, and they went in. A figure rose out of the dimness, asking, "What'd ye want?"

"Are you Coleman's caretaker?" John asked. Coleman was the name of the bankrupt.

"Yep," said the man.

So this was the mill.

"We've bought him out," said John. "Want to have a look at the plant."

"Help yourself."

They walked about silently on the earthen, scrap littered floor. A nail mill, as nail mills were at that time, was not much to look at, and a cold iron working plant of any kind has a bygone, extinct appearance. Thane had never seen a cold mill. He was horribly depressed. Gradually their eyes grew used to the dimness. The equipment consisted of an overloaded driving engine, one small furnace for heating iron bars, a train of rolls for reducing the bars to sheets the thickness of nails and five automatic machines for cutting nails from the sheet like cookies, —all in bad to fair condition.

"Won't look so sad when you get her hot and begin to turn her over," said John.

Thane said nothing. Having examined the machinery and the furnace thoughtfully he stood for a long time surveying the mill as a whole. There was no inventory to speak of. The raw material, which was bar iron bought outside, had been worked up clean. They looked into the small sheds and then it began to be dark. As they drove away Thane spoke. It was the first word he had uttered.

"When do we start up?"

"Right away," said John. "I'll contract some iron tomorrow."

"Give me a couple of weeks," said Thane. "There's a lot to be done to that place."

"What?"

"She's all upside down," he said. "The stuff ain't moving right. No wonder they had to shut up."

That night at supper Agnes questioned her puddler.

"What is your mill like?"

"A one horse thing."

His manner was preoccupied and she let him alone. After supper he went to his room, removed his coat, waistcoat, collar and shoes and sat with his feet in the window, thinking.

They had three rooms, —two bed chambers and a living room between. She sat in the middle room sewing, with a view of him through the door, which he left ajar. He did not move, except to refill and light his pipe. He was still there, slowly receding beyond a veil of smoke, when she retired.

Before he went to bed the little nail mill was all made over and the stuff was moving right.

Thane at this time was twenty-five. He had lived nearly all his life in the iron mill at New Damascus. He could not remember a time when its uproar and smells were not familiar to his senses. His mother died when he was three. He was the only child. Then his father, who was a puddler and loved him fiercely, began to take him to the mill. It was a wonderful nursery. When the shift was daytime he was the puddlers' mascot and playmate. At night he slept on a pallet in some gloom hidden niche from which he could see his father, satanically transfigured in the glare of the furnace. Then he went to school, but spent all his playtime in the mill. The thrill of it never failed him. When he was old enough to carry water he got a job. At nineteen he became his father's helper and delighted to vie with him in the weight of pig iron he could lift and heave into the maw of the furnace. The normal carry was one pig. He began to carry two at a time and his father matched him. But one day his father stumbled. As they stooped again side by side at the iron pile he picked up one pig. The old man gave him a queer, startled look and did the same. After that it was always one pig, and they never spoke of it. When his father died Alexander took his place, and as he drew his first heat, Enoch watching, the fact stood granted. He was the best puddler in the mill.

He had it in his hands. Of iron, for coaxing, shaping and compelling it, he had that kind of tactile understanding an artist has for paint or clay, or any plastic stuff. He seemed to think with his hands. It is a mysterious gift, and leaves it open to wonder whether the brain has made the hand or the hand the brain. Besides this intuitive knowledge that belongs to the hand Thane possessed a natural sense of mechanics and a naïve way of taking nothing for granted because it happens so to be. All of this was to be revealed. It was John's luck.

XXIII

While Thane was thinking how to set the nail mill in order, John, sitting in the hotel lobby with his feet in the window, gnawing a cigar, was reflecting in another sphere. His problem was the nail industry at large. It was in a parlous way. Although cut iron nails had been made by automatic machines for a long time there had recently appeared a machine that displaced all others, because it made the nail complete, head and all, in one run, and was very fast. This machine coming suddenly into use had caused an overproduction of nails. The price had fallen to a point where there was actually a loss instead of a profit in nail making unless one produced one's own iron and got a profit there. The Twenty-ninth Street plant had to buy its iron. The probability of running it at a profit was nil.

His meditations carried him far into the night. The lights were put out and still he sat with his feet in the window, musing, reflecting, dreaming, with a relaxed and receptive mind. An idea came to him. It will be important to consider what that idea was for it became afterward a classic pattern. It had the audacity of great simplicity. He would combine the whole nail making industry in his North American Manufacturing Company, Ltd. Then production could be suited to demand and the price of nails could be advanced to a paying level.

He took stock of his capital. It was fifteen thousand dollars. Maybe it could be stretched to twenty. In his work with Gib, selling rails, he had acquired a miscellaneous lot of very cheap and highly speculative railroad shares, some of which were beginning to have value. But twenty thousand dollars would be the outside measurement, and to think of setting out with that amount of capital to acquire control of the nail making industry, worth perhaps half a million dollars, was at a glance fantastic. But one's capital may exist in the idea. John already understood the art of finance.

Leaving the Twenty-ninth Street plant in Thane's hands, with funds for overhauling it, he consulted with Jubal Awns and set out the next morning on his errand.

The nail makers were responsive for an obvious reason. They were all losing money. In a short time John laid before Awns a sheaf of papers.

"There's the child," he said. "Examine it."

He had got options in writing on every important nail mill in the country save one. The owners agreed to sell out to the North American Manufacturing Co., Ltd., taking in payment either cash or preferred shares at their pleasure. The inducement to take preferred shares was that if they did they would receive a bonus of fifty per cent. in common stock.

"But they will take cash in every case," said Awns, "and where will you find it?"

"They won't," said John. "I'll see to that. What have you done with Gib?"

Awns had been to see Enoch. The New Damascus mill produced in its nail department a fifth of all the nails then made. There was no probability of buying him out. John well knew that. Yet his nail output had to be controlled in some way, else the combine would fail. So he had sent Awns to him with alternative propositions. The first was to buy him out of the nail making business. And when he had declined to sell, as of course he would, Awns was to negotiate for his entire output under a long term contract.

"He wouldn't sell his nail business," said Awns.

"I knew that," said John.

"But I've got a contract for all his nails," said Awns, handing over the paper. "The price is stiff, —fifty cents a keg more than nails are worth. It was the best I could do."

"That's all right," said John reading the agreement. "We are going to add a dollar a keg to nails. This phrase —'unless the party of the second part,' (that's Gib), 'wishes to sell nails at a lower price to the trade' —who put that in?"

"He did," said Awns. "I couldn't see any point in objecting to it. No man is going to undersell his own contract."

John handed the agreement back and sat for several minutes musing.

"There's a loose wheel in your scheme, if I'm not mistaken," said Awns. "If you add a dollar a keg to nails won't you bring in a lot of new competition? Anybody can make nails if it pays. These same people who sell out to you may turn around and begin again. You'll be holding the umbrella for everybody else."

"Anybody can't make nails," said John. "I've looked at that."

"Why not?"

"Nail making machines are covered by patents. There are only four firms that make them. I've made air tight contracts with them. We take all their machines at an advance of twenty-five per cent. over present prices and they bind themselves to sell machines to nobody else during the life of the contract. So we've got the bag sewed up top and bottom. They were glad to do it because there isn't any profit in machines either with the nail makers all going busted."

Awns stared at him with doubt and admiration mingled.

"Well, that is showing them something," he said. "If you go far with that kind of thing laws will be passed to stop it."

"It's legal, isn't it?"

"There's no law against it," said Awns.

"We're not obliged to be more legal than the law," said John. "Tell me, what do you know about bankers in Pittsburgh? I've got to do some business in that quarter."

Pittsburgh at this time was not a place prepared. It was a sign, a pregnant smudge, a state of phenomena. The great mother was undergoing a Caesarian operation. An event was bringing itself to pass. The steel age was about to be delivered.

Men performed the office of obstetrics without knowing what they did. They could neither see nor understand it. They struggled blindly, falling down and getting up. Forces possessed them. Their psychic condition was that of men to whom fabulous despair and extravagant expectation were the two ends of one ecstasy. They were hard, shrewd, sentimental, superstitious, romantic in friendship and conscienceless in trade. They named their blast furnaces after their wives and sweethearts, stole each other's secrets, fell out with their partners, knew no law of business but to lay on what the traffic would bear, read Swedenborg and dreamed of Heaven as a thoroughfare resembling Wood Street, Pittsburgh, lined with banks and in the door of each bank a grovelling president, pleading: "Here's money for your payrolls. Please borrow it here. Very fine quality of money. Pay it back when you like."

They were always begging money at the banks. When they made money they used it to build more mills and to fill the mills with automatic monsters that grew stranger and more fantastic. Many of these monsters, like things in nature's own history of trial and error, appeared for a short time and became extinct. When they were not making money they were bankrupt. That was about half the time. Then they came to the banks in Wood Street to implore, beg, wheedle money to meet their payrolls.

There is the legend of a man, afterward one of the great millionaires, who drove one mare so often to Wood Street and from one bank to another in a zigzag course that the animal came to know the stops by heart, made them automatically, and could not be made to go in a straight line through this lane of money doors.

The bankers were a tough minded group. They had to be. Nobody was quite safe. A man with a record for sanity would suddenly lose his balance and cast away the substance of certainty to pursue a vision. The effort to adapt the Bessemer steel process to American conditions was an irresistible road to ruin. That process was producing amazing results in Europe but in this country it was bewitched with perversity and it looked as if the English and German manufacturers would walk away with the steel age. Fortunes were still being swallowed up in snail shaped vessels called converters, not unlike the one Aaron had built at New Damascus twenty-five years before.

Of all the bankers in Wood Street the toughest minded was Lemuel Slaymaker.

"All the same," said Awns, "I should try him first. His name would put it through and he loves a profit."

Awns knew him. They went together to see him. Slaymaker saluted Awns and acknowledged his introduction of Mr. John Breakspeare not otherwise nor more than by turning slowly in his chair and staring at them. He had a large white face, pale blue eyes and red, close-cropped hair. The impression he made was one of total sphericity. There was no way to take hold of him. No thought or feeling projected.

John laid out his plan, producing the papers as exhibits, A, B, C, in the appropriate places. Lastly he produced data on the nail trade, showing the amount of nails consumed in the country and the normal rate of annual increase with the growth of population, together with a carefully developed estimate of the combine's profits at various prices per keg. When he had finished the idea was lucid, complete in every part and self-evident. Therein lay the secret of his extraordinary power of persuasion. He seemed never to argue his case. He expressed no opinion of his own to be combatted. He merely laid down a state of facts with an air of looking at them from the other man's point of view.

"And what you want is a bank to guarantee this scheme," said Slaymaker. "You want a bank to guarantee that if these people want cash instead of stock the cash will be forthcoming."

This was the first word he had spoken. The papers he had not even glanced at. They lay on his desk as John had placed them there.

"That's it," said John. "Guarantee it. Very little cash will be required."

"How do you say that?"

"To make them want stock instead of cash," said John, "you have only to engage brokers to make advance quotations for the stock, here and in Philadelphia at, say, par for the preferred and fifty for the common. If you do not know brokers who can do that I will find them. The scheme is sound. The stock will pay dividends from the start. A bank that had guaranteed it might very well speak a good word for it here and there. The public will want some of the stock."

Slaymaker gazed at a corner of the ceiling and twiggled his foot. Then he turned his back on them.

"Leave the papers," he said, "and see me at this time tomorrow."

When they were in the street again Awns said: "You got him."

And so the infant trust was born, —first of its kind, first of a giant brood. Biologically they were all alike, but with evolution their size increased prodigiously. The swaddling cloths of this one would not have patched the eye of a twentieth century specimen delivered in Wall Street.

Slaymaker's lawyers and Jubal Awns together verified all the agreements. The stock of the N. A. M. Co., Ltd., was increased enough to make sure there would be plenty to go around. Slaymaker took a large amount for banker's fees, John took a block for promoter's services and another block for the Twenty-ninth Street mill, the lawyers took some, and a certain amount was set aside for Thane, —for Agnes really. John was elected president and the combine was launched. Before the day came on which the options of purchase were to be exercised the preferred stock was publicly quoted at 105 and the common stock at 55, and there were symptoms of public interest in its possibilities. As John predicted, nearly all the nail manufacturers elected to take stock in the new company, with Slaymaker's name behind it.

Everyone at length was more enthusiastic than John. He kept thinking of that phrase in the contract with Gib —"unless the party of the second part wishes to sell nails to the trade at a lower price." No one else had noticed it, not even Slaymaker. Nobody else would have had any misgivings about it. Who could imagine, as Awns said, that a man would undersell his own contract? There is a law of self interest one takes for granted.

XXIV

Thane had been reporting laconically on the Twenty-ninth Street mill. It now was in action and the nails were piling up. John had not been out to see it. Their contacts had become irregular; generally they met by accident in the hotel lobby, rarely in the dining room. This was owing partly to John's absorption in his scheme and partly to the resolve he had made to avoid Agnes. He had not once been close enough to speak to her since that third morning when his haggard true self met his anti-self in the mirror, saying: "She is his." The only way he could put her out of his mind at all was to involve himself in difficulties. Trouble was a cave of refuge. As during those two nights of struggle with his anti-self, when it had almost conquered him, he played absently at faro and increased his bets to make the game absorbing, so afterward in business, wilfully at first and then by habit, he preferred the hazardous alternative; he seemed to seek those situations in which the chance was all or none. This made his ways uncanny. Luck seems to favor one who doesn't care. Or it may be that one who doesn't care sees more clearly than the rest, being free of fear.

"Better come and sight it," said Thane, one morning in the lobby. "I'm worried where to put the nails."

"We'll go now," said John. "Anyhow, I want to talk to you. I don't know about this Twenty-ninth Street mill. It's a poor layout. Maybe we'd better shut it up. Now don't get uneasy. Wait till I'm through. The company —(and, by the way, you are a director and there's some stock in your name) —it has bought nearly all the nail mills there are. Over a hundred, big and little, all over the place. The idea is to combine the nail industry in one organization and put it back on a paying basis. I want you to go around with me and have a look at mills. Some of them we'll throw away. The trouble was too many of them."

He went on talking to take up Thane's injured silence. That he was a director in the company, that he had stock in it, that his salary was to be doubled, —none of this availed against the puddler's pride in what he had done with the Twenty-ninth Street mill. The thought of now shutting it up hurt him in his middle. John on his side was disappointed in Thane's inability to rise to an opportunity. So they came to the mill.

"Sounds busy," said John.

Thane held his thoughts.

On beholding the scene of action within, almost at a glance, John placed the puddler where he belonged. Here was the work of a master superintendent. Nothing was as it had been except the engine and furnace. Everything else had been relocated with one aim in view, which was to eliminate all unnecessary human motion and shorten the train of events from the raw material straight through to the finished nail packed in the keg and stored. Besides the physical achievement, which alone was very notable, there was a subtle psychic relation between Thane and his men. They worked on their toes and liked doing it for him.

"Shake," said John, holding out his hand. "No, we won't shut her up. We'll take her as a pattern. If you can do this with all the mills we'll walk away with it. Have you figured your costs? They must be fine."

"In my head," said Thane.

They stood at a little greasy box-desk screwed to the wall under a window dim with cobwebs.

"I'll show you how to figure them," said John. "Iron, so much; fuel, so much; kegs, so much; oil, and so forth, so much; wear and tear of tools and plant, so much; labor, so much; total, so much. Then kegs of nails, so many. Divide that by that and you have the cost per keg. Let's see how it will work out."

It worked out nearly as Thane had it in his head and John was sentimental with pride and satisfaction.

"Come on," he said, impatiently. "Leave a man in charge of this, and we'll see the other mills."

Starting with more than a hundred mills, they scrapped twenty outright, saving only their contracts, raw material and stock on hand; others they consolidated. In the end they had fifty well equipped plants strategically placed to supply the trade by the shortest routes. They had all to be overhauled according to Thane's ideas. He turned the Twenty-ninth Street plant into a training station and sent men from there to work the other mills. It was a large and complicated program. He carried it through so skillfully that he was appointed vice-president in charge of manufacturing, and John was free to organize the company's business and function executively.

He raised the price of nails, first twenty-five cents a keg, then fifty, then seventy-five cents, and stopped. At that price there was a good profit. Thane was steadily reducing costs by improving plant practice and that increased profits in another way.

A dividend was paid *on* the preferred stock in the third month. The omens were fine. Still, John was uneasy. No New Damascus nails had been received under their contract with Enoch. The making of nails had not stopped at New Damascus. He made sure of that. No New

Damascus nails were coming on the market, either, for John knew everything about the trade. Then what was to be expected?

The answer when it came did not surprise him. He had guessed it already.

One day the nail market was knocked in the head. Enoch was offering nails to the hardware trade at a price seventy-five cents lower than the combine's price. That meant he was selling them for fifty cents a keg less than the combine had agreed to pay him for his whole output. He had never tendered one ten-penny nail on that contract. Instead, working his plant at high speed, he had accumulated thousands of kegs expressly for the irrational purpose of casting them suddenly on sale to break the combine's market-John Breakspeare's market —*Aaron's market!* John was the only person who understood it. Everyone else was dazed.

Slaymaker sent for John.

"What's the matter with that man at New Damascus?"

"He's out of his mind," said John.

"Better buy him up at his own price," said Slaymaker. "That's what he wants."

John knew better. However, to satisfy Slaymaker, he sent Awns to see Enoch again.

"You're right," Awns reported. "The old man is clean crazy. He won't sell at any price. All he would do was to point to that stipulation in the contract and laugh at me."

The combine stood aside until the trade had absorbed the New Damascus nails and then tried to go on without reducing its own price; but the trade became very ugly about it, the combine began to be denounced, and Congress, hearing from the farmers, threatened to take the import duty off nails and let the foreign product in. The combine had to let down the price and wait.

Three months later the preposterous act was repeated, Enoch flooding the market with nails at fifty cents a keg less than the combine's price. There was no doubt this time that he was selling nails at a ruinous loss, and everyone's amazement grew. Only John knew why he did it.

The combine was now in a very awkward dilemma. If it met Enoch's price it not only would be selling its own nails at a loss but selling them at a price far below that at which it was obliged to take Enoch's entire output in case he should choose to deliver to the combine instead of selling direct to the trade.

"Whipsawed," said John to Awns, "if you know what that means."

For the N. A. M. Co., Ltd. from then on it was a race with bankruptcy, Gib pursuing. He sold Damascus nails lower and lower until it was thought he would give them away. He might ultimately go broke, of course, but that was nothing the combine could wait for. He was very rich, —nobody knew how rich, —and nail making after all was a small part of his business.

Under these unnatural circumstances John won the incognizable Slaymaker's glassy admiration, for in trouble he was dogged and enormously resourceful.

"If we've got to live on the sweat of our nails," he said, "we can't afford to buy iron."

Thereupon at a bankrupt price he negotiated the purchase of a blast furnace and puddling mill over which two partners were quarrelling in a suicidal manner. No cash was involved. He paid for it with notes. In Thane's hands, and with luck that was John's, the plant performed one of those miracles that made Pittsburgh more exciting than a mining camp. It paid for itself the first year out of its own profits. Then John turned it over to the N. A. M. Co., Ltd., at cost. On seeing him do this, Slaymaker, who had never parted with his first stock holdings, privately increased them.

There was a profit in ore back of the iron. John went to that. He got hold of a small Mesaba ore body on a royalty basis and had then a complete chain from the ore to the finished nail. There was still one profit. That was in the kegs. So cooper shops were added.

What with all this integration, as the word came to be for that method of working back to one's raw material and articulating the whole series of profits, and what at the same time with Thane's skill in manufacture, developing to the point of genius, the N. A. M. Company got the cost of nails down very low, —even lower as John one day discovered than it was in Europe. This gave him an idea. There was no profit in nails at home, owing to Enoch's mad policy of slaughter, but there was the whole world to sell nails in. The N. A. M. Co. invaded the export field. This was a shock to the European nail makers. They met it angrily with reprisals. John went to Europe with a plan to form an international pool in which the nail business of the earth should be divided up, —allotting so much to Great Britain, so much to Germany, so much to Belgium, so much to the United States, and so on. If they would do that everybody might make a little money.

He returned unexpectedly and appeared one morning in Slaymaker's office.

"Did you get your pool born?"

"Chucked the idea," said John. "I found this."

He laid on the banker's desk a bright, thin, cylindrical object.

"What's that?" Slaymaker asked, looking at it but not touching it.

"That." said John, "is a steel wire nail. It will drive the iron nail out. It's just as good and costs much less to make. You feed steel wire into one end of a machine and nails come out at the other like wheat."

"Well?" said the banker.

"The machines both for drawing the wire and making the nails are German," John continued. "I've bought all the American rights on a royalty basis."

"What will you do with them?"

"I bought them for the N. A. M.," said John.

"If this is going to be such a God Almighty nail why not form a new company to make it?" asked Slaymaker.

"I'd rather pull the horse we've got out of the ditch," said John.

Slaymaker regarded him with an utterly expressionless stare.

"Go ahead," he said.

Enter the steel wire nail. It solved the N. A. M. Company's problem. Enoch could not touch it. The combine steadily reduced its output of iron nails, until it was nominal, and flooded the trade with the others. Enoch could make any absurd price he liked for iron nails, but as his output, though a formidable bludgeon with which to beat down prices, was only a fraction of what the country required, and as the remainder of the demand was met with the combine's new product, wire nails superseded iron nails four or five kegs to one. They could sell at a higher price than iron nails without prejudice because they were different, and John, putting a selling campaign behind them, proved that they were also better. That probably was not so. But people had to have them.

XXV

Still there were difficulties quite enough to keep John's mind enthralled. The steel wire nails soon got the N. A. M. Co. out of the woods. But as the German nail making machines would devour nothing but German wire their food had to be imported by the shipload. The German wire drawing machines, acquired along with the nail making machines, miserably failed when they were asked to reduce American steel to the form of wire. That was not their fault really. It was the fault of American steel. The N. A. M. Co. had either to import German and English steel to make the wire the nail machines ate or import the wire itself. And now for the first time John turned his mind to this great problem of steel. Six or eight Bessemer steel plants had been built in the United States under the English patents at enormous cost and every one had failed. They could produce steel all right, and do it with one melt from the iron ore, which was what they were after. The trouble was that the steel was never twice the same. Its quality and nature varied. The process was treacherous. There were those who said it simply could not be adapted to American ores; that the only way this country could produce true steel was the old long way, which made it much more expensive than iron.

One night John recognized in the hotel lobby a figure that tormented both the flesh and the spirit of Pittsburgh, —the flesh by wasting its substance and the spirit by keeping always before it a riddle it had not solved. He was a frail, bent little man, not yet old, with a long thin mustache and a pleasing, naïve voice that had cost several iron men their entire fortunes. Wood street bankers wished he were dead or had never been born. This was Tillinghast, metallurgist and engineer, who had already designed and constructed four steel plants that were a total loss. He knew in each case what was wrong, —knew it in the instant of failure, —and begged to be permitted to make certain changes. Very simple changes. Quite inexpensive. He would guarantee the result. But as his changes at length involved rebuilding the whole plant and as the last of the steel was still like the first his backers sickened and turned away.

"What's the matter, Tillinghast?" John asked. "You look so horribly down."

It was a long story, incoherent with unnecessary details, technical exposition, expostulation and argument aside, told at the verge of tears. A steel plant on the river, opposite Allegheny, — one that everyone knew about, —had been under trial for a week. It was almost right. It needed only one correction. They were actually touching the magic. Yet his backers were on the point of throwing it up in disgust.

"No more money, maybe," said John.

"Fifty thousand more," said Tillinghast. "I guarantee the result if they will spend fifty thousand more.

They have spent eight times that already." His idea of money in large sums was childlike.

John heard for a while, then heard without listening, while Tillinghast went on and on, thinking to himself out loud. On leaving him John was in a state of vague apprehension. Afterward he could not remember whether he had said goodnight.

All that he had ever heard, here and there, first from Thaddeus and then from others about his father's fateful steel experiment at New Damascus came back to him, fused and made a vivid picture. That was not so strange. But he seemed to know more than he had ever heard. He seemed to be directly remembering, —not what he had learned from others but the experience itself as if it had been his own. He saw it. And presently in another dimension he saw the steel age that was coming. His imagination unrolled it as a panorama. He understood what it meant to increase one hundred fold the production of that metallic fibre of which there could never be enough.

The next morning he went to look at the abandoned steel plant. It was cast on a large scale. Quite four hundred thousand, as Tillinghast said, must have been spent on it.

"They do it in Europe," he kept saying to himself. "We can do it here. There is only some little trick to be discovered."

Later in a casual way he made contact with the owners. They were eager to get anything back. On the faintest suspicion that he might be soft-minded, they overwhelmed him with offers to sell out. At last he got it for nothing. That is, he agreed to take it off their hands flat and go on with Tillinghast's experiment. If success were achieved their interest in it should be exactly what they had already spent on the plant; if not, he would owe them nothing and lose only what he himself put in.

North American Manufacturing Company stock was now valuable. He took a large amount of it to Slaymaker for a loan.

"What's up now?"

John told him shortly, knowing what to expect. Slaymaker's phobia was steel. The word made him mad. He had once lost a great deal of money in that experimental process. He snatched the stock certificates out of John's hands, put a pin through them and tossed them angrily into a corner of his desk.

"I knew it. I knew it. All right. You can have the money. But I warn you. You'll never see that stock again. You'll be bankrupt a year from now."

Nothing else was said.

Tillinghast treated John not as if John had adopted him but as if he had adopted John and his attitude about the steel plant was one of sacrosanct authority. He was really a cracked pot. It took six months to make the changes. Then they fired up. The first run was good steel, the second was poor, the third was good and the fourth was bad. They got so far that the steel made from the raw iron of one furnace would always be good. When they took the molten iron from two or more furnaces successively the results went askew again. Tillinghast cooed when the steel was good and was silent when it was bad. He could not deny that they were baffled and John had sunk two-thirds of everything he owned.

Thane was a constant onlooker. He looked hard and saw everything.

"It ain't what you do to it afterward," he said, breaking a long silence. "That's the same every time. It's back of that. It's in the furnace."

"Well, suppose it is," said John. "What are you going to do about it?"

"Mix it," said Thane.

"Mix what?"

"The molten iron from the blast furnaces before it goes to the steel converter."

"What will you mix it with?"

"With itself," said Thane. "Ore's various, ain't it? Pig iron as comes from ore is various, ain't it? That's why you puddle it so as to make it all the same, like wrought iron's got to be. Here you take a run of stuff from this furnace 'n one from that furnace 'n it ain't the same because it ain't been puddled, but you run it into that converter thing 'n think it's got to come out all one kind of steel. It won't."

"How can you mix six or eight tons of molten iron?" John asked.

"There's got to be some way," Thane answered.

Tillinghast was deaf. It didn't make sense to John. Yet Thane kept saying, "Mix it," until they were sick of hearing him, and the steel persisted in being variable until they were desperate.

"Well, mix it then," said John. "If you know how, mix it."

Thereupon Thane built the first mixer, —an enormous, awkward tank or vat resting on rollers that rocked and jigged the fluid, blazing iron. Now they started the blast furnaces again and molten iron in equal quantities from all three was run into this mixer and sloshed around. From there it went to the converter. After two or three trials they began to get and continued to get steel that was both good and invariable.

And that was Eureka!

They tried the steel in every possible way and it was all that steel should be and is. They fed it to those fastidious German wire drawing machines and they loved it. Never again would it be necessary to import German or English steel to make wire, or German wire to make nails. They had it.

John formed a new company. Slaymaker came in. The men from whom John had taken the plant got stock for their interest. A large block was allotted to Thane for his mixer. John had the controlling interest. It was named the American Steel Company. But John and Thane between them spoke of it as the Agnes Plant.

"Let's call it that for luck," said John.

Thane made no reply. However, the next time he referred to it he called it so.

XXVI

One evening Thane and John were sitting together in one of their friendly silences, after supper, in the hotel lobby. Thane cleared his throat.

"We've got a house, Agnes 'n me," he said. As there was no immediate comment he added: "I suppose you won't be lonesome here alone. We don't seem to visit much anyhow."

John said it was very nice that they had a house; —he hoped they would be comfortable; — had they got everything they needed? He did not ask where the house was nor when they should move; and that was all they said about it.

No. John would not be lonesome. There was another word for it and he couldn't remember what it was. Although he saw her very seldom and then only at a distance, or when he passed her by chance in the hotel and they exchanged remote greetings, still, just living under the same roof with her had become a fact that deeply pertained to his existence. How much he had made of it unconsciously he did not realize until they were gone. Thereafter as he turned in at the door he had always the desolate thought, "She is not here." The place was empty. The rooms in which he had settled them were open to transients. He thought of taking them for himself. On coming to do it he couldn't. Se he went elsewhere to live; he moved about; all places were empty.

From time to time Thane hinted they would like to see him at the house. For some reason it seemed hard for him to come out with a direct invitation. However, he did at last.

"Mrs. Thane wants you up to supper," he said, abruptly.

"Thanks," said John. "I'm ashamed of myself, tell her. I'll stop in some evening."

"You don't know where it is," said Thane.

"That's so. Tell me how to find it."

He wrote the directions down. Still, it was most indefinite. Some evening meant nothing at all. Thane took him by the shoulders and regarded him with an expression that John avoided.

"And I want you to come," he said, with slow emphasis on the first pronoun. "To-morrow."

"All right," said John. "Meet me here at the office and I'll go with you."

It was a small house in a poor street, saved only by some large old trees. This surprised John, because Thane's income was enough to enable them to live in a very nice way, in moderate luxury even. He was still more surprised at the indecorative simplicity of its furnishings. Thane's nature was not parsimonious. He would not have stinted her. Then why had they set up a household more in keeping with the status of a first rate puddler than with that of the vice-president of a flourishing nail trust, receiving in salary and dividends more than twenty thousand a year? Yet simple, even commonplace as everything was there was evidence of taste beyond Thane's. It must have been Agnes who did it.

The first thing Thane did on entering was to remove his collar and place it conspicuously on a table in the hallway by the foot of the staircase. "I forget that if I don't see it going out," he said. He unbuttoned the neck of his shirt, breathed and looked around with an air of satisfaction. "Beats living at a hotel," he said, opening the door into a little front sitting room for John to see. "The only thing I picked out," he said, "was that big chair," referring to an enormous structure of hickory and rush that filled all one corner of the room. "I'll show you upstairs," he added. Coming to his own room he said: "This ain't much to look at but that ain't what it's for. Nobody sees it." It was furnished with a simple cot, another hickory chair and a plain pine table. On the table was a brass lamp ready to be lighted; also, tobacco jar, matches, some technical books, mechanical drawings, pencils and paper.

At the other end of the hall Thane stopped before a closed door. "She's downstairs," he said, at the same time knocking. He opened it softly, saying: "This is hers." John got a glimpse of a little white bed, a white dressing table, some white chairs and two tiny pictures on the wall. A nun's chamber could hardly have been more austere. He turned away. At the head of the staircase he looked back. Thane had momentarily forgotten him and was still standing on the threshold of the little white room gazing into it. Suddenly he remembered John, closed the door gently and joined him.

"We'll see about supper," he said, leading the way through the sitting room into the next one, where the table was spread.

Just then Agnes appeared from the kitchen, bearing a tray. John had another surprise. Her appearance made an unexpected contrast, so striking as to be almost theatrical. She wore a dainty apron. Behind that was an elaborate toilette. She was exquisite, lovely. His first thought was that she had prepared this effect for him. Yet he noticed that Thane was not in the least surprised. He looked at her calmly, taking it all for granted, as if this had been her normal way of appearing. And so it was.

She shook hands with John. Her manner was a little too cordial. "Supper is quite ready," she said. "Please sit down." She had served a joint *of* beef, mashed potatoes browned, some creamed vegetables. Thane surveyed the food.

"Nothing fried?" he said.

"Shall I fry you something?" she asked. "It won't take a minute." Her tone puzzled John. It expressed patience, readiness, even tractability, and yet submissiveness was in a subtle sense explicitly denied.

"I was only fooling," Thane replied. He whetted the carving knife carefully, as for a feat of precision, ran his thumb over the edge and applied it to the roast with an extremely deft effect.

"Did you buy the house?" John asked. "It's very charming."

The note failed. He felt Agnes looking at him.

"Rent it," said Thane. "Mrs. Thane thought we'd better rent a while, maybe as we'd want another shape of house afterward. I want her to get a girl. She says there ain't nothing for a girl to do."

There was a silence. John did not know which side to take. He spoke highly of the food.

"Mr. Thane tells me you also have left the hotel," she said.

"You get tired of it," John answered absently. He was wondering what to make of the fact that they were Mr. and Mrs. to each other. Twice he had been at the point of calling her Agnes. He wished to get one full look at her and tried to surprise her eyes. She avoided him. Then as if accepting a challenge she met his gaze steadily and utterly baffled his curiosity.

This time he could not be sure. A kind of wisdom was in her eyes that had never been there before. It might be only that she was on her guard, knowing the secret he was after.

Conversation suffered many lapses. There seemed so little they could talk about. All the three of them had in common was remniscent; and reminiscences were taboo. After supper they sat as far apart as three persons could in the small front room, —Thane in his big chair, Agnes in a stiff chair with some needlework over which her head was bent. Her knees were crossed. The men were fascinated by the swift, delicate, tantalizing, puncturing rhythm of her needle, and in the margin of John's vision was exactly all she meant to be seen of a small silk-clad ankle and slippered foot.

If it was as he suspected, how could Thane endure it?

"We are very quiet," she said, not looking up.

At that John began to talk about Thane, —of his work and the genius showing in it, of the methods he had evolved, of the things he had invented, of his way with his men and what a brilliant future he had. Agnes listened attentively, even tensely, as he could see, but made no comment; and Thane, sinking lower and lower in his chair, became intolerably embarrassed. He stopped it by beginning of a sudden to talk about John. He knew much less about John's work, however, than John knew about his. For that reason the narrative fell into generalities and was not convincing. Agnes listened for a while and became restive. Suddenly she put her needlework away and asked if anyone would like refreshments. John looked at the time. It was past eleven o'clock and he arose to go. Thane would have detained him; Agnes politely regretted that he had to go so soon. Still, when she shook hands with him at the door her manner was spontaneous and warm and she pressed him to come again.

John walked about in the night without any mind at all. When his thoughts became coherent he found himself saying: "No. They are not man and wife. They are strangers. I wonder what goes on in that house. Why does she do it?...Why does she do it?"

Why did she?

XXVII

As the door closed behind their visitor Agnes turned without speaking and went back to the front room where she sat at a little desk to write in a large black book. This was the last thing she did each day.

Thane leaned against the door jamb looking at her back. It was the view of her that sometimes thrilled him most. It made him see her again as she was that first night, in the moonlight, sitting at the edge of the mountain path, mysteriously averse. Approaching timidly he stood behind her chair, close enough to have touched her, as he longed to do if only he dared. He looked at his hands, turning them in the light; then at himself, downward, and was overcome with a sense of incongruity.

To him she was as untouchable as a butterfly. Her way of dressing so elaborately was at once an insurmontable barrier and a maddening provocation. Never did he see her in less formidable attire, not even at breakfast. Her morning gowns were forbidding in quite another way. Their effect was to put him on his sense of honor. If it should happen that he came home unexpectedly she was always in her room and when she appeared it was like this. Embellishment was her armor. It was constant and never slipped. Yet the need for it was only in those moments such as now when his feeling for her broke down his pride and moved him toward her in spite of himself. This was not often. It had happened only a few times since the first night in the hotel, when after supper she met his impulse by looking at him with such scorn and anger, even horror, that his desire instantly collapsed and left him aching cold. His pride was as black a beast as hers.

For a long time after that they had no way with each other, almost no way of meeting each other's eyes. Then to his great surprise she offered truce, not in words but by implications of conduct. She became friendly and began to talk to him about himself, about his work and by degrees about themselves. It was she who proposed to take a house. She chose it, bought the things that went into it, ordered the pattern of their twain existence within its walls. He was for spending more money, telling her how much he made and how well they could afford having more. She was firm in her own way, asking him only if he were comfortable, and he was.

The only thing she would freely spend money for was clothes. He pondered this and found no clue to its meaning. They had no social life whatever. She never went out alone. Twice in a year they had been to the play and nowhere else. Except for the recurring frustrations of his impulse toward her, which left him each time worse mangled in his pride and filled with rage, shame and self-abomination, he was happy.

He had been standing there back of her chair for so long that he began to wonder if she was aware of his presence when she spoke abruptly.

"Yes?" she said, in a quick, sharp tone.

He quailed, with the look of a man turned suddenly hollow. His pride saved him. Without a word he turned and went upstairs. When his footsteps were near the top she called, "Goodnight." Apparently he did not hear her. At least he did not answer. She went on writing.

The black book was the longer of her spirit's solvency. Each night she wrote it up. There was first a record of all the money received from Thane. Then a record of all expenditures, under two heads, —money spent for household purposes, itemized, and money spent upon herself, for clothes, etc., unitemized. At the end of each month against her personal expenditures was entered, —"Item, to Agnes, for wages, $50." If her personal expenditures exceeded her wage credit she wrote against the excess, —"Balance owing Alexander Thane, to be accounted for."

Some day she would have a fortune of her own. Then she would return everything she had spent above her wages. That was what the record said. Anyone could see it at a glance. The book was always lying there on the desk. Perhaps covertly she wished he would have the curiosity to look into it and see what she was doing. He never did and he never knew. She meant sometime to tell him. What was the point of not telling him? Yet she didn't, and the longer she put it off the more difficult it was, for a reason she was afraid to face. She would not face it for fear it was true. But even more she feared it might not be true.

So it appears that what went on in that house was as much an enigma to Thane as to John; and nobody could answer John's question, —"Why does she do it?" —for Agnes who knew concealed the truth from herself.

XXVIII

Thane became vice-president also of the American Steel Company. Its capacity was greater than the need was for wire to make nails. For this reason the N. A. M. Co. enlarged its scope and began to make steel wire for all purposes, especially for that distinctively American product called barbed wire which ran the first year into thousands of miles of farm fencing. It was cheaper than the rude, picturesque rail fence which it immediately superseded and at the same time appealed in an unaccountable manner to the Yankee sense of humor.

Steel wire was indispensable to the steel age. There were bridges to be cast in the air like cobwebs, chasms to be spanned, a thousand giants to be snared in their sleep with threads of steel wire, single, double, or twisted by hundreds into cables. Enough of them would make a rope strong enough to halt the world in its flight if one end could be made fast in space. There could never have been a steel age without steel wire. But the steel age required first of all steel rails to run on. John saw this clearly. Iron rails wore out too fast under the increasing weight of trains; besides, the time had almost come when they simply couldn't be made in quantities sufficient to meet the uncontrollable expansion of the railroad system. The importation of steel rails over the high tariff wall was increasing. American steel rails had been made experimentally, were still being made, but they were variable and much distrusted. When they were good they were excellent. They were just as likely to be very bad. They could not be guaranteed, owing to the variableness of steel obtained in this country by the Bessemer process.

This factor of variability was now eliminated by Thane's celebrated mixer. For the first time there was the certainty of being able to produce American steel rails that would not only outwear iron as iron outwears oak, that would not only not break, that would not only be satisfactory when they were good, but rails that would be always the same and always good. It was natural that the American Steel Company should turn to rails. John knew the rail business upside down. He believed in railroads. When other people were thinking railroad building had been overdone he said it had not really begun. He imagined the possibility that the locomotive would double in size.

It did. Then it doubled again. It could not have done so without steel rails under its feet, and if it had not doubled and then doubled again this now would be a German world. Democracy even then was shaping its weapons for Armageddon through men who knew nothing about it. They were free egoists, seeking profit, power, personal success, everyone attending to his own greatness. Never before in the world had the practise of individualism been so reckless, so purely dynamic, so heedless of the Devil's harvest. Yet it happened, —it precisely happened, —that they forged the right weapons. It seems sometimes to matter very little what men think. They very often do the right thing for wrong reasons. It seems to matter even less why they work. All that the great law of becoming requires is that men shall work. They cannot go wrong really. They cannot make wrong things. The pattern is foreordained.

Knowing what difficulties lay in the path of the steel rail, —knowing them very well indeed, since many of them were of his own work, —John executed a brilliant preliminary maneuver. The point of it was to create his market beforehand. With that in view he persuaded the officials of several large railroads to take ground floor shares in the North American Steel Company. Its capitalization was increased for that purpose. Thus not only was capital provided toward the building of a great rail making addition to the plant but powerful railroad men now had a participating interest in the success of the steel rail.

Meanwhile others also had discovered true steel formulas. As usual in such cases many hands were pressing against the door. Once the latch is lifted the door flies open for everyone. And then it appears that all the time there were several ways to have done it. Thane's way was not the only way. He had been the one to see where the cause of variableness lay. After that there could be several methods of casting it out. So the American Steel Company had competition almost from the start. However, as its rails were all bespoken by the railroads whose officials were stockholders, and as in any case the demand for rails was increasing very fast, there would have been prosperity for everyone if Enoch Gib had not been mad.

No sooner had the American Steel Company begun to produce rails than Enoch did with iron rails as he had done before with iron nails. He began to sell the famous Damascus iron rail at a ruinous price. The steel rail makers had to meet him. Then he lowered his price again, and again, and still again, all the time increasing his output, until there was no profit in rails for anybody.

John knew what it cost to make Damascus rails. Enoch was selling them actually at a loss.

The fact that puissant railroad officials were stockholders in the American Steel Company counted for less and less. Though they might prefer steel rails for both personal and intrinsic reasons, still they could not spend their railroad's money for steel rails with the famous Damascus rail selling at a price that made it a preposterous bargain. There was a panic in Pittsburgh.

John's emotions were those of Jonah riding the storm with an innocent face and a sense of guilt at his heart. He made no doubt that Enoch had set out deliberately to ruin the steel rail industry and would if need be commit financial suicide to accomplish that end. Nobody else knew or suspected the truth. John could not publish it.

Other steel rail makers quit. They could not stand the loss. And there it lay between Enoch and John. Enoch's mind was governed by two passions. One was his hatred of steel. The other was his hatred of John, who symbolized *Aaron*. He had the advantage of a fixed daemonic purpose. His strength was unknown. How long he might last even John could not guess.

In the fight over nails John's rule had been defensive. It had to be. But here there was choice. His resources now were so much greater that a policy of reprisals might be considered. If Enoch were determined to find his own breaking point the sooner the end the better for everyone else. The American Steel Company could slaughter rails, too, increasing both its own loss and Enoch's, and thus foreshorten the agony. But when it came to the point of adopting an offensive course John wavered. He could not bring himself to do it. Never had he hated Enoch. So far from that, his feeling for him was one of unreasoning pity. The old man probably would not survive bankruptcy. It would kill him. "Therefore," said John, "let him bring it about in his own time."

And so it was that a lone and dreadful man, stalking day and night through the New Damascus iron mill like a tormented apparition, goading his men to the point of frenzy, using them up and casting them off, yet holding them to it by force of contempt for fibre that snapped, —that one man in a spirit of madness frustrated the steel age and made it to limp on iron rails long after the true steel to shoe it with had been available. In all the histories of iron and steel you read men's blank amazement at the fact that it took so many years for the steel rail, once perfected, to supersede the iron rail. They cannot account for it.

At about this time a committee of New Damascus business men went forth to investigate the subject of steel. Enoch caused this to be done. His mood was one of exulting. Many had begun to believe that steel might overthrow iron. He was resolved to put that heresy down. He chose the right time. The committee going to and fro saw steel rail plants lying idle; it found the steel people in despair, terrorized by Enoch. It returned to New Damascus and saw with its own eyes on Enoch's books how the output of iron rails was increasing. Who would go behind such evidence? The committee reported that steel would never supersede iron. Except perhaps in some special uses, iron was forever paramount. It adopted a resolution in praise of Enoch, who had made New Damascus the iron town it was, and disbanded.

The sun of New Damascus was then at its zenith and the days of Enoch were few to run. He lived them out consistently. No man saw him but in his strength. His weakness was invisible like his nakedness. His end was as that of the oak that once more flings back the storm, then suddenly falls of its own weight. Never had his power seemed so immeasurable as at its breaking point.

For all that John could or could not do, the American Steel Company came itself to the brink. It could not forever go on making steel rails at a loss. How far short of bankruptcy would it give up the struggle and stop? The rocks were already in sight. Seeing them clearly, John did not act. He stood still and waited as if fascinated. The longer he waited the more desperate was the chance of saving the company.

Its credit was sinking. All of this he saw. "Then what am I waiting for?" he would ask himself, and postpone the answer. Twice he had called the directors together to lay before them a plan of salvage, which was the abandon rail making and convert the plant to other uses; and each time at the last minute he changed his mind.

One morning at breakfast he was electrified by a single black line in his newspaper.

"Damascus Mill Closes"

Beneath it was this dispatch:

"New Damascus, June II. —The Damascus mill closed down last night in all departments for the first time in its history. There is no explanation. Enoch Gib is understood to be ill."

John knew what this meant. The end had come. Having verified the news by telegraph he went to Slaymaker and told him for the first time enough of the history of New Damascus and its people to illuminate what had been going on.

"Why do you tell me this now?" Slaymaker asked.

"Isn't it a great relief?" said John. "The ghastly game that's nearly ruined us is at an end."

"There's some other reason," Slaymaker insisted.

"You have lost a lot of money with me in American Steel," John said. "Now of course it will all come back. Still, you might be able to turn this information to special advantage. There are two or three idle rail mills that could be picked up for nothing."

Slaymaker took time to reflect.

"Go ahead," he said. "I'll help."

John shook his head.

"It's an apple I don't like the taste of. If I were in your place I'd know what to do. That's why I have told you. But leave me out of it entirely."

"I can't for the life of me see why you shouldn't," said Slaymaker.

"Neither can I," said John. "There's no reason. Say I'm superstitious and let it drop."

"There's nothing the matter with the apple though?" asked Slaymaker.

"Not for you," said John.

He left the banker on the edge of his chair. When he arrived at his own office Thane was there waiting.

"We've got a telegram Enoch is dying. Thought maybe as you would go along with us."

"How does Mrs. Thane take it?"

"Cold and still," said Thane. "But you can't tell."

"Does she want me to go?"

"She knows I'm asking you," said Thane. "There's just time. She's at the depot."

John turned and went with him.

XXIX

It was six hours by train from Pittsburgh to New Damascus. The last hour was from Wilkes-Barre down the valley, the railway now running with the turnpike on which Agnes passed her wedding night between Thane and John over the flying heels of a pair of bays. Not one of them had seen it since. Surreptitiously watching for signs and landmarks they became silent and solitary. Memories in which they were intimately associated instead of drawing them together caused separate states of reverie.

Agnes sat at the window with her face averted. John and Thane were together in the opposite seat. Her eyebrows were a little raised, acutely bent and drawn together, and in her forehead was a Gothic cross. This muscular tension never for a moment relaxed, not even when she spoke and smiled. In her eyes was an expression of strained and baffled interrogation, inward looking.

Two years were gone since that night of John's first supper with the Thanes in their trial abode. In this time she had changed at the base of her personality. The girl of her had vanished almost without trace.

What becomes of the being we have ceased to be?

That Agnes of the tantalizing armor, half of ice and half of flame, part disdain and part desire, who froze the impulse she provoked and singed the pride that saved her, —she was gone, entirely gone. This Agnes knew her not. This Agnes was a woman who knew bitterness and the taste of dust. When she had been ready... willing... dying... to give her pride to save her love the door was closed. The shop was dark.

The light went out that night she let him stand behind her chair in an agony of longing, pretending not to know he stood there, and then broke him with a hard, glissando "Y-e-s?" It was ominous that he did not respond from the top of the staircase to her careless goodnight. She regarded him particularly the next morning and began to wonder. Never again did he look at her in that way she ached for and dreaded. The more he didn't look at her in that way the more she ached for it and the less she dreaded it, until she couldn't remember why she had dreaded it and forgot why she had ever repulsed him.

She had repulsed because her vanity required it. He had got her to wife without wooing her. She had been thrust upon him. The thought was a sleepless scorpion in her breast. It poisoned her dreams. Well... but before he could touch her he should have to want her and prove it. She would attend to that. To reach her at all he should have to overcome a great barrier. This she resolved and so she repulsed him. Each hurt to his pride was a stone added to the barrier, and she set no limit to it, for the higher it was the more it would prove if he ever got over. Then she would see what her own feelings were.

He on his part, after that night, once and for all accepted the only inference he could draw from her behaviour. He was hateful to her; he filled her with loathing and disgust. Well... he could no more help that than he could help the fact of their being married: but he could avoid those moments on the rack. They left him limp and useless for days afterward. He could lock the impulse up. Its getting loose was what drew her scorn upon him. So he chained and locked it up.

At first, seeing the door was closed, she walked to and fro before it, thinking he would read in her manner a sign of remorse. He saw nothing. Then she began to knock. He did not hear. She thought he was making her pay. She was willing, even greedy, to pay. She went on knocking. Presently she realized that he was blind and deaf. In a panic she beat upon the door, hurled her weight against it, crying out her wish to surrender. But she had seared his heart. He could see only with his eyes and hear but with his ears, and totally misapprehended her woman's gesture.

She imagined that now *he* repulsed HER, not in revenge, not to trample on her, —that she could easily have endured, —but coldly, with undesire.

This completed the irony. Thereafter she held aloof and began to fear him. She put away her glittering armor, staining it with tears of rage and chagrin, and he never noticed even that. He was always gentle, always absent, always cold. He grew on her in this aspect, assumed colossal proportions, and began to seem as inaccessible to her as she had seemed to him. They changed places again. She stood in awe of him. What he wished for was. He spoke of a way of living more in keeping with their circumstances. She moved them to a larger house and organized their lives according to such dim suggestions as she could get from him, one of which was that she should "stay out of the kitchen." There had to be servants. Evenings were so much worse on that account that they began to go out more, often alone, sometimes together. By a law of contradiction, the more they concealed themselves from each other in the tatters of their pride and the further they went apart, the more polite they became and the easier it was to be friendly.

Her outwardness had changed no less. A wilful, pouting mouth had found the shape of wistfulness. Her eyes had lost their defiant glitter; they were softer, deeper and full of recognition. Into her movements had come that kind of gentle dignity, loftier than pride, lovelier than loveliness, which is idolized of men above the form and sign of beauty.

"Almost there," she said, settling back in her seat.

"How strange the mill looks! —cold," said Thane.

Agnes did not look.

"Five years," said John. "What a long time!"

"Six," said Agnes.

"Six," said Thane.

The Gib carriage was waiting at the station. "I'll be at the inn," said John. "It will take no time to bring me if I'm wanted. If Enoch-if you don't stay at the mansion I'd like you to have supper with me."

"I'll send you word," said Thane.

XXX

On the last terrace the carriage was stopped by two men who detached themselves from a sullen group on the lawn and stood in the driveway with their hands upraised. Thane recognized them. The two who halted the carriage were puddlers with whom he had worked side by side in the mill. The others, to the number of six, were heaters and rollers, all men of long service under the tyrant.

"Want a word with you, Thane," said the taller one of the two puddlers.

He got out of the carriage and stood for an instant hesitating whether to let Agnes go on to the house alone or have her wait. Suddenly a scream of mindless, futile fury kanted through the air. Everybody shuddered.

"Him," said the puddler, answering Thane's startled look.

Deciding then not to let Agnes go on alone he took her out, led her to an iron bench in the shade, and returned to hear what the men were so anxious to tell him.

"You heard him," said the tall puddler. "That's at us. We ain't a going to do it. Nary if nor and about it, we ain't. It's against God, man and nature. It's irreligious. What's moreover the men won't have it. They got to work there, don't they? No sir. They won't have it."

"What does he want?" Thane asked.

"He takes on that a way and says as he can't die until's we promise. But we ain't a going to promise."

"What does he want you to promise?" Thane asked, patiently.

"No sir," the puddler went on. "Nobody's a going to. Not so as you could notice it. Ain't it bad enough to have him always on our necks alive?"

"You ain't told him yet," said the second puddler.

"'Tain't Christian," said the tall one, walking off by himself. "It's heathen," he mumbled. "It's unbelieving. It's...."

"You tell me," said Thane to the second puddler. "What does Enoch want?"

"Wants us to burn him up in a puddlin 'furnace,'" said the second puddler. Trying to say it calmly, even lightly, and all at once, he lost control of his voice. It squeaked with horror on the last word.

"Is that all?"

The puddler recoiled. The group behind him fell back a step.

"Is that all he wants?" Thane asked again.

"That's what he's a screaming at us for," said the puddler, sharply.

Thane went back to Agnes. He had time to tell her before they reached the mansion.

"If he wants it, and you have no will to the contrary, I'll promise to do it," he concluded.

"It strikes one with terror," she said. "If he wants it that's enough."

Just as they were admitted they heard the dreadful scream again. The door, closing, seemed to cut it off. Inside there was no sound of it.

The family doctor anxiously received them. He talked rapidly, addressing Agnes in a manner tactfully to include Thane, whom he had never seen before. The two best consulting physicians in Wilkes-Barre were present, he said. There had arrived within the hour also an eminent alienist from Philadelphia. Four men nurses had been provided. Everything possible to be done had been thought of almost at once.

"But what is it?" Agnes asked. "What has happened?"

The doctor was sympathetic. Naturally she would want to know what it was and how it happened. Those were questions anyone would ask. Alas! who could answer them? He, the doctor, had attended the late Mrs. Gib; it had been his happiness to know Agnes before she could possibly know herself; but Mr. Gib, as they all knew, lived to himself. He had, so to speak, no pathological history. Three days before it happened he had begun to behave strangely at the mill. The men noticed it. He interfered with their work by having them hold the furnace doors open while he committed papers, bundles and various unidentified objects to the fire, thereby spoiling several heats of good iron. It was not a doctor's business to know these things. He had taken it upon himself, nevertheless, to make inquiries.

On the third day there had been a conference between Mr. Gib and his lawyers. What took place at this conference a doctor would probably not understand if he were told; however, he had not been told. The lawyers were reticent to the point of being rude, not knowing, of course, how important it was for a doctor to be able to reconstruct the events that have immediately preceded the seizure. Mr. Gib, he had learned, never returned to the mill from that conference with his lawyers. The notice of the mill's closing was posted by the lawyers; it was signed by them with power of attorney. Mr. Gib went straight home and was next seen in a state of frenzy. When the doctor arrived he was in a paroxysm of rage, very dangerous to himself but otherwise harmless, since it seemed to vent itself upon imaginary objects. This state was followed by others, in rapid, alarming alternation-despair, exultation, terror. It had been necessary, as they could realize, to put him under restraint. Two men nurses were by him constantly.

What was it? The Wilkes-Barre consultants had agreed upon one diagnosis. The patient, they said, had been attacked by delusional mania. If the attack subsided he would recover; if not he would die of exhaustion. That might be a matter of weeks. The Philadelphia alienist had only just now seen the patient; yet his mind was made up. He pronounced it a kind of progressive disintegration of the brain matter, with sudden, catastrophic lesions. Death would take place in a few hours. And it certainly was true that all the symptoms grew worse.

"What is your opinion?" Agnes asked.

"My own?" said the doctor, casting glances around. He lowered his voice to a nonprofessional tone. "We have different names for it," he said. "That is scientific. No matter. We are all talking about the same thing....He...is...possessed."

Agnes shuddered.

"What does he want from these mill workers outside?" Thane asked.

Yes, yes. The doctor was just coming to that. Mr. Gib had lucid, coherent intervals. They were decreasing in frequency and duration and that was an ominous sign. In the very first of these intervals he seemed to be facing the thought of death and revealed an extreme horror of natural interment. He had in one such interval either conceived a way or remembered one of cheating the earth, which was to be cremated in one of his own furnaces. Thereupon he began to call for certain old puddlers and heaters by name and when they were brought up to him he demanded of them a promise to dispose of his body in that extraordinary way. While he looked at them they had not the strength to say outright they would not; but he could not make them promise, and each time he failed it was very bad for him. The state of terror returned, and if this continued the consequences would be fatal.

"Would it relieve him if I promised?" Thane asked.

"Promised what?" the doctor asked moving uneasily.

"To do what he wants done with his body," said Thane.

"But who would do it?" the doctor asked.

"I would," said Thane.

The doctor looked away in all four directions. "Certainly it would relieve him now," he said, vaguely, as if that were not the point.

Thane suggested that Agnes be permitted to see him in the next lucid interval, and that afterward, in the same interval if possible, and if not, then in the next one, they should try letting him promise to carry out the old man's cremation wish.

The doctor agreed. However, he was not to be held responsible for the consequences. He had been responsible until now for everything because there was no one else. He could not be unaware of the fact that there had been an unfortunate family episode. No one could tell how Mr. Gib would be affected by the unexpected sight of his own daughter. He had not asked to see her. However, she *was* his daughter and there Was no one else, —no one. How extraordinary!

He left them to ascertain and report.

Agnes, putting off her hat and gloves, sat facing the window. Thane took several turns about the room, came up behind her chair, laid his hand gently on her head. She sat quite still and reached over her shoulder for his other hand. They did not speak. The doctor returned in haste, saying: "If Mrs. Thane will come now, at once, very softly, we may try." Agnes and the doctor walked up the staircase together, Thane following. Her feet were as steady as his own. He was suddenly swept with a feeling of great tenderness for her.

The Philadelphia alienist and the Wilkes-Barre consultants made a group in the front hall window. They had been arguing technically and stopped to stare a little at Agnes and then at Thane, who fell back and stood leaning against the wall as Agnes and the doctor went on. The doctor opened the door carefully and peered in. Standing aside he motioned Agnes to enter.

Her father lay in a great four-poster on his back, extended to his full length, his feet together and vertical, his head slightly raised on pillows, —and their eyes met as she crossed the threshhold. He recognized her instantly. She was sure of it, —sure he was in his right mind. Yet he gave not the slightest sign of his feelings. She was surprised that he was not more shrunken. His bulk was intact. But he was the color of sand. His aspect was sepulchral. She advanced slowly, holding his gaze, hardly aware of two men standing alert at the head of the bed, just outside the line of vision, ready to seize him.

When she was half way to him he began to sit up, lifting his whole trunk from the hips without the use of his arms, his feet at the same time rising a little, under the lower part of the sheet.

"Go away 1" he said hoarsely, and she stopped. "Go away!" he meant to say again, but as his voice rose he became inarticulate and made guttural sounds. He began to repel her with excited gestures. The doctor interfered. "Come," he whispered. She half turned to go, but faced her father again. In a clear, loud voice, she uttered the three words he had once with all his strength demanded and could not make her say. "I am sorry." Their effect was to excite him all the more. He continued to wave her away. When the door had closed behind her he collapsed.

Thane was waiting outside the door. She leaned on him heavily and seemed about to go under. He took her in his arms and bore her downstairs. She revived at once and sharply declined to be made about, even by the doctor, whose smelling salts she put aside. Thane walked with her in the air.

Presently the doctor joined them. The idea of bringing Mr. Thane to Mr. Gib's notice as one who would promise to do the strange thing he desired,- —this idea, he said, had been discussed with the alienist; and it was the alienit's notion first to put the patient under the suggestion that a puddler named Thane had been sent for, the point being that Mr. Gib might remember Mr. Thane as a puddler and forget him as a son-in-law. This seemed to the doctor too subtle altogether; still, as it couldn't do any harm he had consented. It had in fact been done with such success that Mr. Gib now lay in a fever of hope. Would Mr. Thane, the puddler, please come at once?

Thane had never been in a sick room. He had never seen death transacting. He had known two idiots and had an idea of imbecility; insanity he could not imagine. The doctor's long medical discourse on Enoch's disorder had filled him with a vague sense of resentment; and the doctor's private conviction that Enoch was possessed had made him angry. He did not believe in devils. That flash of superstition threw the professional manner into grotesque relief and he was contemptuous of it. His feelings went over and stood with Enoch against these self-important outsiders who by some law of their own had established themselves above him in his own house, were permitted to restrain him in his own bed, who stood about in his hallway disputing as to how and why he should die.

As Thane entered the room the two nurses were leaning over the old man from opposite sides of the bed, and the sight of them deepened his antagonism. They stood back as he approached. Enoch, slowly opening his eyes, gazed at Thane with a look of tense recognition. Otherwise he lay perfectly inert until Thane stood looking down at him. Then his lips began to move as if he were talking. No sound was audible. Thane, bending lower and lower, dropped on his knees and put his ear very close. Enoch was whispering. His words, though faint, were distinct, almost fluent, and dramatically intentional.

What he said was that worse puddlers and lesser men than Thane, men he had known all his life, had refused to do for him that service one cannot perform for oneself and must therefore be permitted to ask as a favor. This service was to dispose of his remains agreeably to a certain wish, which was to be cremated. There was no physical difficulty whatever. It was feasible to be done in a puddling furnace! —his own furnace! —his own mill! —his own body! Why not?

"I will do it," said Thane, removing his ear and meeting the old man's eyes. Enoch's lips continued to move. Thane returned his ear.

It was to be done in Number One Furnace.

Thane met his eyes again, saying: "All right. In Number One. I understand."

Enoch's lips were still moving. Thane listened.

There was one thing more, Enoch said. He had no right to ask it except as a favor for which he would be deeply grateful. Would Thane listen very carefully? In that walnut secretary by the door, in a secret drawer of it that would come open when the moulding above the pen rack was pressed downward-there he would find the key to a room upstairs, directly above the one they were in. He wished to die in that room opstairs, —*by himself*. He knew better than to ask the nurses or the doctors. They already thought him mad. Anyhow they would ask questions and he couldn't tell them why he wished to die in that room alone. He had been saving his strength against an opportunity to give them the slip, intending to lock himself into it. Once in it he would be safe. But his strength had suddenly departed forever. No one knew this yet. It had just happened. The nurses supposed he was resting. The fact was he could not move foot, hand or finger. So now he was utterly helpless and hopeless except for Thane, —and the end was so near.

Would Thane get the key? —carry him over all obstacles to that room above? —set him in a certain chair, taking care not to move it? —then retire and lock the door and keep them all off for an hour? An hour would do it. In one hour he would be out of their reach.

Thane did not pause to reflect. The old man's appeal to be permitted to die as he would in his own house was irresistible. It moved him dynamically. He strode to the walnut secretary, discovered the key, dropped it in his pocket and returned to the bedside.

The nurses were dumfounded! scandalized! to see him suddenly take the old man up in his arms, sheet and all, and start off with him toward the door.

They followed, exclaiming and chattering. They were too amazed to act. At the door occurred a scene of pure confusion. As Thane pulled it open the four doctors, having heard the commotion within, were there in a group on the momentum of entry. At sight of Enoch in Thane's arms they recoiled and stood blankly aghast. The two nurses behind Thane became hysterically vocal, trying all in one breath to exculpate themselves and explain an inconceivable thing.

Thane was pushing through.

"He wants to die upstairs," he said.

Instantly on speaking of it he became aware that the situation had an irrational aspect; and he wondered how he should clear them out of the room in which Enoch wished to die and keep them out, —for of course they would follow. He could not help that. With a resolve if necessary to throw them all downstairs he crossed the threshold. The alienist from Philadelphia and the two Wilkes-Barre consultants fell back. It was not their case. The family doctor barred Thane's way at the foot of the staircase.

"You must be crazy," he shouted, waving his arms. "This simply cannot be permitted. As his physician I order you to take him back."

"Stand aside," said Thane.

"You will kill him," said the doctor. "Do you hear that? This will kill him. I forbid it."

Thane seemed not at all impressed. Probably he would have pursued his purpose in a straight line but that his mind was arrested by a startling change in the heft and feeling of his burden.

It became suddenly so much heavier that he almost lost his balance. And as he looked to see what this could mean there rose out of Enoch a groan unlike any sound concerned with life. With that the body underwent a violent muscular commotion and threw itself into a state of rigid extension. Thane needed all his strength to hold it. Immediately there was another change. The body began slowly to go limp.

"It's over," said the Philadelphia alienist.

What Thane held in his arms was no longer Enoch, but a distasteful object, fallen in one breath from the first person *I*, from the second person *you*, to the state of a pronominal third thing which is spoken of —*that!*

Thane carried it back to the bed.

All of this had taken place in less than half an hour. Thane found Agnes as he had left her, on an iron bench in the maple shade.

"He is dead," she said, on looking at him.

He answered by sitting by her side in silence.

She asked him nothing about the end, and he was glad, for it had been extremely harrowing. Still, he was surprised at her want of curiosity, and had a moment of thinking her callous. He had somehow mysteriously arrived at an understanding of Enoch, was shaken by a sense of loss, even grief, and yearned to share his emotion with Agnes.

Having been for some time withdrawn in thought she started slightly. "Did you promise?" she asked. "Was there time for that?"

"Yes," he said. "Don't let it upset you," he continued gently. "You won't have to think about it. I've got it worked out in my mind. There can be funeral services here like they have sometimes when nobody goes to the grave or when there ain't going to be any burial. Then I can go alone with him to the mill. There's nobody at the mill, you know. It's shut."

She regarded him with a troubled, unbelieving expression.

"Alone!" she said.

"I'd rather to," he said, "with everybody being so superstitious about it."

"But I shall go," she said.

"May take a long time," he said uneasily. "I'll have the furnace going, of course, but it's got to be kept going and watched I don't know how long."

She met these difficulties with a scornful gesture.

"All right," he said. "He'll be pleased you feel that way."

XXXI

Late that night Thane was telling John how Enoch died and how his remains were to be disposed of. He had to tell someone. It was a weight on his mind and he was tormented with misgivings about his own conduct. When he came to the key he remembered having it in his pocket still and produced it associatively. John took it out of his hand and continued to regard it thoughtfully long after the narrative was finished.

"Was I right?" Thane asked, anxiously.

"Admirable!" said John, a little off the point as it seemed to Thane. He added thoughtfully: "The fate that amuses itself with our lives knew what it wanted when it tangled you in."

"Seems there's a lot as I don't know," said Thane, a faint edge to his voice.

"It's hard to get at," said John. He continued: "This place, if you know, was founded by General Woolwine, my great grandfather, whose partner was a younger man named Christopher Gib, this Enoch's father."

So he began, as if opening a book. Some of it was missing, parts were illegible, yet the shape of the drama stood vividly forth. When he came to the end-to where the invisible writing stopped, —it was sudden and for a moment bewildering, almost as if they had forgotten who they were and had been unexpectedly let down in the middle of a story. They sat a while musing.

"To be continued by the three of us," said John. "I should like to know what is in that room."

"Let's go see," said Thane.

He had come to the hotel only to talk to John and was returning to the mansion. John went with him.

Enoch's body lay where it was in the second floor bed chamber. They passed it without stopping and went on to the third floor. On the landing was a little table with a lighted glass lamp, which John took up.

"That would be it," he said, indicating a certain doorway. The key fitted the lock, but to their surprise the bolt was already drawn. John held the light. Thane went first. He had but crossed the threshold when he started back, recoiled rather, with a movement so sudden and involuntary that John immediately behind him was thrown off his balance, and dropped the lamp, which burst and harmlessly petered out. They were then in darkness. There was no other light on that floor.

"Match," said Thane, now standing quietly.

John had matches and he divided them by a sense of touch. Each struck one and held it out.

What had startled Thane was the figure of a woman. As they saw her now in the flickering light of their matches she stood at the other side of the room, her back to the wall, facing them. John recognized her at once as the woman who met him in the front doorway, holding an oil light over her head, the night he carne seeking Agnes and encountered Enoch at the gate. She was dishevelled. Her thick black hair had fallen on one side and her face was distorted and swollen from weeping. Her eyes were alight with a kind of wild animal defiance. As they approached her she began to move along the wall, sideways, her arms a little spread. In one hand she held a coil of small rope.

"Who are you?" Thane asked.

She did not speak, but continued slowly to edge along the wall, staring at them angrily. They lit fresh matches from the dying ones and pursued her in this way, asking her who she was and what she did there, and she answered only with that wild look, until with more presence of mind than they were able to summon she had worked herself to a position between them and the open door. Their matches gave out and she disappeared in the dark. They heard her go down the back stairway.

"We'll have to get a light," said John.

They groped their way downstairs, both absurdly unnerved, found some candles and returned to the room. Both had the same thought. From what they had glimpsed of the interior in the light of their matches by a kind of marginal vision it seemed quite empty. And so it was. There was no trace of what had been there, except dust, which on the floor showed evidence of much moving about. The only object of any kind was a key that evidently the woman had dropped. It was a duplicate of the one in Thane's possession. They examined the room with silent curiosity. The walls gave a dead, solid sound to the rap of their knuckles. The windows were double and grated inside with iron bars.

Now they went in search of the woman, knowing nothing about her, not even her name. She was probably the housekeeper. Agnes would know. But they hated to disturb Agnes. She was at the other side of the mansion and it was very late. Besides, they had a feeling that the sequel might be distressing.

The woman had vanished. They could find no trace of her, nor could they raise any servants indoors, for the reason afterward disclosed that latterly Enoch's menage had consisted of three persons, —housekeeper, gardener and stable man.

"Let's try the stable," John suggested. "There must be somebody alive."

On their way to the stable they stared curiously at a great unsightly heap of ashes, still smoking and glowing in spots, on the back terrace, as if a miscellaneous lot of things had been gathered hastily together and burned.

"Strange place for a fire," said Thane, with an unspoken intuition that John shared.

The stable-man was sitting up, smoking, with the look of a man whose eyes have seen more than mind can grasp. He knew Thane and seemed comforted by the advent of human society.

"Nobody in the house. What's the matter?" Thane asked.

"I ain't the housekeeper," said the stable-man. "No, thank God, I ain't her. She's on her way."

"Way where?"

"Wherever," he said, with the air of a man who for cause has newly resolved not to meddle with things that will be.

"What do you know about her?" John asked.

They had only to listen and piece it together. He was full of it. The woman's name was Ann Sibthorp and she came from nobody knew where, —most likely from some place where they had ceased to speak well of her. She had been Enoch's housekeeper for many years and at last his only house servant. She was not a woman you could get acquainted with. You wouldn't if you could. So it wasn't that anybody cared, but that she gave herself airs about her station, became oppressive and drove the help away. She did much that Enoch probably knew nothing about. Yet she had her way, even with him, and it got so nobody dared to cross her. For several days she had been going strange. When the old man died she seemed to lose her mind. She looked without seeing. There was no sense in her eyes. A little while before dark she began to carry things from the house and pile them out there on the terrace. He could not say exactly what they were, —some pieces of furniture, a chair, a bed no doubt; yes, and some clothes, a pair of white slippers and little what-not objects. When he saw her pouring oil on them he protested. She didn't hear him. She wasn't natural and he was afraid to do anything except to draw a lot of water in case something caught fire. Then she lighted the pile and watched it burn, fairly standing in the flames, poking them with a stick, rubbing her hands in them, taking on like a witch. It made a God-fearing person sick to see her. After that she went in and he didn't see her again until just now when she rushed out of the house and disappeared among the trees.

"She's a going to do herself a damage, that woman," he predicted, calmly. "Found this in the edge of the ashes," he remembered, drawing from his pocket a small square brown case, badly singed at one corner. "Maybe you would know what it is."

It was a daguerreotype in a faded leather case. Thane opened it and held it for John to see in the light of the stable lantern.

"I recognize it," said John. Thane gave it to him.

That was all from the stable-man. And that was all that was ever known about Ann Sibthorp. She was never seen again, dead or alive.

"You know the picture?" Thane asked, as they were parting at the gate.

"It's a portrait of my mother," John answered.

"Esther that you just told me about?"

"Yes."

XXXII

At daybreak smoke was seen curling out of one of the cold mill stacks. Everybody in New Damascus knew that Enoch's body was to be burned in a puddling furnace.

"There he goes!" one said. "There goes old Enoch now."

"Not yet," said another. "Take a hotter fire than that. Don't you see it's just started. That's his puddler son-in-law getting it ready for him."

It takes eight or ten hours, starting with it cold, to get the maw of a puddling furnace white hot. In this case it would take even longer since Thane had it all to do alone and would be unable to stoke the fire steadily. There were other duties. Simple obsequies would take place at the mansion in the afternoon. That was all the public was permitted to know. Only Thane and Agnes knew at what hour the cremation would begin. The point of keeping it secret was obvious.

All day long people watched the smoke with fascinated horror. Crowds gathered on the mountainside and at points overlooking the mill to witness this weird translation of the symbol that was Enoch, —symbol of iron, symbol of indestructibility. There were many who believed he would not burn.

After the funeral services had taken place at the mansion interest in the smoke became intense. Changes in its color or density or in the way it twisted out of the top of the stack evoked exclamations of horrendous wonder and cries of "Look! Look! That's the image of him. That's Enoch going up. Don't you see him?" Then news would come, seemingly by a telepathic impulse, that that had been only the son-in-law poking up the fire; the body was still at the mansion. Again it would be rumored that a previous rumor was positively true. The remains had been got into the mill unobserved. Everybody had been fooled. Enoch had got the last laugh. He had been burning up for more than an hour and had already very largely vanished into the sky.... So the whole afternoon and the early evening passed.

An hour after sunset the stable-man drove a spring wagon to the Enoch portal of the Gib mansion. He tied the horse to the ring in the hand of the ironboy hitching post and went indoors. Presently the front door swung open. Thane, the gardener and the stableman appeared bearing the coffin. They slid it into the bed of the wagon over the tailboard. Agnes followed with a black drape. Thane covered the coffin with it. Then he helped Agnes up over the high front wheel, took the lines from the stable-man, got up beside her, and they drove away at a walk.

At the entrance to the mill yard Agnes held the lines while Thane got down to unlock the gate. A number of people were idly gathered there in separate knots, pretending to be non-existent. News of the body's arrival would travel fast. That couldn't be helped. What Thane had counted on was that darkness would cheat the eye of morbidity. But he had forgotten the moon; it was full and coming up. The whorl of smoke rising from the stack looked even more ghost-like by moonlight than in daytime and the watchers, now sure of their spectacle and of Enoch's presence in the smoke, were more gruesomely thrilled than they had hoped to be.

The yard and mill were deserted. Even the watchmen had been sent away until midnight. Agnes still holding the lines, Thane leading the horse, they crossed the yard, picking their way around heaps of rusty pig iron, abandoned castings, rails piled up like cord wood, and came to the rear door of the mill.

"You stay here for a minute," said Thane. "I'll come and get you."

He drew the coffin half way out of the wagon, stooped to get his shoulder under, lifted it, and walked slowly into the gloom, treading cautiously. There was no light and there were many pitfalls, but his feet knew every inch of this ground before they wore shoes. He soon returned, tied the horse, helped Agnes down and led her by the hand.

At first she could see nothing and followed him blindly. Then far off in the crêpe interior she saw a sultry glow. As they drew near she heard the roar of the furnace fire, like the sound at the brink of a cataract. A fire is a cataract upward. It grew louder and louder with each step until she could feel its vibrations in the soles of her feet. She never had been in the mill before.

A puddling furnace is a low brick structure somewhat resembling a double tomb. One side is the fire pit; the other side is the oven. The flames from the fire pit are sucked by draught across the roof of the oven. As you face the furnace you see two iron doors-one is to the fire pit, opening on the grate, to receive the fuel. To the right of that on a higher level is the small square door of the oven. Through the first door when it is open you see the fire. Through the other you see heat, —nothing but heat, —blinding incandescence.

Thane led Agnes to a bench facing the furnace, spread his coat upon it and motioned her to sit down. The roar was so great that conversation in normal tones was impossible. She now began to take in the scene.

The fire pit at the last stoking had evidently been gorged to the teeth. A long iron bar was propped against the door to hold it shut. Gases, smoke and cherry flames were belching through the cracks. The oven door was set in a square halo of exuding white light. And directly in front of this door, pointing toward it head first, was the coffin, resting on a pair of iron horses.

There was no light other than that escaping from the furnace doors, and as it was continually running through unpredictable changes, so perspectives, and the forms, dimensions and relations of objects, were always changing with a very weird effect.

Thane threw off his collar, tie, waistcoat and hat, and seemed to take the furnace by the jaws with his bare hands. First he opened the oven door and was immersed in scalding light. He slammed it to, shaking his head. Kicking away the iron bar, he opened the fire door and immediately banged it shut, still shaking his head. The fire was not hot enough. Rolling up his sleeves he seized a great poker, pulled the fire door open again, and made several passes; then he stopped, slammed the door, and stood for a moment in apparent dilemma. No wonder. Who in a white shirt could bring a fire to its zenith? He disappeared into the gloom and was lost for five minutes. When he reappeared he was in the puddler's rig he had worn earlier in the day, —naked to the middle, trousers rolled at the waist, cowhide shoes, gloves and skullcap. Now be could talk to the fire. As he thrust the javelin into its throat it roared back at him like an angry beast. He made it turn over, lie down, turn over again and rear on its legs. For moments he was swallowed up in smoke and Agnes could scarce restrain a shriek of thrill and terror. Each time he miraculously emerged unsinged. Then he cast in more fuel, working swiftly, with heroic ease and grace, and banged the door shut just in time, for the monster was on the point of lunging headlong forth. With another look at the inside of the oven he came and sat on the end of the bench. She noticed that his chest rose and fell slowly. All that exertion had not forced his breathing. Ten minutes passed. He rowelled the fire again. This time instead of returning to sit on the bench he walked to and fro in front of the furnace.

In Agnes a mysterious excitement was rising. It seemed incongruous with what they were doing; therefore she ceased to be aware of that. The emotion comprehended Thane, centered in him, excluded everything else save the fact of herself in relation to him. As she watched him his figure became splendid, fabulous! Her own ego's importance collapsed. In his power with ideas man is dimly admirable to woman; in his power over circumstances he inspires her with trust; in his power over people he satisfies her taste for grandeur; but in his power over elements, —in that aspect he wrecks her completely, for she is herself an element. In that moment he is god-like; she cannot comprehend him.

She was in love with him. That fact had long been desperate and apparently hopeless, since he had closed the door. But now, in addition to the potential of her love, she felt that sweet, fierce longing for the thing of life, that headlong impulse to perpetuation, with which we are mysteriously seized in the presence of death. This nameless elemental forethought will pierce through grief, affliction and terror. Sir John Everett Millais caught its gesture in the most poignant pencil sketch in the world —"Marrying and Giving in Marriage at the Deluge."

Thane's emotions were parallel. He loved that woman. And the stark enigma moved him in the same way to answer death with life. Being a man he thought himself abominable. Yet the impulse overthrew him.

Breaking his walk before the furnace he strode to the bench where she sat, lifted her free, pressed her to him and kissed her once hotly on the mouth.

Instantly overcome at what he had done, humiliated, chagrined, horribly ashamed of the desire that possessed him, he put her down as suddenly as he had picked her up, roughly, leaving her stunned and limp.

She had been overwhelmed in all her senses. The impact was catastrophic. There had not been time for her to react as her nature listed. For a moment she could scarcely believe it had happened. It might almost have been an episode of phantasy. She rose to run after him.

At that instant he opened the furnace door and the glare blinded her. When he closed it and turned she was at one end of the coffin and he at the other. So they faced each other.

"It is ready," he said. Though she could not hear she knew what he meant. The fire at last was hot enough. As she neither moved nor made a sign, he asked: "Is there anything to say?" That also she understood.

She crossed her arms and dropped her head on the foot of the coffin. Thane looked away.... She raised her head and stood back. Thane flung the door wide open, quickly lifted the coffin by the middle, rested the head of it on the lip of the oven, then took it by the foot and pushed it in. It made a grating sound above the roar of the fire and was instantly wrapped in a flame of burning wood. Seizing an iron bar he pushed it far in and slammed the door.

Hours passed. No word was spoken. Thane gave the fire no peace. He made it rage and bellow. The door of the oven was not opened again. From time to time he unstopped the little round eye through which a puddler kneads the waxing iron and peered in.

It was nearly two o'clock when he gorged the pit once more with fuel, propped the fire door shut, and stood in front of Agnes, saying: "We could go now."

She rose slowly and he took her by the hand to lead her out.

When they came to the air by the door at which they went in he said: "Wait here by the wagon. I want to wash a bit." She caught a white gleam of him in the moonlight as he got out of the puddler's rig and heard him splashing under the tap at the water tank. He was not long, and returned carrying his coat on his arm, otherwise dressed as when he came, except that his collar was missing and the front of his shirt lay open. He offered to help her up.

"I'd like to walk," she said.

One of the watchmen who had returned took charge of the horse and they departed on foot. Although dense smoke still issued from the stack there was very little of Enoch left in it, perhaps not a trace. When Thane last looked there was nothing on the incandescent bed of the oven but an ashy outline fainter than a shadow. The fire as it was would continue to burn for hours.

"Thought you might rather go to the hotel," he said, when they were through the gate, and he had locked it again. "We've got rooms there."

"I would," she answered, "only I've no sleep in me and I'd like to walk."

She was looking toward the mountain and they walked that way. Thane was stirred by an intuition, which he disbelieved, that if he were passive and let her choose they would come to a certain path. And they did. He had a further intuition, most unbelievable, that of her own accord she would stop at a certain place, turn in a certain way, and stand looking into the valley. And she did.

It was the spot at which they first met, the night of his battle with the Cornishman, —a night very like this one.

All the way she had been silent. If they touched, walking side by side, he made it clear without words that the contact was accidental. When they came to the path he stood aside and she went ahead. When at this spot she stopped and turned her face to the valley he went a few paces away, not to disturb her reverie, and stood with his face averted.

The summer night was cool; but the air he breathed was hot, tasteless and suffocating. Memory reconstructed the episode of their original meeting. It went on from there. He saw as in one picture the whole of his life with Agnes and feelings extremely inconsistent assailed him. There was one, —the one he thought he had got control of, —that rose higher and higher, for a reason he seemed painfully aware of and yet for a moment could not recall. Then he remembered. It referred to that moment in the mill when he kissed her for the first time in his life, and by force. He had forgotten it as one might momentarily forget having just committed a murder. He loathed himself for having done it. He wondered that she could tolerate him afterward, could walk with him alone, could speak to him with no sign of disgust. He wondered what she was thinking, so still in the moonlight. Probably thinking of that.

He became aware that she moved. She was coming toward him. He did not turn round. He detested himself so much that he could not bear to look at her, or to be looked at, and stepped out of the path to let her pass. She did not pass.

He felt her standing close to him, —near enough to have touched him. Still he did not turn. She raised her arms, slowly, with a wistfulness he could not have imagined or believed. He knew her hands were stealing around his neck and he could not realize it. Then she clasped him fiercely, hung her weight against him, adhered to him like a vine, saying, "Oh! Oh! Oh!" Turning in her embrace he tried to kiss her. She buried her face in his neck, sobbing deeply, all the time clinging to him frantically as if she expected him to put her off. Lifting her head she leaned far back against the encircling chain of his arms and lay there looking at him, moonbeams in her eyes. Clasping him again she kissed his face, his mouth, his eyes, stopping only to whisper in his ear the most stupendous three words a woman can say.

For a long time he did not let the ground touch her feet. He carried her to and fro in the path, then up the mountain, higher and higher, and at last to the very top.

XXXIII

John, unable to sleep, had risen from his bed and gone walking. He let his feet drift, having nothing consciously in view, and presently found himself in the path where on just such a night six years before he had raced up and down in a panic calling the name of Agnes. It occurred to him to look for the spot at which he had found her things. Unable to make sure of it he idly gave up the effort. The view of the valley impressed him and he sat on a stone at some distance below the path to sense it. He was there when Agnes and Thane arrived. They could not see him; shrubbery above his seat concealed him. He could see them distinctly. His first impulse naturally was to disclose himself. Hesitation arose on the thought that their coming to this place must have been by romantic impulse; and then as the scene between them developed he could only sit still. They should never know he had witnessed it. Long after they were gone he sat there. And when he departed he stumbled straight down the mountain side to the highway lest they should still be near and see him if he went by the path.

He felt strangely exalted. His love for Agnes was hopeless. It had been hopeless as a matter of honor because she rightfully belonged to Thane. Now it was hopeless in a new and final sense because she had learned to love Thane as he loved her. What had been inevitable now was fulfilled, and what had been renounced in fair conduct was beyond temptation. There was also his feeling for Thane which made them closer than brothers.

He waited for them to seek him. That occurred on the second day. They had come to the hotel and Thane asked him to join them for supper. They required his advice. Much to their surprise Enoch not only had left no estate; he was hopelessly bankrupt. The mill was heavily in debt. They had to decide whether to pay off its debts or let it be sold for the benefit of creditors. They were in no state about it. Agnes, it was true, would never come into that fortune of her own out of which she had meant to pay those "balances owing Alexander Thane to be accounted for," according to the black book. That no longer made the slightest difference. As for Thane, he cared nothing about being rich. Besides, his income now was large. Nevertheless, was it not an astonishing fact?

"Had you suspected it?" Agnes asked.

John told them of Enoch's obsession against steel and how the wreck was made. He put it entirely on the ground of Enoch's steel phobia and left himself out of it.

"What would be your guess to do with the mill?" Thane asked.

This question they debated at length.

"It's too late to make New Damascus a steel town," John said. "That opportunity has gone around. However, there will always be a want for New Damascus iron. I'll go halves, if you like, to pay off the debts. We'll form a close corporation and save the mill. Rationally worked it will pay its way."

To this both Thane and Agnes agreed.

John went back to Pittsburgh. Thane and Agnes remained for several weeks, to settle Enoch's affairs, to dismantle Number One Furnace and to arrange for reopening the mill under a superintendent brought by Thane from the Agnes plant.

And New Damascus unawares was delivered to its fate.

XXXIV

Now the steel age was come with its deluge of things.

Man's environment was made over twice in one generation. Nothing was built but to be built again on a greater scale. It seemed impossible to make anything big enough. Wonders were of a day's duration.

In twenty-five years the country's population doubled. In the same time the production of things unto the use, happiness and discontent of people increased five, ten, twenty fold. Man had now in his hand the universal power of steel. It extended his arms and legs unimaginably, grotesquely.

The production of metallic fibre increased more than one hundred fold. Railways were built which if placed end to end and run around the globe would have circled it six times. Those already grown when the steel age came were not yet old when a ton of freight was transported more than 2,500 miles annually for each man, woman and child living on American soil. Food was cheaper and more abundant than ever before in the life of man because the railways, pursuing the sun, had suddenly opened a virgin continent to bonanza farming. So was everything else. Modern cities were made and were no sooner made than torn down and built over again. Chicago grew faster than St. Louis because it had less to tear down. Rivers were moved, mountains were levelled, swamps were lifted up. Nothing was right as God left it.

> *O, bigger! and deeper! and higher!*
> *O, faster! and cheaper! and plus!*

And it is still incredible, like the Pyramids. Men lived in strife by doing. They labored and brought it forth. There was never a moment to think. There has not come that moment yet. What it was toward nobody knows.

Steel was to make men free. They said this who required a slogan. Men are not free. Why should they be? What shall they be free to do? Go to and fro, perhaps. What shall they be free to think? Anything wherein is refuge from the riddles they invent.

The men who delivered the steel age were not thinkers. They were magicians who monkeyed with the elements until they had conjured forth from the earth a spirit that said: "Serve me!"

Those who directly served it were of two kinds.

First were the men who thought with their hands. They were daring in invention. Mechanical impossibilities intoxicated them. They abhorred a pause in the production process as nature abhors a vacuum.

Next were the men of vision, who worked by inspiration, who had a phantasy of things beyond the feeling of them, and ran ahead.

And since men of both kinds are more available here than in Europe the steel age walked across the ocean.

Here were men like Thane whose genius fashioned tools in the guise of sentient creatures, — walking tools, thinking tools, co-operating tools, with eyes and ears and nerves and powers of discrimination. Human tools but that they lacked the sense of good and evil.

Fancy a tool larger than an elephant keeping vigil before a row of furnaces, pacing slowly up and down, apparently brooding, and then at the right moment opening a door and plucking forth a block of incandescent steel weighing many tons, neatly, with not the slightest effort, and nowhere in sight a human being!

Fancy another tool to drudge and fag for this one! It comes running up, stands still while the other gently lays upon its back the white-hot slab, then runs and dumps it on a train of rollers.

That two hundred weight of flaming iron you saw swinging through the gloom of Enoch's mill in hand tongs now is a mass of ninety tons or more, handled, carried hither, delivered there, shaped and forged, all by automatic tools. The ladle no larger than a pot in which the fluid iron was first decanted is now a car on wheels, —no, not one but many in a string, hence called a ladle train, running through the night behind a donkey locomotive, slopping over at the turns, on the way from where the ore is smelted to where the mixers mix it and the converters change it into steel.

The Thanes did that.

And here were men like John to say: "Give us a tariff protection of six-tenths of a cent a pound for ten years and we will not only make all our own steel wire hereafter but wire for all the world," —who got it and did it.

Here were men to say: "We spend half a million good American dollars each year in England for tin cans to throw over the alley fence. Give us a duty on tin plate and we will not only make our own but in ten years other people will be throwing our cans over the fence," —who got it and proved it.

Here were men to say: "There is going to be only one steel concern in the world. That's us" —They meant it literally.

They were men who knew not how to stop. They dared not stop. The one who did was lost. Every little while they had to throw away everything they had created, cast it out on the junk heap, because new ideas came in so fast. It was nothing to scrap a million dollars' worth of machinery before it had settled in, a greater, faster engine of production having just appeared. Whereas formerly every new thing came from England, Germany or France, now Europe's ironmongers were continually coming over here to see what the Americans were doing and how and why they had captured the steel age.

Later, when the pace of evolution began somewhat to abate, when original discoveries were fewer and a steel mill would stand awhile, when the wild and reckless youth of the steel age was past and Wall Street found it out, —then all these dynamic, self-paramount men began to get rich. And as you may suppose, they no more knew how to stop getting rich than they knew how to stop anything else. Of that in its right place.

XXXV

No two were more the darlings of the steel age than John and Thane. They were for it and of it, lover and husband to it, remarkably possessing between them the qualities it demanded of men. No part of its mystery was unknown to them. They became miners and smelters of ore, bringers of coal, burners of coke, drawers of wire, rollers of rails, in a very large way. Their wealth in property increased alarmingly. One thing begat another so fast and new opportunities so unexpectedly appeared that their resources were chronically stretched to the utmost and they were continually in need of more capital. John was always buying something they couldn't pay for, —an ore mountain perhaps, a ship to transport the ore down the Great Lakes, a steel plant somebody had blunderingly steered on the rocks. He was like a man on a tight rope juggling more glass balls than he can hold all at once. He has to keep them going in the air. He cannot stop. John never thought of stopping. It wasn't that he wished to be rich; it wasn't that he had a passion for power; he craved excitement. And there was plenty of it.

The steel industry had frightful growing pains for which there was no diagnosis. The trouble was it grew by violent starts and then had fits of coma. The profits were so great when there was any profit at all that the steel maker would pawn his hope of the everlasting to build more mills; and perhaps before they were finished the profit had vanished and his despair was as wild as his ecstasy. The time to buy steel plants was when the sky was visible at Pittsburgh; the time to sell them was when the smoke was so dense that the sun at midday resembled a pickled beet. But at one time no one had the money to buy anything with and at the other time nobody would sell.

These were conditions perfectly suited to the exercise of John's reckless speculative genius. In the sloughs of despond he bought more property, as he had bought the Agnes plant, with his notes of hand and promises to pay. He seemed never so serene as when treading the edge of a financial precipice in a high wind with a swaying load on his back. People watched him with awe. He would do it once too often, they said, as each time he got back to safe ground again. Certainly he was a dangerous man to walk with. In an industry controlled by fatalists he was unique for daring. Yet back of his apparent passion for the gambling chance were saving qualities. He had keen, brooding vision and rare business sagacity. When he told a committee of United States Senators that with a tariff protection of six-tenths of a cent a pound he would make this country independent of the European steel wire makers (this was at the beginning), —when he said that nobody took him seriously. However, they gave him what he wanted. The price of wire was then twelve cents a pound and this country was importing from Europe three-quarters of all it used. A few years later the tables were turned. This country was making more than half the steel wire used in the whole world, selling it heavily even in England, and the price was two cents a pound. So with all things of steel. So with steel rails. When the American steel industry got started at last foreign steel rails were being imported for American railways at $125 a ton. Ultimately American steel rails sold for $18 a ton in this country, in Europe, in Asia and Africa. The United States then had become an exporting nation selling the products of its skill to the four ends of the earth.

Business is warfare in time of peace. Hence its lure for combative men. Its goal is conquest. Let alone it would perhaps wreck itself or enslave the world. No matter. When it is ruthless, knowing no law but its own necessity, then it is magnificent.

Attila, king of the Huns, vowing no grass to grow where his horse had trod the enemy's soil, is magnificent. We can see him in that light now that he is far away in history and not pursuing us.

Business as it was in the last quarter of the nineteenth century also is far away. Nothing like it can ever happen again. It was utterly lawless, free in its own elemental might, lustful and glamorous. The barbaric invasion that overturned Roman civilization was more obvious as a spectacle but no more extraordinary, no more unexpected, and perhaps as it shall turn out, no more significant, than America's economic invasion of the world in the steel age. One stupendous sequel already present is the economic, financial and political supremacy of the isolate American people in the affairs of this earth. What will come of that nobody knows.

The Breakspeares conceived it, imagined it, planned it; the Thanes tooled it. There was of course labor. But labor no more invents the tools that are the means to economic conquest than soldiers invent the weapons of war, and has generally less understanding of ends than soldiers have of the strategy.

The men controlling the steel industry came to be grouped in three main divisions. There was the original Pittsburgh group, under the leadership of a round head named Carmichael; it had founded itself in iron and then gone into steel. It was steady and powerful and had gained some influential support in Wall Street. There was the western group, always falling down and getting up again, very unstable, yet dangerous as competitors.

And thirdly was the Breakspeare group, extremely unpredictable, whose interests lay in every direction.

John naturally attracted men who loved risk and lived easily with danger. Slaymaker learned the attitude, not thoroughly, but sufficiently, and walked doggedly along. His goal was wealth for its own sake. Although John's high adventures often threatened to involve all of them in colossal bankruptcy, yet this never quite happened, and each time it didn't happen Slaymaker took a part of his profit and hid it away, never to be risked again. Jubal Awns, the lawyer, became superstitious about John and followed him blindly. Besides these two, who had been in from the start, there were three others who would be called general partners. They not only were very large stockholders and directors in John's companies; they joined their capital with his in new undertakings. One was Isaac Pick, a wordless man who conversed in gestures and disbelieved everything including the fact of his own existence. He had made a fortune in scrap iron and was brought into the group by Slaymaker at a time when new capital was urgently needed. Another was Col. Wingreene, an exceedingly profane man, one of the railroad officials whom John had induced to take original stock in the American Steel Company when it began to make rails. Wingreene had bought out the other railroad people and now devoted himself entirely to the steel business. A third was Justinian Creed, a Cleveland banker, very obese, who believed in the better way and twice a year was in a grovelling panic about his sins, never thinking, however, to divest himself of the fruits thereof. Thane was a partner, too, only his work was in other material. There were many others loosely affiliated, but these five, —Slaymaker, Awns, Pick, Wingreene and Creed, —were John's own, whom he led, and who came to be known generically as the Breakspeare Crowd.

When the game was hot they worked at high pressure, wholly sustained one would have thought by strong waters; when it was won they let down with a bang. They were men of strong habits, strong wills, strong feelings and strong humor. One of their odd passions was for getting one another's goat. In their practical jokes they were serious, grim and imaginative, with an amazing power of deception. Never was a time when some absurd hoax was not brewing; and if one knew of nothing in pickle for another he began to be uneasy about himself. His defence was to prepare something of his own against the field. They were always on guard and regarded one another askance, with a kind of owlish suspicion. One would have thought, seeing them together, that they were too distrustful of themselves to look away or turn to spit. So they were. But this was personal, part of a game, and had nothing to do with business really.

Their code of conduct was intricate. If the word passed they could trust one another implicitly. Yet they avoided the word so far as possible, preferring in all normal circumstances unlimited freedom of personal action, each fellow for himself. In an emergency they came close together, stood back to back, and presented a solid ring to the world. In all situations John led them. Often he moved them against their judgment. Sometimes he was wrong. Generally he was right. When they acted severally against his judgment, on their own, they were always wrong. His character was perhaps no stronger than theirs; his judgment intrinsically was no better. But he had above all of them a faculty of intuition, and he could change his mind. Creed used to say: "John, he looks where he isn't going and goes where he isn't looking. His eyes are crossed inside."

He said it cynically, and it was distorted by John's enemies, who took it to mean that he could not be trusted by his own crowd. That was not so. He never broke the code. Creed, as it turned out, was the only man who needed watching within the rules.

Fortuity was the stuff they worked in; hazard was what they played with. They were always betting. No game of chance or skill but they had to add stakes to make it interesting. As they grew richer and more easily bored it was increasingly difficult to find a pastime in which the stakes were high enough. John turned the leisure of their minds to horse racing. They would appear in a body on the race track and scare the bookmakers with the size of their wagers. John was their oracle. They never believed him; they only followed him. When he had involved them in enormous loss they were obliged to go on; there was no other hope of getting out but by his star of luck. And it was by no means infallible. Once at Saratoga they had a frightful week. Twice they had telegraphed home for money. Their losses had gone into six figures. Slaymaker met Awns, Wingreene, Pick and Creed on the hotel veranda after breakfast. He was exceedingly sore.

"As long as I live and have my senses I'll never bet on another horse John picks," he said. "He dreams these things. He never had a real tip in his life."

They were all of one mind. They were through. Just then John's voice reached them from the doorway, saying: "We'll get it all back today."

They groaned and turned their backs.

"No, now listen?" he said. "You always get cold feet at the wrong time. This is our chance. It's air tight. It's so secret I can't even tell you what horse it is. Give me your money and I'll bet it with mine."

He sat down and went on with it until Slaymaker said: "I'm an imbecile. If anybody knew what an imbecile I am there would be a run on my bank. This is positively the last time."

They all gave him their money. It was the third race. No more could he tell them. The horses went to the post and still they did not know which one carried their money.

"It's on," said John. "It's down all right. Don't worry about that."

"Lord, no," said Slaymaker. "That's not what we are worried about."

John watched the horses. The others watched him.

A horse named Leadbeater took the lead at the start, held all the way and won by four lengths. John fell back with a blank expression.

"That the horse?" asked Slaymaker.

"Yes," said John. "That's it."

"Then what's the matter?"

"I didn't bet on it," said John.

"You didn't —what!"

"That was the horse," John explained. "Only after we came out here I got what I thought was a better tip and bet all the money on... Now, wait!"

They would not wait. They rose with one impulse and left him alone in Saratoga. That night on the train they began *to* get telegrams from him. Would they authorize him to lay five thousand apiece for them on a horse that was bound to win the next day at odds of 100 to 1? They tore up the telegrams. More kept coming, overtaking them en route all that night and until noon the next day. They would not even reply. But that horse did win and John by himself broke half the bookmakers at Saratoga.

It was the end of their racing sport for that season. The crowd was too disgusted to touch it again and John did not care for it alone. Slaymaker said it was forever; so did all the rest. Yet the next season they did it all over again.

XXXVI

All the men who got rich with John Breakspeare developed strange pathologies from nervous shock and strain. Their eyes became opaque and had that uncanny trick of suddenly and without movement changing their focus while they looked at you, as if something were transacting on the far-away horizon of their thoughts and you for that instant were transparent. They had their luck by the tail and could not let go. They could count their gains; they could not seize them. John was always getting them in; he never got them out. Their wealth was in property to which enormous additions had continuously to be made by an uncontrollable law of growth. Thus the richer they grew the greater correspondingly their liabilities were and there seemed no way either to quit or get out. If you had all the wealth in the world you could not sell it. There would be no one to buy it. In principle that was their problem. If they could sell out they would be millionaires. But where was there anybody with money enough to buy them out? It would take twenty-five millions or more. Once they had begun to look at this dilemma they could not let it alone; it filled them with anxiety. They began to worry John about it. He had got them in. Couldn't he find a way to get them out?

"All right," he said. "I'll show you a way out."

"How?"

"We're like a railroad," he said. "No railroad is privately owned any more. It's too big. It represents too much capital. Only the public is rich enough to own a railroad. It takes thousands of investors putting their money together to build a railroad. Then somebody works it for them and pays them dividends on their shares. We can do that, —put our shares on the New York Stock Exchange and sell out to the public."

So he led them to Wall Street. The motive was theirs; the plan was his.

The American Steel Company was reorganized. Its capitalization was increased to take in properties hitherto jointly owned among them and for other purposes. They agreed to sell no shares except through John in order that all should fare alike. It was a verbal agreement. All of their private agreements were verbal and never so far had one been broken.

Enter John Breakspeare upon the Wall Street scene with something to sell.

The shares of the American Steel Company were duly listed on the New York Stock Exchange, —that is, they were added to the list of securities permitted to be dealt in there and allotted sign and booth in the great investment bazar.

People stared and passed by. It was a strange sign not only because it was new but for the reason also that the public knew only mining and railroad shares. The day of industrial company shares had not come. John was a pioneer in that line. He was a vendor unused to the ways of this fair with merchandise nobody had ever seen before.

He was not disappointed. He knew, if anybody did, that goods must be brought to the buyer's attention. Nothing will sell itself, least of all seven per cent, shares for which there is instinctively neither hunger nor thirst. He knew also in principle how this kind of impalpable merchandise should be displayed. It has no appeal to any of the natural senses. Therefore it must be made to appeal to all of them at once, symbolically. How?

First to be engaged is the sense of sight. The shares move. They go up. People ask: "What is that?" They move again. People ask: "Why is that?" They continue to move, going up, then down a little, then suddenly up a great deal, and people say: "Here before our eyes is something doing, —a chance to make some money." And when once they begin to say that all their senses and appetites are touched with expectation, for money, however derived, is in itself palpable. It is the symbol of all things whatever.

For the art of making shares go up and down in a manner to excite first attention, then curiosity and then an impulse to act for gain, there is a long, inartistic word. The word is manipulation. The stock market manipulator is an illusionist. Perched high upon some eerie crag of the Wall Street canyon, producing enchantment at a distance, he is himself invisible save to the initiate, and even they do not know what he intends or why, because what he seems to be doing is never at all what he is really doing. If it were, the lesser fauna-the wolves, the jackals, the foxes, apes and crows, —would anticipate his ends and take the quarry out of his hands. He makes shares rise when he is selling them and fall when he is buying them. He can take an unnoticed, unwanted thing like American Steel and cause it to become an object of extravagant speculative interest, so that tens of thousands hang over the tape and wait for the next quotation, betting whether it shall be up or down. Moreover, he is a ventriloquist. When he has made certain shares very active by the apparently simple though extremely intricate expedient of buying and selling them furiously through different brokers, no two of whom know they have the same principal, —when he has done this and people begin to ask the question, then answers suitable to his purpose are in everyone's ears, saturate the atmosphere, and although he, the manipulator, is the source of them that fact is as little known as the fact that he was himself the solitary source of all the buying and selling that started the excitement. Not only is the public deceived; the fauna, too, will often be caught. All is flesh that rises to his lure. His work is sometimes legitimate, as when he creates a public demand for shares the proceeds of which go to build a railroad or some other great economic work so vast that the capital could not have been obtained in any other way; it is sometimes predatory, sometimes wanton.

At this time the pendragon of manipulators was one Sabath, —James Sabath, —feared by the wicked and righteous both. He was not a member of the Stock Exchange for he did not wish to be bound by the rules. There was no name on his door nor was his name in any directory or book of celebrities. Yet it was constantly on the lips of all men concerned in gains and losses from speculation. One might have asked in every bank in Wall Street who and where this Sabath was and one's inquiry would have been received with utter blankness. Yet there would have been hardly a banker in Wall Street, certainly no very important one, who had not had transactions with him of an extremely intimate and delicate nature. Such is the way of men in the money canyon.

For example, there was Bullguard. He was the great private banker of his time, —a kind of Caesar's wife to the institution of American finance. His authority was absolute, his power was feudal and tyrannical. For him to have been seen in the society of Sabath would have been scandalous. Nobody would have known what to make of it. Yet in the pursuit of his ends he often engaged Sabath to do things he could not risk doing for himself. That again is the way of men in the little autonomous state which is Wall Street.

John sought an audience with Sabath. After long delay and much unnecessary mystery he was received in that strange man's lair. Besides himself there was nothing in it except a ticker, some chairs and a worn Turkey carpet. The room was without windows, therefore lighted artificially in daytime. Twice during the interview he rang a bell and each time a boy appeared with one glass of whiskey in his hand. Sabath drank it at a gulp, with no here's how or by your leave. He sat in an arm chair and combed his beard upward from its roots with his fingers, or for change twisted it with the other hand. His head was continually moving; sometimes he threw it far back to start his fingers through his beard; no matter what he did with his head his eyes all the time were perfectly still and held John in a blue, vise-like gaze. He looked at people in a way to make them feel full of holes. His head was very large; his body was neat and small; his voice was sarcastic, thin and shrill.

John explained his errand. He wished Sabath to take hold of American Steel shares and create some public interest in them. Sabath said nothing, but continued to look at him. John went into details, telling about the company, what it owned and what it earned. Still Sabath continued to gaze at him in silence. John told him at length how the shares had been pooled in his hands by his associates, none to be sold except through him. And Sabath said nothing.

"Does it interest you at all?" John asked at last.

"Come back tomorrow," said Sabath. He made a gesture toward the door without looking at it. As John went he sat still, but for his head, which turned slowly in a reptilian manner.

To John's surprise Sabath was vocal the next day and asked many questions in a high, twanging voice. Some of his questions were oblique and some apparently quite irrelevant. Suddenly he said:

"And so you know that God-fearing Creed, do you? You must know him very well. How much of this precious stock has Mr. Creed got?"

John told him. Sabath tweaked his beard, saying: "Who would imagine I'd ever be found in the same alley with a he-cat like Creed."

"What's the matter with him?" asked John.

"I say nothing against him," Sabath answered. "I only say I'd hate to go into a room with him alone."

There was a third interview, then a fourth and a fifth. Terms were stated. It seemed to be all ready for the signatures and as there weren't going to be any signatures John couldn't understand why Sabath kept postponing the final word. Then one day out of a painted sky he said: "We seem unable to make a trade, Mr. Breakspeare. I cannot allow myself to waste any more of your valuable time. I'm not interested."

John was amazed.

"However," he said, "I suppose I can trust you to keep to yourself the information you have obtained in the course of these interviews?"

"That's what we live on down here, —trust," said Sabath. "We couldn't do business without it."

With that he turned his back and stood looking at the ticker. John, thus rudely dismissed, was at the door with his hand on the knob when Sabbath spoke again, without turning around, without moving his head, as if he were thinking out loud.

"What did you ever do to Mr. Bullguard?"

"I don't know him," said John. "Why?"

"He knows you," said Sabath, still reading the tape. "He says you are a gambler. Is that true?"

"I don't know what he means," said John. "It would be absurd to talk about it. I have some business to transact in Wall Street. How does that concern him?"

Sabath now turned and walked with him to the door. His manner was both ingratiating and menacing; his voice was ironic, and yet there was a suspicion of friendliness in his words. "Because if you are," he continued, as if John had not spoken, "I would urge you to keep all that talent for the steel business. I understand the steel business needs it. We don't like gambling in Wall Street. You are a young man. I have wasted your time. Now I offer you my advice. Don't try anything in Wall Street. Gamblers don't go far down here. We eat them. Mr. Bullguard would swallow you up at one bite." He made an exaggerated bow. "Let me know if there's anything I can do for you before you go back to Pittsburgh."

"Thanks," said John. "When I want to be amused I'll look you up. Tell Mr. Bullguard I've been eaten up so often that I like it. Sometimes I fairly hunger for it. Why did you change your mind?"

"How could I have changed my mind?" Sabath injuredly asked. "How can you say that? It had never been made up."

"Why did you change your mind?" John insisted.

"You would be betrayed," said Sabath. "I should be betrayed, too, of course; but I'm used to it and you're not. The only man you don't suspect is always the one who betrays you."

"Did Mr. Bullguard call you off?" John asked.

"You might never get used to it," Sabath continued, vaguely, ignoring the question. "You wouldn't know what to do. I've been betrayed so much that I know it before it happens. And I know what to do. You never get through a deal like this without being betrayed."

He turned sadly and walked back to the ticker. The interview was closed.

John reacted to this experience with thoughtful curiosity. He was baffled and chagrined and at the same time deeply interested, for he perceived that here was a province of the dynamic mind in which subtlety was carried to its ultimate point. After long reflection he was still of the opinion that underlying Sabath's diabolism lay a vein of well meaning; also of the opinion still that the puissant Bullguard had interfered. But why? What could his motive be? This was presently to be discovered. John explored the matter adroitly and learned that Bullguard was about to do for the Carmichael crowd what John lone-handed had attempted to do for his crowd, —that is to say, capitalize the steel business and introduce it to the public. Naturally Bullguard desired the field to himself and took a high-handed way against the interloper.

Nevertheless, John resolved to go on. He would be his own manipulator. Why not? The stock market was nobody's private preserve. He had as much right there as Bullguard or Sabath. Besides, where was the risk? He controlled all the shares of the American Steel Company.

So he engaged a broker, who engaged other brokers, and buying and selling orders, both issuing from John, began to be executed in American Steel. For a while he was delighted. It was so easy to make the shares active, to make them go up and down, to create the illusion of excited bargaining, that he began to wonder why anyone should pay manipulators large fees to do this simple trick. He wondered, too, what Sabath was thinking of his performance. He could almost feel Sabath watching him. He imagined him at the ticker, tweaking his beard, sneering at the amateur quotations that were appearing on the tape for American Steel.

They were beautiful quotations, rising from 80 to 85, then to 90, then to 95 and at length to 100; they were also very costly quotations. Commissions to brokers who executed his orders began to run into large figures and there were no offsetting returns. That is to say, real buyers were not in the least intrigued. After several weeks John himself was the only buyer and the only seller. He discussed it with his broker who thought what he needed was publicity. He ought to get American Steel written about in the newspapers.

Financial writers to the number of twenty were invited to meet the president of the American Steel Company. Six came. John received them in his broker's private office and spoke eloquently and earnestly of the company, its merits, earnings and all that. They stared at him incredulously, then began to look very bored and went away. The American Steel was not written about except in one newspaper, which told of the solicited interview in a way to make it ludicrous.

Now a most improbable thing happened. John's broker reported that someone was selling American Steel shares.

Selling them? Who could be selling them? Nobody had any to sell.

Nevertheless, it was true. Well, next best to selling the shares to the public, which he hadn't succeeded in doing, was to buy them from speculators who would sell them without owning them, for in that case when the sellers were called upon to deliver what they never had then they couldn't and John would be in a position to squeeze them. He would have them in a corner. So he gave orders to buy all the American Steel anyone offered to sell. The selling steadily increased. How strange that professional Stock Exchange gamblers, the canniest men in the world, would sell themselves into a corner in that silly manner! Yet what else could it be? Still sure the sellers were selling what they couldn't deliver John continued to buy until very large sums began to be involved.

One afternoon his broker informed him that the selling had been traced to Sabath. This John had already suspected. He was now in deep water and wired for his crowd, —Slaymaker, Awns, Wingreene, Pick and Creed. Having laid the cards before them he proposed that they should unite their resources and bring off a corner in American Steel. Clearly they had Sabath cornered. They had only to let him go on selling until he was tired; then they could make him settle on their own terms.

Creed declined. This was John's party, he said. They had authorized him to sell their shares. Instead he had got himself involved in a contest with the most powerful speculator in Wall Street and now expected them to stand under. They would be fools to get into that kind of game. He flatly wouldn't do it.

The others wavered. They hated to leave John in the lurch; they were afraid to stand by. Creed withdrew and vanished.

While the other four were hesitating a sudden panic shook the stock market. American Steel shares fell from 103 to 25 in ten minutes, plunging headlong through John's buying orders. And while this was taking place his broker came to him in a state of gibbering excitement.

"I thought you said nobody had any American Steel to sell?"

"Nobody has," said John.

"Then we're all crazy," said the broker. "More than a million dollars' worth of the stuff has just been delivered to us. We've got to pay for it at once."

"Let's look at it," said John. "I want to see it."

He saw it. The shares that had been delivered to him were Creed's.

John paid for them, though it almost broke his back. He used his own money until he had no more and borrowed the rest from Slaymaker and Pick on his notes. The fiasco was complete. American Steel was indignantly stricken from the Stock Exchange list because it had been manipulated in so outrageous a manner and the newspapers wrote about it most scornfully.

It was all over and John and his crowd, now always excepting Creed, were at dinner in the Holland House, when a reporter from *The Sun* appeared at their table unannounced and asked: "Mr. Breakspeare, how do you feel?"

John went on eating as he replied: "I feel like a dog that's been kicked so much he goes sideways. I've got every pain there is but one. That's belly ache."

This was printed the next morning on the front page of *The Sun,* and Wall Street forgot itself long enough to say: "Not a bad sport, anyhow."

"Now I suppose we'll go back and attend to the steel business," said Slaymaker.

"In a day or two," John answered. "There's something I want to do here yet."

He wanted to find out how it happened. And he did. Bullguard, knowing Creed, had tempted him to part with his shares at a very nice price. These shares Bullguard turned over to Sabath with the understanding that they should be used to club John's market to death. John had no hostile feeling for Sabath. For Creed he felt only contempt. But with Bullguard he opened a score.

His state was not one of anger. He had only himself to blame. "I don't so much mind getting plucked," he said, "but I look so like Hell."

He simply couldn't leave until he had turned the laugh. This he did in the way as follows: One morning at eleven o'clock a small funeral cortege, instead of stopping at Trinity Church as funerals should in that part of the city, turned down Wall Street and stopped at the door of Bullguard & Company. Six men drew from the hearse a silver-mounted mahogany coffin smothered in roses, carried it into the great banking house, put it down on the floor, went immediately out and drove away. It was so swiftly yet quietly done and it was so altogether incredible that the door attendant knew not what to do or think. His wits were paralyzed and while he stared with his mouth open the pall-bearers disappeared. So did the hearse and carriages. A great crowd instantly gathered. The nearest policeman was called. As no one could say how the coffin got there or what was in it he refused either to move it or to let it be moved until the coroner should come to open it. He was a new policeman and could not be awed. He knew his duty and no manner of entreaty availed. For an hour it lay there on the floor. Police reserves were summoned to keep a way for traffic through the gaping throng. Somewhere inside the banking house, out of sight, was Bullguard, surrounded by his partners, apoplectic and purple with a sense of unanswerable outrage. The coroner was accompanied by a group of reporters.

When the coffin was opened, there upon the white satin pillow lay a rump of a pig, rampant, tail uppermost; and in the curl of the tail was twisted and tied like a ribbon the few feet of ticker tape on which the last quotations for American Steel were printed

It was a freak story and the newspapers made much of it. Wall Street rocked with glee. John went back to Pittsburgh with a smile in his midriff, leaving the wreck of a fortune behind him.

XXXVII

John's Wall Street disaster was personal. He assumed all liabilities. Therefore it did not involve his partners, save that he owed Slaymaker and Pick nearly half a million dollars on his notes. Nor did it touch Thane and Agnes. He took good care of that.

On the day of his return to Pittsburgh he had dinner with them. They had moved again, to a house of their own, one they had built on an unspoiled eminence among some fine old trees. They exhibited it with the pride of children. It was large and expensively made, with an unpretentious air, and one of its features, saved until the last, was an apartment for John. They hardly expected him to adopt it. However, it should be his always, just like that, whenever it might please him to come, and it had pleased them to do it.

The evening meal was no longer supper. It was dinner. Thane at last was comfortable in the society of servants, even in the brooding, anonymous presence of a butler.

Agnes now was in full bloom. Life had touched her in its richest mood. There were moments in which her aura seemed luminous, like a halo; or was that a trick of John's imagination? He had not seen her for above a year. She was more at ease with him than she had ever been, spontaneous, friendly, quite unreserved, and by the same sign infinitely further away. There was no misunderstanding her way with Thane nor Thane's with her. They had achieved the consonance of two principles. They were the two aspects of one thing, separate and inseparable, like right and left, like diameter and circumference. What one thought the other said; what one said the other thought. They conversed without words.

Agnes pressed John with questions about the Wall Street episode. They had read a good deal about it in the newspapers. His narrative left much to be vaguely imagined.

"But you yourself-how did you come out?" she asked. "Nobody else appears to have got hurt. What happened to you?" For on that point he had been evasive.

"I did get rubbed a bit," he said. "Don't worry about it. I'm all right."

She looked at him thoughtfully.

"Tell him what we've been doing," she said, turning to Thane.

"Remember," said Thane, "you said once we'd see ore go in at the top of a blast furnace and come out rails at the other end of the mill without stopping?"

"Yes," said John, sitting up.

"That gave me an idea," Thane continued. "We've done it. It's experimental yet but we can do it. Take the steel ingots straight out of the soaking pit and put them through the rolls with no reheating."

"Does anybody know it?" John asked.

"Just ourselves," said Thane.

Agnes took it up there, described the process in detail, and told how Thane had evolved it through endless nights of trial and failure. John was amazed at the extent and accuracy of her knowledge. Thane anticipated his question.

"She knows," he said. "She could run a mill."

It was literally true. John was thrilled to hear how at night, in cap and overalls, she had been going with Thane to the mill to watch his experiments. Not only did she learn to understand them; she could discuss them technically, and make helpful suggestions. She had taken up the study of metallurgy in a serious way. She spent her days digesting scientific papers in English, French and German and was continually bringing new knowledge to Thane's attention. Later to her immense delight she saw phases of this knowledge translate itself through Thane's hands into practice at the mill.

"It's in the blood," said John, bound with admiration.

It was a cherishable evening. After dinner they sat on the veranda. Below them was a bottomless sea of velvety blackness, with no horizon, no feeling of solid beneath it, sprinkled at random with lights and intermittently torn by flashes from blast furnaces and converters many miles away.

"It's like looking at the sky upside down," said Agnes.

They could feel what was taking place off there in the lamp-black darkness. Men were tormenting the elements, parting iron from his natural affinities, giving him in new marriage without love or consent, audaciously creating what God had forgotten —*steel! steel! steel!* There in that smutted deep were tools walking about like fabled monsters, obedient and docile, handling flaming ingots of metal with the ponderous ease and precision of elephants moving logs. There amid clangor and confusion shrieking little bipeds were raising gigantic ominous shapes from shapelessness. There an epic was forming.

These three sitting on the veranda were definitely related to all of this. It had never ceased to thrill them. Much of it they had imagined before it was there. Some of those Leviathan tools were Thane's own. He was thinking of them, not boastfully, yet with a swelling sense of having created them. They were his ectoplasm, his arms and legs and sinews externalized in other forms. Seldom did he review his work, being normally too much absorbed in the difficulty at hand. Now, as he gave way to it, a tingle of satisfaction stole through his blood. It made him wish to touch Agnes. His hand reached for hers and it was near. She seemed to know what he was thinking.

John was thinking of the steel age, of what it yet required, of its still unimagined possibilities. Every railroad then existing would have to be rebuilt with heavier rails and bridges. Cars would come to be made of steel. Street railways were a new thing: they would take immense quantities of steel.

They had been silent for a long time.

"That's the Agnes plant... way over there... that blue flame. There!" said Thane.

"I had made it out," said John.

"What did you call it?" Agnes asked.

Sheepishly they told her that from the beginning, for luck, they had called it the Agnes plant. "How nice!" she said.

From that their conversation became more personal, even reminiscent. They found they could speak naturally of incidents always until then taboo. They talked of Enoch, of their arrival and beginning in Pittsburgh, of the mill at Damascus which was doing well, and of each other, how they had changed and what it was like to be all grown up.

When Agnes rose to leave she shook hands with John, saying: "Alexander will give you the key. We don't press you. But it's there for you whenever you have the impulse to come. Day or night. Any time. And even if you never come it will please us to keep it always ready for you."

With that she was gone, so suddenly that John had been unable to get any words together. He had not even said good-night.

"That place we've fixed for you means something," said Thane, lunging out of a silence. "I can't find any way to say it. We know how it was when you brought us to Pittsburgh and how there wasn't any job for us until you bought the little nail mill. We know all about it. It's lucky for all of us, —lucky for Agnes and me, I mean, —I didn't know enough to see it then. There ain't no way to say how we feel about it. You can just understand that's what this key means."

John took it, turned it over in his hand, then put it in his pocket and said nothing.

"The reason Agnes was asking you so close how you came out in Wall Street," Thane added, "was we thought you might-a got skinned. We've got a lot of money. We think it's a lot. And we want you to know —"

"Don't!" said John. "That's enough. Now stop it. Stop it, I tell you."

"A-l-1 right, a-1-1 right," said Thane. "I'm through, I ain't a going on, am I? I've got it all said."

"I'm going," said John. "Walk down to the gate."

At the gate they shook hands and lingered.

"You've got it all wrong," said John. "There's nothing you two-what I mean —"

"I know, I know," said Thane.

"You don't know anything," said John. "Let me say something. I owe you a damn sight more than you owe me. I couldn't have done anything without you. You're the axle tree. I'm only the wheel. This one new wrinkle, if it proves out, is worth millions."

"Well, don't lose that key," said Thane.

They shook hands again and pushed each other roughly away.

XXXVIII

The steel industry was a giant without lineage, parentage or category. Nobody knew how big it should be nor could tell by looking at it what stage it was in. Not until afterward. It was measurable only by contrast with itself. It was supposed to be already grown up when John brought the American Steel Company back from Wall Street. But it was still in the gristle. Bone and sinew had yet to be acquired.

"What, my God! if we had sold out then," Slaymaker would say again and again, with the aghast and devout air of a man whose faith in the deity dates from some miraculous escape. "We should probably never have got in again," he would add.

If they had got out then they would have been able to count their wealth in millions. But they had to go on. And when at last they did get out in the golden harvest time years later they counted it in scores and hundreds of millions.

Thane's new method, which proved itself in practice, gave the American Steel Company a whip hand in steel rails. It could make them at a lower cost than anyone else in the world, owing to the saving in fuel. Nobody ever knew what that cost was. No matter at what price the Carmichael people sold rails John could sell them a little lower if he needed the business, and he became for that reason a burning thorn in the flesh of Bullguard, who had capitalized the Carmichael properties and brought the shares out in Wall Street. They had a wretched career. Everyone who touched them lost money. This was not only because of the American Steel Company's competition; the steel industry as a whole was running wild. There was no controlling it. For a year or two the demand for steel would exceed the utmost supply at prices which made a steel mill more profitable than a gold pocket. Then new mills would appear everywhere at once and presently, although there never could be enough steel really, the bowl would slop over from sheer awkwardness.

There were still the three great groups, —the Western group, the Carmichael group and John's —all growing very fast. Minor groups were continually springing up at precisely the wrong time. They generally smashed up or had to be bought out by the others to save themselves from ruinous competition. The steel age cared nothing about profits. All it wanted was steel-more and more and more.

Next was the phase of specialization. One mill made rails exclusively, another merchant steel, another structural shapes for bridges and skyscrapers, another sheet steel, another steel pipe, and so on. That only intensified the competition.

Then trusts began to be formed, precisely as John had formed the nail trust years before, and for the same purpose, which was to regulate the output and keep prices at a profitable level. Somebody would go around and get options on nearly all the mills of this kind, of that kind and then get bankers to make them into a trust with shares to be listed on the Stock Exchange and sold to the public. So there came to be a steel pipe trust, a sheet steel trust, a bridge and structural steel trust, a tin plate trust, a trust for everything; and matters became a great deal worse because some of the biggest mills, such as John's, were never in a trust and if the pipe trust or the structural steel trust got prices too high the independent mills would begin to make pipe or structural steel. Besides, each trust was a law unto itself and the steel industry was still anarchic.

Now finance began to be worried. The shares of these trusts having been floated in Wall Street and the public at last having begun to buy them, an outbreak of disastrous competition among the trusts, or between the trusts and the independents, or an overrunning of the steel spool, caused a panic on the Stock Exchange. Enormous sums of capital had become involved. Every such panic caused a general commotion, like a small earthquake. Something would have to be done to stabilize the steel industry. That was the word; everybody began to say, *Stabilize it!* Gradually there crystallized the thought of a great trust of trusts to embrace everything. Not otherwise could the steel industry be stabilized. Any such colossal scheme as that would have to consider first of all the three dominant groups. But when overtures were made to John directly or through his partners, he repulsed them. To Wall Street's emissaries he would say flatly, "No." To his partners he would say, "Not yet."

His word was final. Having retrieved his fortune in the first year after his inglorious ship-wreck, by the most daring and brilliant selling campaign the steel industry had ever seen, —a campaign that put American rails over European rails in all the markets of the world, —his authority not only was restored: it was increased. Then, having paid off his notes with Slaymaker and Pick, he had got possession of Creed's shares. That made his interest in the American Steel Company greater than that of any three others. There was still the North American Manufacturing Company, in which he was the largest stockholder; it controlled the manufacture of steel wire and nails, and had never ceased to pay dividends.

He enforced one policy of business. That was to make steel continuously under all conditions and never to close a plant except for repairs. Back of him was Thane steadily reducing the costs of manufacture. Sometimes they sold steel at a loss. In the long run, however, this policy paid so handsomely that they were presently able to find in their own profits the capital they needed for expansion. On an ever-increasing scale they devoted profits to the construction and purchase of new properties, —more mines, more ships, more mills. When his partners complained, saying it was time to take something out instead of putting all their gains back again, John offered to buy them out.

So he grew wise and tyrannical and a little grey at the temples. His voice became husky. He lived hard, worked hard, walked steadily on the edge of the precipice, with nothing he cared for in view. On his watch chain he carried the key to Thane's house. Twice he got as far as the gate and turned back.

XXXIX

When the steel age walked across the ocean from Europe a dilemma was created. The will and mentality were here; the labor was there. Until then labor in American mills had been made up of British, Irish, Welsh, Germans, Swedes and, choicest of all, Buckwheats, meaning young American brawn released from the farm by the advent of man-saving agricultural implements. The steel age widened the gap between brain and muscle. It required a higher kind of imagination at the top and a lower grade of labor below. There was no such labor here, —at least, nowhere near enough. Hence an impouring of Hungarians, Slavs, Polacks and other inferior European types, —hairy, brutish, with slanting foreheads.

Nobody thought of the consequences. Nobody thought at all. The labor was needed. That was enough. There was no effort to Americanize or assimilate it. There wasn't time. It had to be fed raw to the howling new genie. It lived wretchedly in sore clusters from which Americans averted their eyes. Where it came from life was wretched, even worse, perhaps; but here were contrasts, no gendarmes freedom of discontent, and a new weapon, which was the strike. These men, bred with sullen anger in their blood, melancholy and neglected in a strange land, having no bond with the light, were easily moved to unite against the work bosses who symbolized tyranny anew. Their impulse *to* violence was built upon by labor leaders and the steel industry became a battle ground. Strikes were frequent, bloody and futile, save for their educational value, which was hard to see then and is not at all clear yet.

This was all in the way of business, —big business. We imported labor and exported steel. We flung Slavs into our racial melting pot and sold rails and bridges in Hungary. One can easily imagine an invisible force to have been at work, a blind force, perhaps. The centers of power were shifted in the world. Greatness was achieved. The rest is hidden.

One advantage the Breakspeare mills had was almost complete immunity from labor troubles. In every reign of terror destruction passed them by. For this there was Thane to thank. He handled all labor problems. In disputes between the workers and the steel companies the question of wages was seldom the basic matter, even when it seemed to be. The trouble was much more subtle, or more simple, as you happen to see it, turning upon the ways and hungers of humanity. Thane knew men, he knew what drudgery costs the soul and how little it takes beyond what is due to overcome its bitterness. He knew, besides, how and in what proportions to mix different kinds of men so that the characteristics of one kind would neutralize those of another kind by a sort of chemistry.

Seven miles down the river from the Agnes plant had been built a magnificent new plate mill, called the Wyoming Steel Works. It had every element of success save one. The manager had no way with labor. He was continually engaged in desperate struggles with the Amalgamated Unions and the plant for that reason had involved its New York owners in heavy loss. These troubles, becoming chronic, culminated in a strike that spread sympathetically over the whole eastern steel industry. At the Agnes plant the men went out for the first time. They had no quarrel of their own. That was made very clear. But they felt obliged, as all other union workers did, to take up the quarrel of the men at the Wyoming Works and settle it for good; they would if necessary tie up every steel plant in the country in order to bring pressure to bear upon their arch enemy, the Wyoming manager, to whose destruction they had made a vow.

Not only did the strikers seize the Wyoming Works, as was the first step in hostilities; they took possession of the town that had grown up around the plant and organized themselves on a military basis. An Advisory Committee of workers declared martial law, mounted a siren on the town hall to give signals by a secret code, put sentinels around the works, around the town, up and down the river front, and held a mobile force of eight hundred Hungarians, Poles and Slavs in readiness for battle at any point. No one could enter the town on an unfriendly errand. Trains were not permitted to stop. The telegraph office was seized. The Advisory Committee announced that any attempt on the part of the owners to retake possession of their property, —say nothing of trying to work it with non-union labor, —would mean an abundant spilling of blood.

This was the situation when Thane received a telegram from John in New York, as follows:

"Can buy Wyoming Steel Works for a song. Will close transaction at once if you will say labor trouble can be straightened out with the plant in our hands."

Almost without reflection Thane answered:

"Yes. Go ahead."

He had no doubt that the mere announcement of their having bought the works would end the violent phase of the strike. The rest would be a matter of peaceable negotiation. He might have made the announcement in Pittsburgh. The strikers there would have communicated it fast enough. He might have telegraphed it to the Advisory Committee. He might have done it in one of several ways. But his natural way was to go himself and see to it. He knew the strike leaders; he talked their language. An hour after answering John's telegram he was in a launch going down the river.

There had been no news from the scene of passion since the afternoon before. No one knew what was taking place in the Wyoming Steel Works town.

In the night two barge loads of Pinkerton men, recruited in Philadelphia, had silently drifted down the river past Pittsburgh. The manager was resolved to get possession of the plant by force. The plan was to land the Pinkerton men before daylight on the river bank. Once inside the works they could stand siege until the state authorities could be persuaded to send the militia in. But the barges were sighted by the Advisory Committee's sentinels a mile above the town. The siren blew an alarm. Men, women and children tumbled out of bed. The armed battalion was rushed to receive the Pinkerton men.

In the darkness a running fire was exchanged between the strikers on shore and the barges; however, the barges did land at the works and the leader of the Pinkerton men signalled for a parley. He told the strikers he had come to take possession of the works and meant to do it. The strike leaders dared him to try. He did. He formed his men and started them off the barges. They were stopped by a volley from the Slav battalion entrenched behind piles of steel in the yard, —and fled back to the barges. Daylight came. The Pinkerton men, unwilling to venture forth a second time, hoisted a white flag. The strikers scoffed at it and went on firing at the barges. They became discouraged. They could see the holes their shots made in the planks; they couldn't be sure they were hitting the men inside. So they floated burning oil down the river and sent tanks of burning oil down the bank against the barges. That was ineffective. Pinkerton men would not burn on earth. Someone thought of dynamite. Cases of it were brought, and the lightest of arm among the strikers calmly attached fuses to the sticks of dynamite, lighted them, and hurled them at the barges, like firecrackers. Once in a while they made the target, tearing a great hole in the barge planking. Then there would be a volley of shots at the Pinkerton men suddenly exposed. Two cannons were brought. They were handled so awkwardly that they did little damage *to* the barges and took off one striker's head. The use of dynamite increased. In some fashion the Pinkerton men fought back. When a striker fell groans were heard. When a Pinkerton man was hit cheers went up from the strikers and were repeated by the spectators, —women, children and noncombatants, —who gorged the spectacle from afar.

And that was what had been going on for hours when Thane's launch appeared, speeding down the middle of the river, He was steering it himself; his boatman lay flat on the bottom. Having recognized him the sentinels above the town passed word down their line, so that the strikers at the works knew who he was before he had come within rifle range. Firing ceased. He steered the boat in, shot it high on the bank, and stepped out.

At that instant there appeared from behind one of the steel piles the figure of frenzy personified. This was not a striker. It was one of those weak, anaemic creatures who are intoxicated by participation in the lusts and passions of others and go mad over matters that do not concern them. He was a clerk in a dry goods store and taught a Sunday School class. It must be supposed that the cessation of firing made him think the strikers were weakening He brandished a rifle, shrieking:

"Citizens! There are the men who wreck our homes, assault our women, take away our bread. Kill them! Kill them without mercy I" He was unnaturally articulate. "Cowards!" he cried. "Follow me!"

He levelled his rifle at the barges. The only man in sight was Thane, walking up the bank. The insane neurotic fired and Thane fell in a crumpled heap.

Several men together leaped at the assassin and disarmed him. He disappeared.

Thane was unconscious. There was no doctor, no ambulance. They took him to Pittsburgh in the launch.

John arrived the next morning. He looked once at Agnes and knew the worst.

Thane lived through that day and into the night. Shortly before he died he wished to be alone with John. They clasped hands and read each other in silence. Once the doctor opened the door and softly closed it again. Thane beckoned to John to bring his head nearer.

"Take... Agnes," he said. "That's... all... everything... Let her... come back... now."

Only Agnes knew when he died. At daylight the doctor went in and she was still holding his form in her arms.

XL

For John the sense of loss in Thane's death was as if part of himself had broken off and sunk out of sight.

To Agnes it was as if the whole world were gone. She seemed to have forgotten there was ever anything in it but Thane. Her life had inhabited his.

She went on living in the house, almost as if he were still there, often calling his name and answering aloud to an audible memory of his voice. She saw no one but John. She hardly knew anyone else. And she saw him only because she was aware of his great feeling for Thane and they could talk about him.

This was a bond between them and led to a companionship without which both would have missed the Autumn and gone directly from Midsummer to the Winter of their lives. It was impersonal, yet very sweet, and they came to rely upon it much more than they knew. Agnes had neither kin nor friends. John was that solitary being who has many friends and no brothers among men.

Agnes began to fade. John induced her to travel. She went to Europe. He joined her there. They went around the world together. When they returned she seemed much improved in spirits. She had begun to smile again. After a month in the house among the trees she became terribly depressed. He coaxed her to New York and settled her luxuriously in a hotel apartment. She disliked it and stayed on. More and more of John's time now passed in New York for business reasons. He told her this.

"We've no one else to visit with," he said. "Let's stay in the same town."

She said nothing. Often he surprised her looking at him with a thoughtful, far away expression as if trying to remember what it was he reminded her of. Suddenly she made up her mind to go to New Damascus and build herself a house there. It would be something to do John said at once, and that was what she needed. The house, which was small but exquisite, occupied her for a year. Before it was finished she had conceived the idea of building in New Damascus the finest hospital in the state.

Journeys to New Damascus now became John's sole recreation.

And so the Autumn stole upon them.

XLI

High in the financial heavens stood a sign, —sign of cabal, sign of rapture, sign of gold. The time had come to form the trust of trusts. Lords and barons of the steel industry began to settle down in Wall Street. They brought their trusts along. One day the Western crowd loaded six trusts on special trains, —brains, books, good will, charters and clerks, —and trundled them thither, banners flying, typewriters clicking, business doing on the way. They took the top floors of the newest steel skyscrapers and preferred solid mahogany furniture with brass mountings.

Wall Street said: "Here is the fat of money! It walks into our hands. How shall we divide it?"

But Wall Street had much to learn. These men, brash, boastful and boisterous, were also very wise. They did not come to play Wall Street's game. Most of them, like John, had sometime meddled with it and cared not for it. Now they were strong enough to play their own game. They brought their brokers with them, from Chicago, Cleveland, and Pittsburgh, —men whose tricks they knew, —and bought them seats on the New York Stock Exchange.

"Oh," said Wall Street. "That's it, is it? Well, well," and lolled its tongue in relish. It knew very little about steel and nothing yet about steel people.

"Now, gentlemen," said the steel people. "Red or black. High or low. Any limit or none. Let's shoot."

Using their own brokers to buy and sell the shares of their own trusts they began to make the canyon howl. For a while the play lay between Wall Street and the barbars, and the barbars held all the cards. If Wall Street sold steel shares for a fall the dividends were increased in the night. If it bought them for a rise suddenly the mills were shut up and dividends ceased. Wall Street was outraged. This was worse than gambling. It was a pea and shell game. The steel people were haled to court on the charge of circulating false information about their properties to influence the value of shares.

Nothing to it! Nobody could prove the information to have been false. Merely the steel people had it first, as they naturally would, and acted upon it in the stock market, as everybody would who could. So they all went back to Wall Street and the play waxed hotter and steeper. No one had ever seen speculation like this. At conventions, unwritten rules, limits, the steel people simply guffawed. They invented rules. Nobody was obliged to play with them. Their creed was, "Nothing in moderation."

After hours they played bridge for ten dollars a point. En route from Wall Street to the Waldorf, which was their rendezvous, they would lay bets in hundred-dollar units on the odd or even of numbered objects, like passing street cars. Whiskey was their innocuous beverage. There was one whose drink was three Scotch high-balls in succession. As the third one disappeared he would slowly rub his stomach, saying: "That one rings the bell." Yet all the time they attended strenuously to business. They were men of steel, physically and mentally powerful. Carousing was an emotional outlet. Gambling on the Stock Exchange was hardly more than pastime. Night and day they kept their eyes on that sign in the heavens.

They had delivered the steel age. The steel industry was their private possession to do with as they damn pleased. They could make a circus of it if they liked. They did. Their way with it had become a national problem. The steel industry was much too important to be conducted in that manner. It kept the country in a state of nerves. These wild, untamable behemoths would have to be bought out. They were willing to sell. There was a ludicrous fiction among them that they were weary of doing, whereas they were only sated with it. However, as they were willing to be bought out and as to be rid of them had become a public necessity, there remained only the question of how. It would take all the spare money there was in the country. Yet it would have to be done. That is what the sign meant.

John called his crowd together saying: "This is the tall goodbye if we want to get out."

They did. He pledged them in writing to leave everything in his hands and then returned to Wall Street where for months past he had been preparing his ground unobserved. In one of the new steel skyscrapers he had established himself an office. On the door was his name —

John Breakspeare

under that

American Steel Company
North American Manufacturing Company

and nothing more. Inside was a private room of his own with a stock ticker and a desk with a lot of telephones on it. Beyond was a large meeting room furnished with a long table, chairs, brass cuspidors, a humidor and a water cooler. From the window was a panoramic view of New York harbor. A very simple establishment one would think. Yet it was the center of a web radiating in all directions. Nothing much could happen in Wall Street without causing an alarm on his desk, for he had made some very excellent and timely connections. His private telephone wires reached the sources of information. One of them, it would have surprised everyone to know, ran to the office of John Sabath, with whom he had come to confidential terms. So it was that perhaps no one man, save only Bullguard, knew more than he about what was invisibly taking place under that sign which stood higher and higher in the money firmament.

What was visible had by this time become very exciting. The newspapers were giving astonished publicity to the doings of the golden bulls. What they did in Wall Street was recorded by the financial writers; what they did at large was written by the news reporters. And the public's imagination was inflamed.

Incipient Napoleons of finance, greedy little lambs, comet riders, haberdashers' clerks, preachers, husbands of actresses, dentists, small business men, delicatessen shop-keepers, jockeys, authors, commuters, winesellers, planters, prizefighters, crows and jackals clamored together at the Wall Street tickers. From ten to three they watched steel shares go up and down, betting on them, trying to out-guess the steel men who ordered their fluctuations. In the evening all this motley appeared at the Waldorf Hotel, sitting in rows along Peacock Alley, walking to and fro as if at ease, peering in at the dining-room doors to glimpse the lords and barons of steel at their food and drink.

Everybody loved it. This was the Steel Court, —a court of twenty kings, with its rabble and fringe and jesters, sycophants in favor, men of mystery passing, the unseen lesser deeply bowing to the greater, sour envy taking judgment at a distance, greed on ass-ear wings listening everywhere. One might hear a word to make him rich to-morrow. And the Machiavelli, too. That was Sabath, his beard now grey, otherwise the same, sitting always by himself, darting here and there his piercing eyes.

This court made news. Often the steel men, bored with gaping admiration, would extemporize a midnight stock market and buy and sell their shares among themselves. Each morning as addenda to the regular stock market reports would appear: "Transactions at the Waldorf." The newest rumors floated here. No financial editor was safe to go to bed until the Waldorf grill room lights were out, for it was generally late at night that the steel men spilled their secrets. One was overheard to say:

"There's a billion dollar steel trust on the way."

What tidings!

The remark had gone around the world before daylight, and at the opening of the stock market in London people began to sell American securities. Those Yankees, they said, always a bit mad, now were drunk with the arithmetic of their wealth. Wall Street was vaguely uneasy, too. There was no such thing as a billion-dollar corporation.

Rumor for once in its life was below the truth. The great steel trust was to be capitalized at a billion and a half. There had to be room for everybody. Bullguard was to be its deity. There could be no other. The charter had been applied for. Famous lawyers had reconciled it with the law. All these facts came out gradually, mostly in the form of midnight rumors. In the highest circles of the steel court an extremely curious fact was already privately known. Sabath was to be the manipulator. If he could not perform the unimaginable feat of selling the shares of a billion-and-a-half dollar corporation to the public nobody could. Yet how strange that Bullguard and Sabath should sail a ship together.

At length all the salient probabilities had been established, and nothing happened. A week passed. Then another. Wall Street was strung with suspense and the nightly Waldorf swarm buzzed with adverse rumors. Time was priceless. The public was in a fever of excitement. If ever there was an opportunity it was then. Why did Bullguard wait? What unexpected difficulty had been encountered?

There was but one obstacle and that was John. The Breakspeare properties were too important to be left out. A trust of trusts without them simply could not be. Bullguard sent for all the other lords and barons first, and they were quick to come. Then one day John received a telephone call from the office of Bullguard & Company. Would he be pleased to come to their office for a conference? His response was to mention his business address. Next day one of Bullguard's partners called in person.

"Mr. Bullguard wishes to see you," he said.

"If I wished to see Mr. Bullguard, I'd look for him at his office, not mine," said John.

"I beg your pardon?"

John repeated it. The partner went away, deeply offended in the name of Bullguard.

Sabath came to see him. He had been sent. John knew it and Sabath knew he knew it.

"When are you going to see Mr. Bullguard?" he asked.

"I'm here nearly every day," said John.

"Mr. Bullguard is performing a great public service," said Sabath, with not a twinkle, as if they did not understand each other down to the ground. "He's trying to get all you gamblers out of the steel business and bring some peace to the country. And because he spanked you once when you were in knee pants, now you're as proud as a pig with a ribbon in its hereafter. I'll tell him what I've said."

"Except the pig allusion. I'll lay odds you won't repeat that."

"I will," said Sabath, departing. "I will."

John's partners began to be alarmed. He kept nothing from them. When they importuned him to bend a little, thinking his obduracy might have disastrous consequences for all of them, he would say: "It amuses me and it will pay you."

One morning Sabath's voice called him on the telephone, saying: "The great mountain is walking. You damn gamblers! Do you want everything in the world?"

"Thanks," said John.

Twenty minutes later Bullguard appeared. He walked right in, sat on the edge of a chair, crossed his arms, leaned forward on his stick, and glared. When he glared the world was supposed to tremble. He was rather awful to look at. His purple face was of a strawberry texture; his nose was monstrous, angry, red, bulbous, with hairy warts upon it; his eyebrows were almost vertical.

Three words were spoken, —all three by Bullguard.

"How much?" he asked.

John drew a pencil pad out of his desk and wrote slowly in large, owlish characters, this:

> If you smile —
>
> $300,000,000
>
> No smile
>
> $350,000,000

Having written it he stopped to gaze at it thoughtfully for a minute, then pulled out the slide leaf of his desk, tossed the pad there for Bullguard to see, and leaned back.

Bullguard glanced at it and stood up.

"That!" he said, tapping the $350,000,000 with his forefinger, and stalked out.

Slaymaker, Awns, Wingreene and Pick were waiting in the big room. John walked in and threw the pad on the table.

"There are the terms."

Knowing John they understood the pencil writing.

"Did he smile?" they asked as one.

"No," said John.

"My God!" murmured Slaymaker. He sank into a chair and wept.

Two-fifths of it was John's. His share included the Thane interest which amounted to nearly twenty millions. Slaymaker, Awns, Wingreene and Pick divided $170,000,000. The balance went to thirty or forty minor stockholders in the Breakspeare companies.

XLII

So the fabulous Damosel of the Dirty Face, rescued from the goat herds who had found and reared her, was clothed in what she should wear, christened in due manner, annointed in the name of order, and presented to the American people. Or, that is to say, the steel industry was bought from the barbars and sold to the public.

Auspicated by Bullguard and Company, manipulated by Sabath, advertised by common wonder, the shares of the biggest trust in the world were launched on the New York Stock Exchange. Popular imagination, prepared in suspense, delivered itself headlong to the important task of buying them. A craze to exchange money for steel shares swept the country. That seemed to be only what people got up every morning to do. Such manias, like panics inverted, have often occurred. They have a large displacement in the literature of popular delusions. This one, although of a true type and spontaneous, was fomented in an extraordinary manner by Sabath, who for the first time in his life had all the power and sanction of Wall Street behind him. The hand of the Ishmaelite that everyone feared now strummed the official lyre and the tune it played untied a million purse strings.

The steel people removed their hats and bowed.

"We were amateurs," they admitted.

For weeks and weeks they sat behind piles of steel engraved certificates, fresh from the printer, and signed their names until they were weary of making pen strokes at ten thousand dollars each. Before the ink of their signatures was dry the certificates were cast upon the market to be converted into cash, —the market Sabath made. There seemed no bottom or end to it. The capacity of that market was unlimited. The public's power to buy was greater than anybody knew.

When it was over, when Sabath's sweet melody ceased, when the public owned the steel industry and the barbars were out, then steel shares began to fall. For several years they fell, disastrously, and the public howled with rage. The trust went near the rocks.

All who had had any part in the making of it faced a storm of wild opprobium. There is much to be said in reproach. However, given the problem as it was, how else could anyone have solved it? The trust got by the rocks. The steel industry was stabilized. And ultimately the shares were worth much more than the public originally paid for them.

This eventuality few of the great steel barbars lived to witness. A little touched with madness anyhow, as heroic stature is, the Wall Street harvest finished them. They were of a sudden Nabobs with nothing on earth to do. Their wealth had been in mills and mines and ships, and business was a very jealous mistress. Now it was in money and they were free.

In the first place they didn't know what to do with the money itself. Some of them bought banks of their own to keep it in. Then what could they spend it for? What could they invest it in? The only thing they knew was steel and they were out of that. Some of them began to buy railroads. They would say: "This looks like a pretty good railroad. Let's buy that." And they would buy it offhand in the stock market. Then Wall Street, controlling railroads without owning them, was struck with a new terror. It wasn't safe to leave control of a railroad lying around loose. There was no telling what these men would do next with their money. They had got control of several great banks and railroads before anyone knew what they were doing.

But after they had invested their money in banks and railroads they still had nothing really to do. They built themselves castles, in some cases two or three each, and seldom if ever lived in them because they were so lonesome. One transplanted a full grown forest and it died; he did it again with like result, and a third time, and then he was weary. He never went back to see. They got rid of their old wives and bought new and more expensive ones. Even that made no perceptible hole in their wealth. They tried horses and art and swamped everything they touched. Gambling they forgot. One developed a peacock madness, never wore the same garments more than an hour; his dressing room resembled a clothing store, with hundreds of suits lying on long tables in pressed piles. One had a phantasy for living out the myth of Pan and ceased to be spoken of anywhere. One travelled ceaselessly and carried with him a private orchestra that played him awake and attended his bath. He died presently under the delusion that he had lost all his money and all his friends, which was only half true.

They disappeared.

Blasted prodigies!

Children of the steel age, overwhelmed in its cinders.

XLIII

John like all the others signed steel trust certificates until his hand became an automaton. If he noticed what it was doing it faltered and forgot. He sat in the big room at the long table, a clerk standing by to remove the engraved sheets one by one and blot the signature. Suddenly he saw it all as for the first time, in an original, unfamiliar manner.

"What are we doing?" he asked the clerk.

"Signing the certificates, sir. They want this lot before 2 o'clock."

"Yes, but what does it mean?"

"What does it mean?" the clerk repeated. "I don't know, sir. What do you mean?"

"I don't know either," said John. He threw the pen away, got up, reached for his hat.

"You're not going now, sir? They are waiting for these certificates."

"Let them wait."

"What shall I say when they call for them?"

"Anything you like. Ask them what it means."

Up and down the money canyon people moved with absent gestures, some in haste, some running, some loitering, all with one look in their eyes. Bulls were bellowing on the Stock Exchange. Steel shares were rising. Sabath was in his highest form. To the strumming of his lyre men of all shapes and conditions turned from their ways and came hither and wildly importuned brokers to exchange their money for bits of paper believed to represent steel mills they had never seen, would never see, had never heard of before. What did it mean?

As John gazed at the scene it became unreal and detached. He was alone, as one is in some dreams, there and not there, somehow concerned in the action but invisible to the actors and to oneself. It was like a dream of anxiety, full of confusion and grotesque matter.

He was lonely and very wretched and accused Agnes. He would accuse her to her face. That was what he was on his way to do, perhaps because there was no other excuse for seeing her in the middle of the day. He would tell her how selfish and unreasonable she was. They were two solitary beings in one world together. Their hours were running away. He loved her. He had always loved her. And at least she loved nobody else. Then why should they not join their lives?

Three times he had asked her that question. Each time she had said: "Let's go on being friends. That's very nice, isn't it?"

A year had passed since the last time. He had watched for some sign of change. But she was always the same, except that after having been gently though firmly unwilling to say either yes or no she seemed to come nearer in friendship and baffled him all the more. If she had any feeling for him whatever beyond friendship he had been unable to detect or surprise it, and fate would bear witness that the possibility was one he had stalked with all patience and subtlety. In fact, he really believed that if he pressed her to the point she would say no, —that she had not said it already only because she hated to hurt him. This notion tormented him exceedingly. It would be a relief to know.

She had been for some weeks in town, at the Savoy, where he detained her on the pretext that her presence was necessary in her own interest. It was only a little past twelve when he arrived there and called her on the telephone, from the desk, asking her down to lunch. She was surprised and pleased and answered him in a voice that had a ring of youth.

The sound of it echoing in his ears evoked memories and caused the years to fall away. He waited, not there in the hotel lobby, but in a boxwood hedge, surreptitiously, and saw her as a girl again, plucking flowers, pretending not to know he was there, yet coming nearer, always nearer, with a thoughtful air; and for a moment he forgot that anything had happened since.

"Business or pleasure at this time of day?" she asked, coming up behind him.

Instantly, at the provocation of her voice, an impish, youth-time impulse took possession of him. It provided its own idea complete and he did not stop to examine it. His mood seized it.

"Personal," he said.

"But you look so serious."

"It is serious-for me."

They sat at a table in the far corner of the dining room.

"Out with it. Lucky it isn't murder. You'd be suspected at first glance."

"What shall we eat? Pompano. That ought to be good....Don't look at me like that. I'm so happy I can't stand it. That's all that's the matter with me....Filet of sole. How about that?"

"Anything to cure such happiness. Sole, salad and iced tea for me, please. Now then."

"A sweet? Or shall we decide about that later?"

"Later. I may be too much surprised by that time to want a sweet."

She was regarding him intently, with a very curious expression. He avoided her eyes.

"Yes, it may surprise you," he said. *"Here, waiter! ...* Of course you know —(*Sole, hearts of lettuce and tomato salad, French dressing, iced tea for one, large coffee, sweets later*) —what an emotional animal I am. —(*Two salads, yes.*) —Or romantic. Whatever you like to call it. (*Sole for two.*) After all, I don't know why —(*No, hot coffee for one.*) —Why I should be so self-conscious about it. The fact is simple enough. I'm going to be married."

"Oh! How exciting. When?"

"When? When, did you say? Why, right away. This evening perhaps."

"Who is the lady?"

"I'd rather not tell you yet."

"Yet? But it's to be this evening, you say."

"You would know her name at once and you might be prejudiced in spite of yourself. I can't very well explain it. But I want you to meet her first."

"This afternoon?"

"Or this evening. I'm coming to that. I very much need your help. It's an extraordinary thing to ask. I'm anxious to keep it very quiet, both on her account and my own. Not the fact afterward. That must come out. But it's taking place, when and where. Then of course we can go away, for a year, two years; live permanently abroad perhaps."

"Yes?"

"I say I can't explain it very clearly. You'll just have to take a good deal of it for granted. The newspapers are so curious and impertinent. I'd like this to happen without anyone knowing it until the notice is published and we are gone. She has no home. I mean, she lives at a hotel. I have no home either. At a church or any public place like that we'd be noticed at once."

"Will you ask the waiter to bring some more butter, please. Yes, go on. What can I do to help?"

"Take mine. I hoped you'd guess by this time. There's no one else I can ask."

"Thanks. No, I can't guess."

"Well, if you would let the ceremony take place in your apartment here and sort of manage the fussy part I'd never know how much to thank you."

"Yes, indeed. I'd love to do it. Why did you make such a bother of asking? I'll have some decorations sent in. What will she wear? What colors does she like?"

"I'll have to find out."

"And the time?"

"I'll let you know."

"As soon as you can. And that's what you were so glum about? Now cheer up. Men are such lumps when they are happy."

"You are very sweet about it."

"Don't mind me. Only go as fast as you can and get the details. You don't know how important they are. I'll expect to hear from you within an hour. You will call me up?"

"Yes."

The next he knew he was in the Central Park Zoo looking at the monkeys and wondering why they were so mystified. What had they to be puzzled about? Then there was a little brown bear that precisely expressed the absurdity he felt in himself. He did not mind feeling absurd. No, that was even comforting. A pain in the ego counteracting one in the heart. Clumsy as the device was it had served his purpose. He had found out. But it was no relief whatever. In the way he hoped she might she cared less than not at all-less than a foster sister or an old maid aunt. He could not be mistaken. He had watched her closely. She had betrayed not the slightest sign of self-concern. He had that same diminished, ignominious feeling with which he retired from the boxwood hedge on the evening of their first youth-time encounter.

What an asinine thing to have done!

When he called her on the telephone two hours later, as he had promised to do, this conversation occurred:

"This is John."

"Yes. Now tell me all about it. You've been a long time."

"Hello."

"Yes. What time?"

"Hello."

"Yes, I'm here."

"Agnes, it's too much of an imposition altogether. I can't imagine how I could have asked you to do it. Thanks all the same, but we'll call it off."

"Nonsense. You're not telling me the truth. Something has happened."

"Maybe so. Anyhow, I withdraw the request."

"Where are you?"

"Near by. Not very far."

"Meet me in the tea room downstairs. I'll be there in ten minutes."

Not waiting for him to answer she closed the wire. She was there waiting when he arrived.

"I'm sorry if anything has happened," she said, most sympathetically. "Can you tell me about it?"

"It's off," he said, feeling secretly and utterly ludicrous. "That's all."

"Oh, that can't be," she said. "Suppose I talk to her. I shan't be modest about you. I'll not promise to be even truthful."

"No use," he said. "I've said everything there is to say for myself. She knows me well enough-too well, perhaps. That may be it."

"Tell me about her. What is she like?"

"Cold. You wouldn't think so, but she is. The fact that a man loves her means nothing-not a thing."

"Is she so used to it?"

"I don't know. No. That isn't it...."

"What?"

"I was going to say selfish. I ought not to say that. I'm selfish to want her. She wants to keep her life to herself. It's her own life."

"But it's only postponed. She doesn't say no, does she?"

"Worse than that. She says —"

"Yes. What does she say?"

"She says it's nicer as it is. We shall go on being friends. Friendship is all right. It blooms in the next world."

"Let me talk to her, please."

"No. It's hopeless."

"I'd not urge you if I weren't so sure I could change her mind. The fact is, I think I know her."

John started and became rigid with astonishment. He regarded her fixedly with a groping, incredulous expression. She stirred her tea very thoughtfully and kept her eyes down.

"If she's the person I think she is," Agnes continued, still looking down, "what you say about her is probably true. And yet —"

"Agnes! Be careful what you say."

"I'll be as careful as I know how to be. Trust me."

"How long have you known her?"

"In one way, of course, you deserve to be wretched. It isn't all on one side. Do you think it's nice —?" "How long have you known her, I ask?" "A long time. Longer than you have," she said.

* * * * *

Note from the society column of the New York *Times,* November 6, 1901:

Mr. and Mrs. Breakspeare are passing their honeymoon in Mediterranean waters on Mr. Breakspeare's yacht, the "Damascene."

THE END

www.ingramcontent.com/pod-product-compliance
Lightning Source LLC
Chambersburg PA
CBHW071429300726
48976CB00004B/1279